THE CULT

K.M. SCOTT

THE CULT

All you've ever wanted is yours for the taking. All you have to do is believe.

When Lara Simpson's sister goes missing, the only clue to her whereabouts is a pamphlet in Rina's apartment about a new self-help group in town, The Golden Light. Convinced they will lead her to Rina, Lara poses as a new member seeking guidance.

The charismatic leader of the group, a man named Micah who promises enlightenment, seems to care about his followers. However, Lara suspects that the real purpose of The Golden Light isn't helping people at all, but something far more insidious.

The more Lara learns, the more she doubts that Rina left of her own accord. As Lara descends deeper into the group's hidden world, she begins to question her own sanity—and wonders if she'll make it out alive.

Because once you join The Golden Light, you're a member forever.

The Cult is a work of fiction. Names, characters, places, and events are the products of the author's imagination. Any resemblance to events, locations, or persons, living or dead, is coincidental.

2025 Eight Feathers Press LLC

Published in the United States

ISBN: 978-1-947705-08-1

1

NASH

"EVERYTHING YOU WANT IS yours to have. Do you believe that? Because I do! And I can show you thousands of people who've gotten all they want by simply believing!"

The leader of The Golden Light spreads his arms out wide, as if he's welcoming guidance from the heavens above, and looks up toward the ceiling. His tanned body and dirty blond hair in front of the royal blue curtains hanging behind him please the eye and make it hard to look away. It's like he's some modern day messiah come to save us all from the ugliness of life.

When he lowers his head to look at the crowd again, he smiles, and it's like the entire room is suddenly brighter. "I know what you're feeling. Trust me. I do. I felt it too once, but I can promise you all you desire is yours for the taking. You just have to believe."

Micah is in rare form today. Not that he isn't usually

mesmerizing, but as I scan the audience this morning, I'm impressed by how they're watching him in rapt attention. One guy looks like he's going to have a seizure any minute now by the way his expression is contorting into that pained yet amazed look. The woman at the end of his row is practically levitating over her metal folding chair.

The leader never fails to get the crowd going. I bet in a past life he was one of those carnival barkers. Or maybe some crazy world leader. Then again, maybe he comes by his charisma naturally since I've heard him claim his great-grandfather was Jim Jones.

He moves to the left side of the dais and points at the young blond woman seated in front of him. Ramon gives me a tiny smile and then quickly returns to looking stoic, just as we're supposed to during these things. That grin tells me he understands his job here, though. When Micah gets his treat after he's done, Ramon's place will be safe.

"Do you believe?" Micah asks her, staring into her eyes in that mesmerizing way that never fails to work on new recruits. "Stand and join me. Find your power deep inside."

I know how he talks about the women here when they aren't around, so it takes everything I have to not smirk. Power is the last thing he wants her to have.

That's only for him.

She takes his hand and joins him on the stage, gazing up into his eyes like she's madly in love. I'm always amazed at how easily they fall for him. All it takes are a few well-chosen words about power and believing in themselves and they're goners.

"Tell me your name. Say it so the Universe can know you're ready to receive all you desire," Micah commands in a voice as smooth as silk.

The seduction plays out in front of everyone in the audience, and I have no doubt every person, male and female, would give anything to be in that blond woman's place. She opens her mouth but nothing comes out, so he takes her by the shoulders and smiles, shaking his head as if to say, "Don't worry. You can do this." I've always thought he looked like a surfer guy or some sixties hippie at times like this.

"It's okay. Channel that power of belief deep inside you and introduce yourself to the Universe."

She hesitates for a few seconds, her lower lip quivering as every single person in the room waits to hear her tell Micah her name. Finally, she takes a deep breath and softly says, "Katie."

He slides his hands from her shoulders to her face and cradles her cheeks. "I want you to know, Katie, that the Universe wants you to have all you want. Are you willing to believe that? Can you give yourself over to it so you can have all you've ever desired?"

The way he speaks, all breathy and soft at times and then booming and powerful at others, is nothing less than intoxicating. I look around the room again and see each person here, including some of my fellow guards, hanging on every word Micah says. Those of us who've been here a while are used to the show, but others like

Ramon still find everything the leader says utterly enthralling.

"I am!" she says, practically sobbing. "I believe, and I'm ready to have all I've ever wanted!"

That breaks Ramon out of his near trance, and he turns to look at me with an expression full of relief. He may be new here, but he's seen what happens when we don't succeed at a task Micah's given us. He watched Simon being led to the box last night after he failed to do what the leader wanted. He heard the screams coming from there for hours until I'm guessing Simon passed out from the agony of his punishment. Everyone heard it. It's one of the reasons why Micah uses the box.

Fear is only useful when it's used.

Micah and Katie turn to face the audience and smile. "Do you want to experience the bliss the Universe has given this sister of The Golden Light? If you do, say it loud! Let the Universe know you're ready to do what it takes to have all you've ever dreamed of!"

As always, this part of the show becomes loud and raucous. Everyone jumps up, throws their hands in the air, and begins to profess their belief that all they want will come to them because they believe. Over and over, Micah tells them they need to show the Universe they're ready, and each time, they react with screams and yelps.

"I believe!" some cry out. "I'm ready to receive!" others scream. Some even begin to shake uncontrollably and collapse to the ground in their enthusiasm.

It would be unnerving if I hadn't seen this hundreds of times. I knew it was the first day I sat in the audience and listened to Micah talk about how we could all have anything our hearts desire as long as we believed and followed him.

That last part is key. Believing is not enough. Only the leader can help us have what we desire.

Ramon slowly moves over toward where I stand and stops a few inches away. "Should we do something for them?" he asks as he looks over at one guy writhing on the ground.

I shake my head without turning to face him. "No. It's all part of the process."

That's what I was told the first time I saw one of Micah's audience members begin to have a fit. I remember wanting to help the woman. She looked like she was having an epileptic attack, but the more seasoned members of the group told me, "This is how it's supposed to go. Let the process do what it's supposed to do."

When I saw her later that day, she was fine, so I guess they were right. She had the same reaction to Micah every time I saw her after that, too. Some people just can't handle what he says.

"Join me, my children, and find the light!" he calls out from the dais.

And with that, he walks out the door behind the stage like he always does at the end of one of his shows, leaving the audience sobbing and swearing only he can give them what they need. It's quite a thing to see.

Ramon waits for me to move and follows me when I begin walking toward the door. He's far more timid than most of Micah's guards, but he's an okay guy. How he's going to handle some of the others who love to inflict pain on anyone they think is weak we'll have to see.

"That's the fourth time I've witnessed, and it's just as exciting as the first day," he says breathlessly once we're outside and walking toward Micah's rooms.

I glance over at him and smile. "It's definitely him at his best."

We make our way in silence to the cabin farthest away from the main building where we were and file in with the other guards and those group members closest to Micah. When we find our spots, all the guards bow to him.

He sits in his blue chair with gold arms and legs that has always reminded me of a throne and steeples his fingers in front of him. Wearing only black pants like usual, he's shirtless, also something he likes to do. I don't blame him since it's got to be in the mid-nineties today. I wish he'd let the rest of us do the same, but he insists each guard wear our usual uniform of a black T-shirt and black pants along with our black shitkicker boots.

To say it's hot is an understatement.

On his right stands Nadine, the only powerful woman in the group. Some think of her as Micah's right hand or his girlfriend, but I'm not sure what position she holds here. All I know is he's the leader, but she possesses far more clout with him than any of us.

Dressed in her usual dark gray dress that looks like something a strict German headmistress of some school for wayward teenage girls might wear and matronly black shoes, she scowls at all of us like we're enemies of the state of Micah. I've never understood why she always looks like she hates us.

Behind her stand her own guards that protect only her. I'm not sure why Micah allows that, but if he has an issue with anything she does, he doesn't show it.

He spreads his arms out wide and takes a deep breath in, expanding his muscular chest. Nadine watches like a proud girlfriend or mother. I can't decide which.

"What a wonderful day it is. That was a very good session, don't you think?"

I've always taken these questions he poses to the guards as rhetorical, but Ramon quickly answers, "Oh, yes! It was wonderful, Micah!"

Nadine's eyes flash the purest anger I've ever seen, their darkness nearly on fire as she glares at the new guard, and my heart pounds in my chest as I wait to see what might happen next. I've seen her lash out at anyone she's decided isn't conforming to the rules, so it wouldn't be surprising for her to order her guards to take poor Ramon out and teach him how to behave. I don't think he'll get the box, but it could be bad for him.

Not a single one of us says a word as we wait for Micah to react, and it feels like I'm holding my breath the whole time. I look down at the wood floor and hope whatever happens won't involve me, but Nadine has seen me talking to Ramon more than once today.

Finally, Micah chuckles, and I lift my head to see him wearing a broad smile. Relief washes over me, and I silently thank God that didn't turn ugly like it definitely could have.

"Ramon, I love that you're so enthusiastic!" he says,

and I take my first breath in what seems like forever. "You did well, my child. You're officially my favorite guard today. How does that feel?"

"Thank you!" Ramon answers. "I'm so happy. Thank you, Micah."

Once more, Nadine glares at the poor guy. Why is she so particularly surly today? Even as I think that, I know we won't have to wait long to find out. What that will mean only God knows.

"Everyone, you did well today. Go enjoy some food and get some exercise. I'll call for you later."

I turn to walk out, but Micah adds, "Nash and Adam, you two stay."

My stomach clenches when my name hits my ears. Being ordered to face Micah is never a good thing. Quickly, everything I've done in the past few days races through my mind, but I can't find anything that would warrant this private meeting.

Everyone else hurries out of the room, no doubt thankful their names weren't the ones Micah spoke, but Nadine and her four guards remain. As Ramon reaches the door, he looks back at me with genuine terror in his eyes.

Maybe he's not as naïve as I thought.

Micah waves us forward to stand in front of him, so I walk up to his chair and bow. I don't give a damn about what Adam does. He mostly gets on my nerves, so thinking about him is the last thing I need right now.

When the two of us stand up, we wait to hear what the leader of The Golden Light has to say to us. I stay away from this guard as much as possible because of his temper, so I can't imagine what Micah wants from the two of us.

Nadine studies Adam and then me, never cracking even the tiniest hint of a smile. Her guards stare over our heads as they've been ordered to. It's an odd requirement she forces on them, but none of the four men who protect her ever make eye contact with anyone in the group when she's around.

Micah turns to her and sighs. "I want to speak to my guards privately. Please take your men and leave for the time being."

That gets the two of us one final nasty glare before she bows to him and spins on her heel to leave with her guards. I'm more at ease now that she's gone because I have a feeling despite being Micah's biggest supporter, Nadine has a bad effect on his mood most days.

The stifling heat of the day begins to get to me, and I wipe my forehead of sweat beads that are forming at my hairline. I've never been jealous of the leader of The Golden Light, but I'd give anything to be shirtless like him at this moment.

"Gentlemen, we have a problem."

My stomach drops at those five words. What problem could he be talking about? Adam and I rarely spend any time around each other, and I've racked my brain to think of what I could have done that would deserve reprimand. I've come up with nothing.

Micah is a master of manipulation, and meetings like this show his particular ability to keep people on edge. He stares at us without saying a word, and I don't know about Adam, but terror builds inside me second by second until it's almost unbearable.

I've seen what happens to people when Micah is displeased with them. The box. Whipping. Sometimes a person will just disappear. One day they're adoring him in every way required of a Golden Light member, and the next they're gone and no one dares ask where they are or what happened to them.

Questions are not part of life here.

Finally, Micah smiles, and the effect is like the sun appearing after days and days of nothing but dark clouds and rain. "Maren has left our loving embrace. I want her back here with us, along with that little friend of hers. Go get them for me."

I can't explain how much I want to laugh or cry or simply show some kind of emotion at this moment. I don't because it's not allowed, but it takes every ounce of self-control to keep my expression placid like it needs to be.

Nodding, I bow but say nothing. There is no response required. When Micah tells you what to do, you do it without comment and hopefully the way he wants you to. If not, then surely punishment will follow.

"Nash, you take the lead. Adam, he's your superior and acting on my behalf. Remember that."

Talk about an emotional rollercoaster. A minute ago, I feared I'd done something to displease Micah and wondered what punishment I'd have to endure. Now he's just made me the boss for this job, ensuring that Adam must follow my orders or suffer the consequences.

Adam and I both say in unison, "Yes, Micah. As you

wish," and then wait for him to dismiss us. With a wave of his hand, he sends us on our way, and I hope as I make my way to the door it isn't obvious how much I want to get the hell out of this room right now.

Just as I walk outside, I turn around and see that pretty blond girl named Katie being escorted in through the back door. Ramon leads her to Micah and is quickly excused, giving me a smile as he hurries out the way he came.

With her big eyes full of awe as she stares at the leader, she's exactly the kind he likes. I leave before I see anything happen between them, but it's the worst kept secret here what he expects from her.

2

LARA

MY SISTER'S phone rings and rings like it has for the past two days whenever I call. I silently pray this will be the time she answers, but just as every other time, I hear her soft voice say, "Leave me a message, and I promise to get back to you as soon as I can. Thanks!"

I pull the phone away from my ear and jam my finger into the red button that says END. Frustrated, I toss it onto the couch and lean back against the cushion, sighing in frustration. Where could she be? It's entirely unlike Rina to not call me when she sees I've left a message. It's almost Pavlovian the way she has to answer, even if it's with only a text to let me know she's crazy busy but she'll call when she can.

The past few weeks flash through my mind while I attempt to find some answer as to where she is. That idiot boyfriend of hers sent her confidence crashing to the floor three months ago. Correction: ex-boyfriend, the jackass who threatened to kill her when she told him she planned to go away to college in the fall. I never liked him, but she was crazy about him, and I'd never seen her so terrified as when he said he couldn't live without her so he was going to kill both of them.

I didn't think much of Jamie, but I wouldn't have guessed he'd ever say he'd kill her because she wants to get a good education. Not that long distance relationships usually work, but he could have at least tried.

Then again, maybe he knew the Rina train was leaving the station and had no place for him on it. One semester of college and she would have been way out of his league.

Truthfully, he probably did her a huge favor by showing his true colors. She'll see that someday. Now, though, I know she's hurting.

That's probably all that's going on. She's laying low, hanging out with some rom-coms on Netflix and enough butterscotch brickle ice cream to last a month. Typical Rina behavior to treat a broken heart.

I think I'll stop over and check up on her. She could use a visit from her big sister. I just have to swear I won't start bashing that asshole ex-boyfriend of hers.

AFTER KNOCKING on her apartment door for nearly five minutes, I turn to my last resort. My sister and I have a longstanding rule of never calling our parents unless it's something serious. We love our mother and father, but once they get a whiff of anything to worry about with either of us, they become the world's worst helicopter parents. No twenty-year-old needs that kind of concern constantly hovering over every phone call and visit, and I know Rina would be furious with me for taking this drastic step.

My mother's cell phone rings twice before she answers nearly out of breath. "Hello?"

"Why do you sound like you were running? You don't run. You barely move, unless you have to," I say, knowing my mother would prefer to have a hot poker stuck up her behind than actually exercise.

"I do move around, Lara. I'm not completely seden-tary. You know, you could take a page out of my book. My doctor says that I get just enough exercise to keep me young. All that yoga and nonsense you do to your body is only going to make you old before your time."

Rolling my eyes, I sigh, already unhappy with how this call is going. "Mom, yoga is one of the best ways to keep your body limber and young," I explain, feeling the need to educate her once again on why my chosen form of exercise is, in fact, good for a person.

Something she knows already since we've talked about this very topic dozens of times.

"Then why does every woman over forty who does yoga look like their faces are covered in weathered leather?" my mother asks with a chuckle.

She's met a total of one yoga instructor in her entire life, and that's what she bases her beliefs on. I could explain to her for the umpteenth time how that one particular practitioner liked the sun too much and that isn't a common theme with most yoga instructors, but I quickly decide that's not a windmill I want to tilt at today.

Changing the subject, I say, "Mom, I'm over at Rina's. She's not here. Do you know where she is?"

I make sure to keep my voice calm and my attitude as casual as possible to avoid her overreacting. I know my mother. The woman jumps to conclusions like Superman leaps over tall buildings. It's like second nature for her.

"Hmmm...let me see. What did she tell me the other day? She mentioned something about that girl she met in town who loved daisies. God, I have no idea why. Daises are the poorest of the flower kingdom. I've never understood why anyone would carry daisies, of all things, in a wedding bouquet, but nowadays, anything goes, I guess."

She'd talk about how bad this particular flower is for the rest of the day, so when she takes a breath, I quickly ask, "Do you remember her name? I don't think she told me anything about her. Is she from that group Rina was telling me about a few weeks ago? What is it called? Golden something?"

All I can think of is golden arches or golden showers, neither of which is right.

"The Golden Light," my mother answers with a huff. "I bet they do yoga."

The smugness in her voice is hard to ignore. I swear in a past life my mother must have died doing something involving stretching. Maybe she was stretched on the rack in medieval times. I can see her mouthing off to some church official and ending up being tortured back in those days.

"Okay. I'll talk to you later, Mom."

"Is that all you called me about? To ask me about your sister? You two talk far more than she and I do. Is something wrong, Lara?"

Quickly, I answer, "Oh, no. Nothing's wrong. I just loaned her a sweater a few months ago, and I need it."

That lie doesn't really make much sense considering the time of year, but she caught me off guard with that question.

"A sweater? Lara, all the weatherman could talk about is how much hotter this July is than any other July in history, and you want to bother your sister about a sweater?"

She isn't buying my fib. She's probably a minute or two away from starting up that helicopter of hers, so I need to calm her down in a hurry.

"You know how I hate air conditioning, Mom. Not everyone is like you and loves the fake cold."

That's always the best policy with her. The off me and on you trick. It never fails to make her focus on herself and not on me.

"I'll have you know that air conditioning is sometimes the only thing that keeps me sane since these damn hot flashes became a part of my life. You'll see. Give it thirty years and you'll be a fan of air conditioning. I hope I'm still around to see it so I can say, 'See? Air conditioning isn't a bad thing.' Trust me, Lara. It's a godsend."

And with just a simple mention of my dislike of air conditioning, my mother is off to the races and not even thinking about my sister. Good. Now to escape this conversation and find out what's going on with Rina.

"Mom, I need to go. I've got another call coming in.

I'll talk to you later," I lie before pressing END on my phone's screen.

Calling my mother was actually the second to last resort. The true last resort is using the key to my sister's apartment that I promised I'd only use in cases of dire emergency. I'm not actually sure this situation is dire, but I'm worried enough to go into her apartment uninvited. If she's in there safe and sound, then I'll apologize and happily go on my way.

I turn the doorknob and open the door before slipping the key back into the special pocket in my purse. Listening for any sounds, especially the TV, I hear nothing but silence. It's deafening and makes a chill race down my spine. My sister always keeps her TV on when she's home. She says it's like background noise and makes her feel like she isn't alone.

As I slowly walk through her apartment, I look around the living room and see nothing out of the ordinary. A half-full glass of soda sits on the coffee table in front of that green couch she got from Goodwill. Thank God my mother isn't here with me because I'd have to endure another round of her complaining about how furniture should never be secondhand.

Everything looks the same as it always does in this room, and when I take another glance at the glass I see no mold growing on top of the cola, thankfully. That means it hasn't been sitting out for days and days.

I take a sip and nearly gag. It's flat and warm. Does that mean she was here recently? Since her apartment is always a comfortable seventy-two degrees year round, not necessarily. All it means is sometime recently she was home and had a glass of soda.

As I turn to walk toward her kitchen, a terrible thought fills my mind. What if she's here and I'm about to find her lying on the floor hurt? Or dead?

Oh, God. I don't think I could handle that. Rina and I are best friends in addition to being sisters. For all but two years of my life, she's been at my side as we grew up with parents who instilled in us that no matter who we meet in this world, each of us has a best friend for life because we're sisters.

No, I can't think of her being hurt or worse. Rina's okay. I know she is.

I gingerly step into her kitchen and look around. There's no sign she's been here for much time recently, but that's not surprising. My sister hates cooking, and she ends up eating more meals out than here in her place. Her kitchen basically serves as the spot for her refrigerator since it holds the soda she drinks constantly.

Opening up her refrigerator, I see the evidence of that. Four bottles of Coke, one bottle of ginger ale that's been in there since that New Year's Eve party she had, and an unopened bottle of water take up the top shelf, and below on the lower shelf a block of yellow cheese sits alone.

So far, nothing is out of the ordinary here in her apartment. Well, other than the fact that Rina is nowhere to be found.

But I haven't checked her bedroom yet.

Dread fills me again as I take the first few steps

toward her room. Please don't let her be hurt or dead. I don't know what I'll do if she's not okay.

I stop just outside her bedroom and take a deep breath. Everything's okay. I should be worrying about waking her and getting an earful about breaking our rule about not intruding on one another's private space.

Reaching in through the doorway, I flick on the light switch. Relief washes over me when I see her bed made. I walk around to look on both sides and see nothing but light brown carpet. Thank God.

As I check her closet, I find nothing odd. Except she's not here. That wouldn't be strange normally, but since she hasn't answered my calls for two days, I know there's something off. I don't know if anything's wrong, but something isn't right.

I sit down on her couch and exhale a breath of frustration. Where could she be?

Out of the corner of my eye, I see something yellow and gold on the end table. I turn to look at what it is and notice a sheet of paper with a picture of the sun with rays of light shooting out. Leaning over, I grab it.

Scanning the words under the sun, I find out it's something from that Golden Light group. As I read, I understand this group is one of those New Age types that focus on positivity and self-actualization. It's all incredibly touchy-feely, and I have a hard time imagining my sister buying into any of it.

At the bottom of the page I see an address that's right in town. Maybe she's there. I doubt it, but at least it's something for me to go on for now.

3

As I WALK down Main Street, I see the usual suspects hanging out like they always have during the summer. There's old Mr. Loftus sitting in his chair outside of his antique store like he has all of my life. It doesn't matter how hot it gets. He's always there as some kind of sentry in front of his store.

I see Sylvie Mattern and wave to her as she straightens the flower display outside her florist shop. She's a new addition to the Main Street business district, but like the older proprietors, she's taken to being outside whenever she can during the summer.

Manford Standish, the owner of the most popular watering hole in town, smiles at me as I walk toward him. My parents' age, he likes to joke that he's a descendant of the Miles Standish we learned about in grade school. I highly doubt that, but then again, who knows?

"Hello, Lara. How are you today?" he asks, and I notice how red his nose looks this afternoon.

He swears he never drinks while everyone who comes to his bar drinks like there's no tomorrow, but that rosy nose of his says otherwise. He's an adult, so he can do as he wants, but why lie? It's not like anyone would care if he enjoyed a drink or two.

"I'm good. You living the dream?" I ask, using the answer he gives when people ask him how he's doing.

The bar owner's expression falls, like he's hurt I stole his favorite sentence and now he doesn't know what to say. "You know how it is."

I give him another smile and look down at the sheet of paper in my hand. The Golden Light pamphlet gives an address on the next street over, so I turn left at the intersection and head down Mulberry Avenue toward Ravine Street to find the building. I don't exactly know what to expect, but when I see it, I have to admit I'm surprised.

The red brick building looks like many in this area filled with early American buildings. It's a source of pride for the town council that this town of ours has existed since the late seventeen hundreds, and they make sure to drive that point home on the signs people see coming in and out of town, in addition to on the town's website.

Other than looking somewhat historical, the building where The Golden Light office is located is unremarkable. The windows seem new compared to others in buildings around town, and a sign above the front door with a big yellow sun and beams coming out of it looks new.

I peer through the front window for a long moment before taking a deep breath and walking inside. I can't place why I feel uneasy, but something about this place unnerves me.

It doesn't look like anywhere that should make me anxious, though. The white painted brick walls are covered with posters about positivity and inspiration, so my discomfort can't be from them. Who doesn't enjoy seeing a picture of a kitten hanging onto a rope and saying just hang in there?

Directly in front of me, a young blond woman sits behind an old wooden desk that reminds me of the one the high school principal always had in his office. The man never sat down during any meeting I ever had with him. I once mentioned it to Rina, and she remembered he never sat when she was there either. It's an odd memory, but it fills my head as I make my way toward the woman.

"Hi! Can I help you today?" she chirps with a big smile.

It's a good start, and it makes me hopeful I'll be able to find out something about my sister. Holding up the paper in my hand, I return her smile and point at the sun at the top of the page.

"Hi! I'm wondering if you could tell me if you saw a young woman named Rina come in here recently? I found this pamphlet in her apartment, so I was hoping she may have gotten it here."

The blond woman takes the sheet of paper from my hand and reads it before shaking her head. Giving it back to me, she says, "I haven't, but I don't think that's from here. One of our members had an info session earlier this week. I think this is from that."

Not the answer I was hoping for, but at least it's not a dead end.

"Okay. Can you point me in the direction of where I might find him or her?"

"Sure!" the blond says, taking my question literally and pointing toward the corner of the building. "There's a farm about ten miles outside of town. It's actually really easy to find. You just drive down Main Street until you leave town and then keep going straight. The property is on the right."

For a moment, I try to place the location, but it's been years since I was out that way. All there is in that area are farms, and since I wouldn't know what to do on a farm if my life depended on it, I don't tend to think about that part of the county much.

"Okay. Thanks!"

"You're welcome. May The Golden Light shine on you."

I stop in mid-turn and look back at her innocent expression and wide eyes. "I forgot to ask. What is The Golden Light?"

My question makes her entire face light up as if someone flipped a switch and turned on the inside of her body. I don't think I've ever seen anyone so happy in my life.

"The Golden Light is a self-improvement group, but it's so much more too. We work with people who want to make the most of their lives. Each of us has a special talent, and it's our duty as humans to cultivate that talent to help ourselves and the world. We only have one planet, so we have to do all we can to make this world the best it can be."

Her explanation sounds like a combination of a recruitment ad for the military and some quasi self-help jargon. I have a hard time believing Rina spent any time hanging out with people who are so woo-woo, but it sounds relatively innocuous. There's nothing wrong with positivity. In fact, my sister could do with some after her breakup.

"Thank you for your help. Have a great day!" I say, attempting to be as perky as she was.

"Happy to help! May The Golden Light shine on you!"

As I walk toward the door, I see a tiny red light in the corner of the room. When I turn to look at it, I see a camera. Interesting. What's the camera for?

It seems like a strange thing to have in a half-empty room that only has one woman sitting behind a desk. I didn't get a sense anyone else was in the building, but then again, I didn't look in any of the offices.

Still, something about being watched unnerves me.

ALL OF THIS rolls around in my head as I drive out to the farm the blond woman told me about. I forgot to ask the name of the property owner, a stupid mistake for someone whose job is research. Worrying about my sister is definitely throwing me off my groove.

I follow the directions the woman at The Golden Light office gave me, and when I come upon a farm in the exact place she said it would be, I can't help but be a little surprised. It's unfair, but all that golden light stuff and her unrelenting perkiness gave me the impression she wasn't too bright.

A dirt road leading away from the main road takes me to an old, white farmhouse with a huge wraparound porch complete with white rocking chairs. I don't see any people around or any cars, so I wonder if this trip was all for nothing. Discouraged, I consider simply turning around and driving home, but I park the car and get out, needing to at least try to find out if anyone here has seen my sister.

I knock on the front door, but nobody answers, so I walk around the house looking for anyone. The place seems deserted, but when I peek through the window in the back door that leads to the kitchen, I see a tea kettle with steam coming out of the top on the stove.

Thrilled to know there's at least one person in the house who may be able to help me, I knock on the back door and eagerly wait for someone to answer it. The tea kettle begins to whistle loudly, the shrill sound coming through the door loud and clear.

But still no one comes to the kitchen to take it off the burner.

I look around as I wonder where the person boiling the water could be, and right above the door I see a camera just like the one in The Golden Light office. Uncomfortable I'm likely being watched or recorded at this very moment and hating the sound of that tea kettle whistling away like it's calling out for help, I knock hard on the door and stare through the window hoping to see someone come at any second.

After another minute of that piercing sound filling my ears, I jiggle the doorknob and find it unlocked. I shouldn't walk into a strange house, but that kettle is going to run out of water, and I wouldn't want it to cause a fire.

At least that's what I tell myself as I rush into the kitchen and hurry over to the stove. I take the kettle off the burner, so the whistling ends, thankfully. Someone must be here since they were making water for tea, but I see no one when I look into the dining room.

I'm not sure I should go any further into the house, but curiosity gets the better of me and I slowly walk through the dining room to the living room at the front of the house. The home is clean and orderly, but I see stacks of that same pamphlet as my sister had in her apartment spread out all over the coffee table.

"Hello? I'm sorry I came in uninvited, but your kettle was going off, and I didn't want it to cause a fire."

My words seem to go unheard since no one answers me or comes down the stairs to order me out of their house. I walk over to the foot of the staircase and look up, but something tells me I shouldn't go up there.

A sound like a sob makes my blood run cold, and I spin around to get the hell out of the house. Then a terrible thought occurs to me. Could that have been Rina? I think about that for a few moments and decide it wasn't her. Whoever made that noise might need help, so I need to call the police as soon as I get back to my car.

The sound of a man angrily complaining about something stops me dead. Oh, God. He's in the kitchen. I can't leave that way.

I turn around to head for the front door but see another man walking toward the house. Damn! I'm trapped here. The man in the kitchen sounded furious, so I don't want to run into him. I have no good reason for being in this house, and they'd have every right to not be pleased with my intruding.

Frantic, I look for somewhere to hide and see a closet behind the front door. Hopefully, neither of the men need to look for anything in there, but it's my only choice at the moment.

Rushing over, I thankfully find nothing but a single winter coat hanging on a rod. I close the door, shutting me in the darkness, and crouch down to make myself small, silently praying to God no one finds me.

As I listen, I hear the first man continue to angrily complain about someone screwing something up. His words don't make sense, but I can clearly understand he's enraged. The second man joins him, but he seems less unhappy and more confused about why the first man is so upset. It's hard to make out every word because they're too far away in the dining room, but something bad has happened.

Pressing my ear to the door, I strain to hear their conversation, but then their words come through loud and clear when I assume the two of them stop right outside where I'm hiding. Suddenly, the man's anger becomes all too real, and I shake, terrified he's going to find me.

"I swear I'm going to lose my cool one of these days," the angry man grumbles.

The other man chuckles. "You have to learn to calm down, man. Remember the golden light?"

A sound like a growl fills my ears, followed by the first man's response. "Somebody better tell Maren about the golden light. Her screw up is going to fuck us all, you know."

"All we have to do is get her and the girl and bring them back to the farm. Let's not make it harder than it has to be."

"It wouldn't be hard if Maren hadn't fucking gotten rough with her. You should have heard how she sounded on the phone. I'm not sure what the hell we're going to find when we get up there."

The heavy sound of footsteps going up the stairs makes hearing any more of their conversation impossible. I don't know what they were talking about, but it doesn't sound good. It certainly doesn't sound positive.

No cute cat posters in this place.

I need to get the hell away from here and figure out what to do next to find Rina, so I wait until the footsteps are only on the second floor and then bolt out of the closet. Adrenaline courses through me as I tear through the house and out the kitchen door. I've never run so fast in my life, and a few seconds later I reach my car.

Still terrified someone may have seen me, I get into my car and throw it into reverse to back out of the parking spot. A man appears in one of the upstairs windows, and even yards away, I see the rage in his eyes. God help the woman who has to deal with him up in that room. I wish I could help, but all I can do is drive to the police station and tell them what I heard.

I slam my foot onto the gas pedal and speed down the access road, leaving a cloud of dirt and dust behind me. By the time I get to the main road, my heart is beating so fast I think I might vomit. I don't know what I just heard, but I think someone is hurt and may be in danger from at least one of those men.

Glancing at my watch, I see it's just before two. Good. I'll include that in what I tell the police. I'll tell them that farmhouse is connected to The Golden Light, whatever the hell that is.

Self-improvement and positivity my ass. Something very bad is going on at that house and with these golden light people.

4

NASH

As ADAM FOCUSES his anger on Maren for being stupid enough to bring a new recruit here because she wanted to get some before handing her over to us like she's supposed to, I watch out the window while a car speeds away from the farmhouse. I didn't see anyone but us and Maren with that chick upstairs, but someone must have been hiding downstairs.

I stare at the driver, trying to memorize her face in case she shows up again, but she's too far away for me to make out her features. She has light brown hair that reminds me of that girl I liked in high school. It's odd that I should notice that since most of the time the way a person's hair looks doesn't make much of an impression on me.

"What the fuck are you looking at, man?" Adam snaps at me. "A little help here would be nice."

He's such a dick. As if handling a woman who weighs no more than a buck twenty is work. It's not like the other one is giving him any hassle anymore since he knocked her out. He's as big as I am, and I could carry both of them out of this house with their arms and legs flailing the whole time.

I slowly turn around and look down at him sprawled out on the floor with Maren slapping her hands off his chest. How hard would it be to simply pin her arms above her head to calm her down? Maybe if he didn't make everything a fucking hassle this wouldn't happen to him.

"Which one do you need help with?" I ask and then chuckle. "The unconscious one or the one doing her own idiotic version of shadowboxing?"

Angry, like always, he shoves Maren into the wall before standing up. "Take this bitch. I'll handle the other one."

He grabs the unconscious blond girl and throws her over his shoulder before storming past me. Her head bounces off the doorframe, but he doesn't notice or doesn't care and keeps walking to the stairs.

Maren sobs in the corner, so I slowly approach her to avoid upsetting her even more. She stares at me with madness in her dark eyes, looking like a wild animal someone made the mistake of trapping.

Great. Just what I need today.

"Calm down," I say as I stop in front of her. "There's no need to freak out. You know we have to go back to the farm. Just take it easy, and we'll be fine."

She shakes her head as she wipes the tears and mascara that have run down her face. "I don't trust you. I saw you beat the hell out of someone in the great room the other day."

I nod since she's right. I did have to punish someone, but it's not like I was beating on a woman like her. The guy was nearly my size and had to be at least six feet tall, so I wasn't exactly picking on a helpless victim. Anyway, he broke the rules and knew what would happen when he did. I was just the one who had to impose the penalty.

"Well, I don't plan to beat the hell out of you, Maren. Just behave and we'll do fine."

After taking a deep breath in and letting it out in a rush, she pulls her knees to her chest. "What about him? Something tells me he isn't thinking the same way."

I shrug because she's not wrong. Adam is always up for inflicting pain on people. Male or female, adult or child, if he can take out his rage on someone, he's a happy guy. Thank God he's rarely given permission. He's likely to get grief for the way he acted toward Maren today, but he doesn't care about that.

"Let me handle him. I just need you to come with us. Keep quiet and don't fight, and I'll make sure he doesn't step out of line, okay?"

Looking around for Adam, I'm happy he seems to be waiting in the car. I don't need his bullshit for being kind to her. Just because he doesn't have a nice bone in his body doesn't mean I have to be an asshole to anyone.

Our job is to get her back to the farm. Nobody instructed me to use violence to do it. We're guards for The Golden Light. That doesn't mean we have to go around hurting everyone.

Maren continues to shake her head. "I don't trust you."

I crouch down and look her directly in the eyes. "I don't care. I have a job to do. I need to bring you back so you can find The Golden Light again. It's that simple. I have no interest in hurting you, but if I can't get you to come peacefully, I'll do what I have to. So what's it going to be?"

"He's going to punish me," she says in a trembling voice.

Unsure who she means, I ask, "Adam? I just told you if you don't fight me I won't do a thing. He won't either."

Barely loud enough for me to hear, she answers, "No. Micah."

I blow the air out of my lungs. "Probably. You knew the rules when you joined The Golden Light, Maren."

She lowers her head to her chest so it's even harder to hear what she says. "I just wanted to spend some time with her. We have a connection. Why can't he understand that?"

This is not a conversation I want to have. I know why Micah doesn't allow group members to leave the farm to be together. She does too. She just doesn't want to admit it. It's not like he ever makes his opinion a secret, especially when it comes to members doing things without his permission. She didn't ask to be with that girl, so she broke the rules. It's that simple. Why she wants to draw this out and make things worse is beyond me.

"Come on. It's time to go. If we keep Adam waiting any longer, he's going to come up here, and then we'll both have to deal with what he does to you."

I stand up and extend my hand to help her up, but she refuses to take it. Instead, she pushes herself up on her own, backing away from me when she gets up on her feet.

She makes her way to the hallway as I follow her, but when we begin walking down the stairs, she stops midway, shaking her head again. Jesus, this woman is a goddamned hassle. She agreed to the rules when she joined us, yet now she wants to act like she's fucking surprised she's in trouble.

Maybe I should just let Adam deal with her.

"Keep moving, Maren."

Looking back at me, she starts to cry. "I don't want to go into the box. Please tell Micah I wasn't bad for you. He might not put me in there."

She's confused if she thinks anything I say will help her. I'm just one of his guards. Nothing more. As for the box, that's where his favorite punishment happens, so she's going in. She should just accept it and deal instead of dragging her feet like this.

But since she's going to be a pain in the ass if I make her see the truth, I force a smile and say, "I will."

That seems to put her at ease, and she begins walking down the stairs again. By the time we reach the first floor, I'm tired of doing this with her and almost ready to just throw her over my shoulder like Adam did with that other girl to expedite things.

As we walk through the house toward the back door, she mumbles, "I loved living in this house. It was left to me by my grandfather."

Behind her, I say, "And now it's Micah's."

She glances back at me and nods. Maren knows the rules. To be a part of The Golden Light, you have to sign over anything you own to Micah. He knows best how to manage everyone's possessions, especially since they never fail to make people think of life outside the group. She heard all of this the day she joined, so I don't understand why she's acting like this now.

When we reach the kitchen, she stares straight ahead and whispers, "Please tell him I never stopped believing."

I don't respond, so she turns around and looks up at me with a sadness in her eyes that hits me in the center of my chest. "Will you? Please?"

Answering with a nod, I expect her to keep walking, but she stops like she's waiting for me to tell her I will do as she wants. Since we need to get moving, I reluctantly answer her, even though I have no intention of getting in the middle of this mess.

"Sure. I will."

Relief seems to wash over her, and although she has nothing to be happy about at this moment, she gives me a tiny smile. "Thank you."

Personally, all I can think of is how relieved I'll be when we finally get in the car. At least then I'll know she's accepted what's going to happen.

When we step out onto the porch, the heat of the day hits me like a brick wall. Summer in the mid-Atlantic is always steamy, but this is stifling. Thank God I don't have to do anything physical today. I don't think I have it in me.

No wonder Maren's terrified of the box. It's going to be over a hundred and ten degrees in there.

Her foot hits the first step on the way down to the

yard, and in an instant, she's off like a shot across the grass before I even realize what she's doing. Damnit! And here I thought she understood how this had to go.

I watch her run like a madwoman for about ten seconds before breaking into a sprint to go after her. Sweat pours down the sides of my face because of the heat and humidity, but there's no way I'm going back to the farm without her. I'm not going to suffer because she's lost her goddamned mind.

"Maren! Don't make it worse than it already is. Stop right now!" I call out, but she keeps running.

Son of a bitch! She's going to be lucky if I don't let that fucker Adam handle this when I finally get a hold of her.

From around the side of the house, I see him come bolting past me and know this isn't going to end well. I yell to her to stop once more, but it's no use.

This is out of my control now.

A moment later, I watch Adam take out his piece and my heart sinks. He's going to say we were justified in doing it, but Micah isn't going to be happy about her dying.

"Adam! We can catch her," I yell to him, but it's like he can't hear me. "Just get her and put the gun away!"

My words get lost in the heavy air that's making it hard for me to keep running, and a second later, the sound of a gunshot pierces the silence. Maren drops to the ground like a hundred pound sack of dirt. I keep running because I don't know what he'll do to her if he gets to her first. My heart slams into my chest and my thigh muscles feel like they're going to explode from under the skin, but I have to beat him to where she lies.

Thankfully, his passion for inflicting pain evaporates once he sees her go down, and I blow by him. When I reach her, I know she's dead. I still crouch down to check her pulse because something inside me says that's what I'm supposed to do.

My fingers press against her neck, but I feel nothing. Not even a faint heartbeat to cling to for a few moments.

Behind me, Adam grunts out, "Serves her right. Fucking bitch. Scoop her ass up and take her to the car."

The sight of Maren lying there lifeless turns my stomach. Even though I've killed before, something about seeing her dead in the green grass with the bright sun shining down on her feels wrong.

Slowly, I turn around as bile inches up into my throat. Adam looks particularly pleased with himself, which pisses me off more. I want to smack that smug smile off his face right now.

"You do it. You killed her."

As I begin to walk away toward the car, I hear him grumble something, so I spin around to face him. "What? If you have something to say, say it or shut the fuck up."

I don't know where this anger is coming from, but if he wants to push me on this, he's going to be surprised. Adam stares at me in shock, probably confused because I've never pushed back against anything he's ever told me to do, despite the fact that he's not my superior, and I see in his expression that he understands he's standing just on the line. If he wants to step over that line, he better be ready for what's coming at him.

Like a fever breaking, he laughs and shrugs. "Fine. I

don't care. It's not like it's a lot of work for me to carry her to the car. Whatever."

He lifts her in his arms, and her lifeless head flops over his bicep. Her eyes are still open, and it's like she's staring into my soul and silently indicting me for letting this happen to her. I look away and start for the car, sick and tired of this fucking day already.

Adam returns to barking out orders, but I'm not listening. All I can hear is Maren's soft voice in my head asking me to tell Micah she never stopped believing.

5

LARA

OFFICER STALEY LOOKS across his desk at me like I've just told him my lunch order and he isn't impressed with my choice of a turkey club. There's no sense of immediacy in his behavior. He heard me say someone is in danger out at that farmhouse and reacted with nothing.

No shock. No worry. Not even a widening of his eyes with a tiny bit of surprise.

All he can muster is leaning back in his chair far enough that I'm sure it's going to topple over and dump him onto the floor. I say do it, chair. At least it would make me happier than I am now trying to figure out how the hell to get him to give a damn about what I heard out at that farmhouse.

"You've always had an active imagination, Lara. I bet it's why you're good at your job. Are you still at that online magazine? What was it called again?"

His transparent attempt at flattery in an effort to distract me does nothing but irritate me. I've known Dustin Staley since grade school. I even thought he was cute in the ninth grade and considered going with him to the fall dance. I didn't because he came down with strep throat, but for a short time, I actually liked this person and considered kissing him.

Now all I want to do is smack some sense into him. This is what happens when you don't leave the same small town you grew up in to go to college. At least if he had ventured out to the next county for a while, the nothingness of this town wouldn't be so ingrained in his very marrow.

"You know full well I work at Good News, Dustin. Come on. I know you're not completely brain dead like the rest of this police force. You know me. You know I wouldn't come here to report something that I didn't witness. Something's going on out at that farmhouse. Can you just check it out? I think that Golden Light group is up to something there."

Nothing I say sways him. With a shrug, he leans forward in his chair and says, "I'll drive out there in a little while. That's the best I can do."

Truer words have never been spoken.

"Thanks, Dustin. You're a real servant of the people. By the way, I don't know how much good it will do to tell you this, but my sister is missing. I think that has something to do with that weird group."

The mention of my sister perks him up, and suddenly, he's writing down details of my report. "Rina? Where do you think she could be?"

I swear to God this man gets dumber every second I'm here with him.

"If I knew where she was, Dustin, she wouldn't be missing. I found one of The Golden Light's pamphlets in her apartment this morning. I've been calling her for two days but she isn't home."

He stops writing and looks over at me. "Any chance she went back to that boyfriend of hers? He does like to take her away."

I hate this man for bringing up her ex-boyfriend. Everyone in town knows that Rina broke up with him when he threatened to kill her. She got a protection from abuse order from the court because she was so afraid he might follow through on his threat. Dustin knows all of this, and still he thinks she might have gone back to Jamie.

Standing, I turn to leave without bothering to say goodbye or thank you. Why would I bother? He hasn't done a damn thing to help me.

"Lara, come on. Don't go. I wrote down everything you said. I'll drive out there. I swear."

I wave his pathetic efforts away as I walk toward the door. "Whatever, Dustin. Keep serving and protecting."

"As soon as something touches on religion, we can't do a thing about it. You know that, Lara."

Religion my ass.

When I step out into the afternoon sun and the day's heat hits me, I almost feel like giving up. The police aren't interested in what I have to say. I doubt Dustin will even drive by that farmhouse.

Blowing the air out of my lungs, I feel nothing short

of defeated. I want to help whoever that woman is out there, but I have to find my sister. I don't have time to do both.

Then an idea comes to me. My boss is always asking me if I'm going to take any of my vacation time. I've actually thought he might ask me to give him some of mine for his many breaks he likes to take from work. He hasn't gone that far, but he has brought up my taking some time off on more than a few occasions in the past weeks.

Maybe it's time I take him up on that much-needed break. I have two weeks of vacation due me, and I can use that to look for Rina. Hopefully, I find her easily and then we can goof around for a week or so getting tans and watching chick flicks.

I fish out my phone from the bottom of my purse and call Mario. He answers in a rush like he's hurrying somewhere.

"Hello?"

"Hi, Mario. It's Lara."

"Hey, Lara. What's up?"

"I need to take a couple weeks off. My vacation will start today."

To my surprise, he isn't enthusiastic about my news. "I don't know, Lara. You know things get busy around this time. We're planning the October edition, and I swear if I hear one more writer suggest a story about how Halloween costumes have grown into cosplay, heads are going to roll."

"I already gave you my suggestions for articles, Mario. You loved them. Remember? Salem and the witch connection to this area of Delaware? There were others, but that was the one you thought would work best."

He's silent for a long moment before he hums and answers, "Oh, right. Still, two weeks is a lot, Lara."

"You're always telling me I need to take my time off, and when I finally decide to, you're going to give me a hard time? You have my article pitch. I turned in my work the other day, so I'm not behind on anything."

A heavy sigh comes through the phone. "Okay. You're right. So why do you suddenly need to take a couple weeks off?"

"I have a family issue. I will say this, though. You might get the biggest story the magazine has ever had if things work out."

"What does that mean?"

"I can't really tell you right now, but let's just say this time off might not be all about lying around at the pool working on my tan if things go south. Just trust me on this, Mario. I've never let you down before, have I?"

"Well, no, but there's always a first time for everything."

Always the optimist, this guy.

"That's the way to think. Ever tried the glass half full vibe, Mario? It might make you a happier person."

That gets me another sigh. "My ex-wife used to say that all the time. It's just not my style."

"It's okay, Mario. We are who we are. By the way, you probably won't be able to get in touch with me for the next couple weeks, but know that if I can use anything I find out, I promise to give you an article that will knock your socks off."

"Find out? Find out what? What are you looking into?" he asks with a hint of concern to his voice.

"Not to worry. Talk to you in a couple weeks. Bye!"

And with that, I end the call and throw my phone back in my purse. The police don't seem interested in my sister being missing, so it's up to me to find her.

Remembering something Rina mentioned about meeting up with some new friends of hers, I think I know exactly where to look.

6

LARA

YESTERDAY, I decided to check out The Golden Light group to see if Rina is with them. Then I had a head full of steam and the confidence I could do this.

This morning is a completely different issue. The group sounds like a cult. I'm not sure what I'm getting into. But what choice do I have? If Rina is with them, with or without her permission, I have to know. It's not like her to be gone for days without telling me.

It's just that the sound of that woman sobbing out at that farmhouse the group uses still echoes in my head. Something terrible happened there.

Last night, I remembered Rina mentioning meeting some new people in Wilmington, so that's where I have to go today. She didn't specifically mention The Golden Light, but she did say something about how nice these new people were and how they were looking to have people join their group. Hopefully, they know something about where she is.

As I settle in behind the wheel, my phone vibrates and my heart soars. It's got to be Rina. I'll listen to her, but she better have a good reason for scaring me like this. What good is calling me her best friend if she doesn't tell me the important things, like where she's going for days?

Searching for my phone in the bottom of my purse, I feel around until the cool metal touches my palm. I lift it out and answer it without even looking at the name on the screen.

"You better have a good reason for making me worry these past few days, chickie."

That's what we call one another when we're upset. I listen for her to start explaining herself, but instead, I hear my mother's voice.

"What do you mean? Who's making you worry? Are you talking about your sister? I knew you were lying yesterday. You're a terrible liar, Lara. Now tell me what's going on."

I close my eyes and wish to be anywhere doing anything other than this with her. "Mom, it's no big deal. Rina has just been ignoring my calls for a few days. She's probably mad at me. You know how she gets."

Much of that is a lie. While it's true my sister does have a habit of going inside herself when she's upset, it's rare that she pulls that kind of thing on me. We're too close for that. I just don't want my mother freaking out and thinking my sister is missing.

Even if she is.

"What did you do? You know your sister is more

sensitive than you are, Lara. You probably bullied her into doing something she didn't want to do. You've always done that ever since you were a child."

Her words sting, and I try to hold back from saying anything in response, but I fail miserably. "I don't bully anyone, including Rina. Now that you've upset me, I have to go, Mom. Don't worry about her or me. We're fine. I'll call you later, okay?"

"Don't be so touchy, Lara."

"It's okay for Rina to be sensitive, but when I am, I'm a bad guy? Okay. Got it. I have to go, Mom. Talk to you later."

Before she can give me any more grief, I end the call and toss my phone back into my purse. Bully my sister? Where does she get this stuff? The only bully in our family is her.

I need to calm down before I make the drive to Wilmington. Why does she call me if she's going to act that way?

HALF AN HOUR LATER, I park my car and start looking for Rina or anyone with The Golden Light. I still have a hard time believing she'd join their group, even if it is all about positivity. It just doesn't sound like something she would do.

I search street after street and see no one who might help me. An hour goes by, and all I have to show for it are sore feet and my favorite pink T-shirt with the cherries on it drenched and stuck to my skin. Discouraged, I sit down on a bench near the entrance of a park and wonder what to do next.

It's a beautiful sunny day, although the shade from the tree nearby is a godsend since it's nearly ninety out today. Leaning back, I close my eyes. Where could Rina be?

"Have you ever truly known love?" a soft voice asks.

I open my eyes to see a pretty blond girl who looks to be no more than twenty-years-old wearing a pale yellow sundress standing in front of me. Her face looks as innocent as a small child's, so even though I was irritated at her interrupting my rest, I smile up at her.

"Sure."

That's not exactly true since my romantic life has been pretty much a dead zone since my last boyfriend and I parted ways nearly six months ago. She begins to talk about how important love is to the world, and I wonder if someone like her has asked my sister that same question. Rina has been feeling particularly vulnerable after what happened with her ex, and I know how much she wants to meet someone new.

"I'm Melody," the blond girl says. "Isn't it a gorgeous day out?"

I nod, curious about her now. "It is. What are you up to today, Melody?"

She smiles, and with the sunlight behind her, she looks like an angel. "I'm out here today talking to people about love. What's your name?"

For a moment, I consider lying and giving her a fake name, but I dismiss that idea and tell her the truth. "I'm Lara. It's nice to meet you."

"It's so nice to meet you. Would you like to hear about true love and how we can all have it in our lives?"

"Sure, but can I ask you a question first?"

This seems to surprise her, but she nods as she continues beaming a smile. "Okay."

I find a recent picture of my sister on my phone and hold it up for her to look at. "Have you seen this person recently? Her name is Rina. I think she was here in Wilmington recently."

Melody studies the picture of my sister and me when we went out to celebrate my birthday a few months ago and shakes her head. Looking over my phone at me, she says, "I don't think I've seen her. I'm sorry."

Crestfallen, I nod and put my phone back in my purse. "Okay. Thanks."

"Let me ask my friend. I'll be right back."

I watch Melody hurry off to the corner where another blond girl in a similar sundress stands talking to a man who looks less than thrilled at what she's saying. The two females talk for a second, which gives the man a chance to get away, and then they hurry over to where I sit waiting.

"Lara, this is Delilah. She thinks she saw your sister the other day."

My heart skips a beat as excitement courses through me. "Really? Where? Was she okay? What did she say?"

Delilah smiles and takes my hand in hers. "She was full of bliss after I talked to her. She knows love now."

What the hell does that mean?

I stand up and ask her, "Can you show me where she is? It's very important that I find her."

Her smile dims as she shakes her head. "Only if you know love like we do. Would you like to find utter happiness and see the light?"

I know I probably don't want to find out what that really means, but if she can take me to where Rina is, I have to tell her what she wants to hear. "Yes, I would. I want to know love like my sister does. Please take me where I can see her and talk to her."

That makes both Delilah and Melody ecstatic, and they bounce with happiness. "Oh, that's wonderful! We're so happy to have you with us, Lara."

Melody hugs me to her, and I smell the distinct scent of weed on her. No wonder she's so mellow. She's probably as high as a kite.

They each take a hand, and we walk down the street with the two of them singing some song I've never heard before. A niggling doubt that I shouldn't be going with them gnaws at me, but I don't have a choice.

I need to find my sister.

NASH

STANDING at the back of the main building on the farm, I listen as Adam explains what happened with Maren out at the house. He sounds like he's rambling, but if he thinks I'm going to jump in and save him, he's out of his mind.

He shot her. Let him take the heat.

This room, like everywhere else on the farm but Micah's private quarters, has no air conditioning, but if our leader is uncomfortable in these temperatures, he doesn't show it. He simply listens as Adam gives him every damn detail of our trip to Maren's and how she ended up dead in the grass. Surprisingly, he hasn't dogged me out and blamed what happened on me. I expected him to, and I stand ready to jump in and correct any incorrect information he decides to give our leader.

When he finishes, he bows as he must and steps back. Then it's a matter of waiting for Micah to give his opinion and dole out any punishment.

After he confers with Nadine, he looks over toward me and beckons me forward. "Nash, come here. I want to hear what happened from your point of view."

Adam spins around to look at me, frantically staring at me like he's trying to telepathically tell me exactly what to say so he doesn't get into trouble. He's wasting his time. His welfare is not my problem. Maybe he should have thought about the consequences of his actions before he pulled out that damn gun and shot her for no reason.

I stop in front of Micah and Nadine and bow. Then I wait for him to let me stand up straight again.

"Very good, Nash. Now tell me exactly what happened. Leave no detail out."

As I stand up to my full height, I see Micah watching me intently. He thinks I'm going to lie for Adam because we're both guards. Nadine just glares like she hates having me or anyone here interrupting her and Micah.

So I go through every moment we spent out at the farmhouse, concluding with how he shot Maren and then drove back here. When I finish, I bow and step back to wait for his judgment.

"Tell me, Nash, did Maren ask you to tell me anything?" Nadine asks, almost as if she knows she did.

I look at Micah for a moment and then direct my attention to Nadine. "No. She made me promise to tell Micah that she never stopped believing in the light."

"And why didn't you tell me that before?" he asks.

I stand tall and look him directly in the eyes as I answer, "It seemed like it would be a private thing and not something to say in front of anyone but you."

The edge that had been in his voice evaporates when he says, "Agreed. I appreciate your discretion, Nash."

He and Nadine whisper again, and when she steps back, she's smirking. "Adam, you get four hours in the box. Be thankful I'll postpone it until tonight," Micah announces.

Behind me, my fellow guard protests, "But she was running. What was I supposed to do? If anyone deserves punishment, it's Nash. He was supposed to control her. I wouldn't have had to shoot her if he didn't let her run away."

Fucker! I knew I couldn't trust him not to lay this all on me.

Spinning around to face him, I snap, "She was five and a half feet, tops. How far do you think she'd get compared to someone my size chasing after her? I would have caught up to her, but you had to put her down like a rabid dog. This mistake is on you and only you."

I've broken The Golden Light rules by raising my voice to a fellow member, but I'll take whatever punishment Micah gives me in exchange for finally telling Adam the truth. He's dangerous, and everyone needs to know it like I do.

"Enough," Micah says as Adam begins to blame me again. "You'll go in the box tonight. As for Nash, I'll decide what punishment, if any, he deserves."

When Adam won't stop defending himself, Nadine's private guards, who are even more powerful than us, appear in the doorway. She and her men lead Adam away, leaving me alone with Micah. I turn around to see him smiling, which hopefully is a good sign.

"I'm sorry. I shouldn't have spoken out like that, I know. I just didn't want you to believe I'd let Maren die like she wasn't important. But I am sorry, Micah."

Nodding, he sighs like all that's happened weighs heavily on him. "I understand, and I'm happy you appreciate how important every member of The Golden Light is to me. I'm their leader, and it hurts my heart when anyone suffers."

We aren't equals, so I don't respond like we're having a conversation. Micah is the supreme leader of The Golden Light. I'm merely a lowly guard whose job is to protect him and do as he orders, like this morning's job that was supposed to be a simple ride out to a farmhouse to retrieve two members and bring them back to the fold.

He stands up from his chair and stretches his arms above his head. "I just got word that we're getting five new recruits today. I want you to be there when they receive their introduction. I've noticed you're quite perceptive, Nash. I want to know your impressions of the new ones."

Surprised he's given me a new job, especially since Adam and the other guards usually handle new people, I nod and wait for more instructions. When he doesn't say anything more, I ask, "Do you want me to come to see you immediately after they're finished?"

Micah looks up toward the beamed ceiling like he's thinking and then smiles. "Yes. And if you think there are any that I should meet immediately, bring them along. Otherwise, I'll meet them when the time comes."

"Okay."

He focuses intently on my face and asks, "You know what I look for, don't you?"

I don't answer with anything more than a nod. I know what he likes in women. Innocent looking. Small. Big tits. Big eyes. Nice mouth.

There's something about rattling off a laundry list of physical features he wants me to keep an eye out for that feels slimy. That's the main reason I've always been satisfied to be a guard and nothing more.

Micah laughs and slaps me on the back as he passes me by. "You know what I'd love? A redhead. If you see one who has what I like, move her to the head of the line."

He leaves me standing in the main meeting room alone, so I hurry to leave, just in case Nadine comes back. Dealing with Micah is intense enough after the day I've had so far. Having to endure one of her interrogations isn't on my list of things I want to go through again.

Once was enough.

I watch as Nadine gives the usual introduction to the new people. The light means unconditional love. They're chosen ones. All the potential in the world exists in them.

It's all very inspirational and positive. It's also nothing vaguely close to what we do here.

Five women. Three remind me of the girls who work on the farm down the road. Nothing much to look at but they seem like they can bench press a tractor. The other two might work for Micah. Neither is a redhead, but the one looks so innocent she might be a virgin.

As for the last one, on second thought I can't see him wanting her. I can't put my finger on it, but something about her seems far too smart for him.

Or this place.

"We're all about bringing out the best in every one of us here at The Golden Light. Each human being deserves to achieve as much as they can, and we're here to help you with that. You'll each have a few days to acclimate to the group, and if you find it's not for you, then you can leave and take whatever you gained here with you. How does that sound?"

Nadine smiles at the five women, and for a moment, I actually want to think she believes what she just said. The problem is nobody ever leaves here. Not for long, at least. Poor Maren is proof of that.

If only she'd just accepted her fate.

All of the new recruits nod, and Nadine claps her hands like she's thrilled she can be part of them achieving all they can be. That self-help positivity shit is just that. Bullshit. Oh, this group may have started out to be a kind of new age gathering of people looking to improve their lives, but those days are long past for The Golden Light.

None of these new people notice that Nadine doesn't ask if they have any questions. That should be their first clue none of what we do here is to help them be anything but followers of Micah. Instead, they excitedly listen to her talk about how finding your true purpose and greatness in this world is truly finding the highest form of love.

It all sounds wonderful, and their expressions tell me they buy it hook, line, and sinker.

"Okay, the first thing we need to do is get you something to eat and something cold to drink. This heat has been oppressive, but like with everything else here at The Golden Light, we want to set you free, so let's go over to the mess right now."

That should be their second clue. We don't call it a dining hall. It's a mess, just like it's referred to in the military. And just like when you join the service, once you sign your name on the dotted line, your life is no longer your own.

The big difference here is there's no getting out. Ever.

I study each woman as she walks out behind Nadine and silently decide only the one with the virginal look to her is worthy of mentioning to Micah. As for the four others, well, the three muscular ones will be welcome additions to the farm. I have no idea what the fifth one will be assigned to. She's not Micah's type, so I doubt she'll be welcomed as one of his favorites. I imagine Nadine will find something for her to do. She always does.

As I follow behind them on my way back to his quarters, that last one looks around like she's searching for something. Her head swivels left and right with each building they pass on their way to the mess while the others simply look straight ahead. What's she so curious about?

The women file into the building near the center of the compound to get their first taste of The Golden Light food and drink. They have no idea that's the first step to keeping them here forever, whether they like it or not.

Micah walks out of his rooms and waves me over to him, so I hurry to where he's standing on his porch and bow. Pointing toward the mess, he asks, "What did you think of them?"

I answer him directly and without including any of my opinions about the women. "Very much like the usual new recruits. Enthusiastic. Eager to find their highest potential."

"Any I'd like?" he asks, cocking a single eyebrow.

Nodding, I answer, "One, possibly. Maybe a virgin. She looks it. The others I don't think so. Three look like they can lift me over their heads, and the other one..."

Before I can find the right words to explain how she seemed a little too curious, he shrugs. "Oh, well. One out of five isn't bad. Twenty percent, right?"

I smile, unsure what that percentage has to do with anything. About a hundred yards away over near the garage, the group member who drove the bus into town so the girls could find the new recruits unloads the other important cargo he had to get while he was away from the farm. With each brown paper bag he takes out of the back of the bus, he sets it down carefully on the dirt before grabbing the next one.

"Did Nadine tell you about the stuff she found that's going to work even better than the stuff we've been using in the food?

I shake my head. I'm the last person she'd tell anything to. Whenever she wasn't gushing about how much we all can't wait to help them reach their full potential and be the people they've always been meant to be, she was glaring at me as I stood in the back of the room as Micah ordered.

He doesn't elaborate about what the bus driver brought back and turns to walk back into his quarters. "Bring the virgin when she's done being fed."

"Yes, Micah," I say and bow as he closes his door.

8

THE OTHER WOMEN Melody and Delilah convinced to join The Golden Light sit down next to me in a large building full of long wooden tables and benches on each side. The setting reminds me of summer camp Rina and I attended every year growing up. When a little girl who looks no more than six or seven with short but wild curly blond hair sets a silver pitcher and a stack of red plastic cups in the center of the table, it definitely makes me think of those weeks I spent at Camp Tioga.

I smile at her to silently say thank you for the drink because the heat of the day has made my mouth parched. She smiles back but then a look of pure terror comes over her, and she hurries away. Looking around for what could have frightened the poor child, I see the woman named Nadine who just gave us our introduction to the group staring in her direction, her dark eyes narrowed as if in anger.

Quickly, I look away, sensing her expression is only a hint at her temper. I don't need to make any waves while I'm here. I want to try to fly under the radar while I'm looking for Rina, so the last thing I need to do is draw attention to myself by noticing something I don't think I was supposed to.

With a hint of rage still showing in her eyes, she says in a sickeningly sweet voice, "Ladies, please eat and drink as much as you'd like. I know the bus ride was long, and in this heat, I'm sure it wasn't the most comfortable hour and a half you've ever spent. There's more than enough to eat and drink, and I see little Kinley coming right now with a tray of cookies her mother made this morning. Enjoy!"

I look around to see a different young girl who looks slightly older than the other one but with the same unruly curly hair. Kinley's is longer than the other girl's and even blonder. She's dwarfed by a huge platter she struggles to carry, but Nadine doesn't move an inch to offer any assistance.

As she attempts to walk as fast as possible to deliver her mother's cookies, I watch in horror as she trips over her little feet, and the platter with all its goodies flies out of her hands and lands on the floor, scattering the cookies all over the place. I hurry over to her expecting her to break into tears, but she simply looks petrified and stares up at Nadine in utter terror.

"I'm sorry. I didn't mean to do it," she says in a tiny, trembling voice.

Worried Nadine might scold her or worse, I turn to look at the woman and stare her down. This child did nothing wrong. I will not let her be punished.

For a second, it's like the whole world is frozen in place. No one moves, including Nadine, but I see in her eyes she's furious even though her smile hasn't faded at all. I've read that homicidal maniacs act like that with expressions that don't match their eyes. I don't know if she's dangerous, but I can see quite clearly she's fighting with everything she has inside her to pretend she isn't angry.

Then, as if someone starts the world again, she says in that same sickeningly sweet voice, "It's okay, Kinley. Here, let me make sure you're okay."

I know I should move and let her get close to the little girl, but the terror in the child's eyes makes me stay put next to her as the woman crouches down to inspect her knees. They're a little red but not scraped, thankfully, and Nadine gives her a kiss on the cheek to make her feel better.

"A-OK. Run along now and go to your mother, okay? Tell her we need more cookies."

Kinley nods and then jumps up before running away. As I stand to rejoin the group, Nadine smiles at me, but it's the kind of grin that a crocodile gives someone right before devouring them.

"She'll be fine."

"I was worried she may have hurt herself. Perhaps she should have some help with the next tray. I'd be happy to walk with her. Just tell me where to find her and her mother," I say as sweetly as I can, hoping she can't tell how much I disapprove of her right now.

"Thank you, Lara. She'll be fine."

Again with the fine. God, I hope her mother helps her this next time because if poor little Kinley drops another tray of cookies, I have a feeling Nadine isn't going to be able to hide how furious she'll be over another mistake.

As I sit down next to the other women, the girl comes walking into the dining hall all alone once again with a plate of cookies. This time the tray's a little smaller, so she has no problem delivering her treats to our table. She smiles up at Nadine, but even as she gets a kind look from her, I swear I see terror in her eyes.

"Please, enjoy these cookies and some lemonade. It's been very hot today, so we don't want anyone to become dehydrated or get sick. I'm going to thank Kinley's mother for her wonderful baking, but I'll be back in a few minutes."

She walks away behind the little girl, and we all reach for a cookie from the pile on the blue platter. Each one is shaped like a star, and I have to say I'm a little surprised they aren't in the shape of that sun with beams coming out I've seen on nearly everything associated with this group so far. Then again, maybe that would be too hard to make into cookies. I'm sure the star shape is meant to symbolize something, like we're all capable of being superstars in the world.

My first bite of Kinley's mother's cookies surprises me with how delicious they are. Buttery and light, they're instantly addictive. Everyone around me gobbles them up, and I can't deny how tasty they are. Even though I didn't think I was hungry, I take a second and then a third one.

After a couple minutes, one woman stands up from the bench and grabs the silver pitcher in the center of the table. Tall with wide shoulders that seem big for a female, she looks around at all of us and asks, "Would anyone like some?"

We all nod and reach for a red cup, and she pours for each of us. Lifting her cup in the air, she smiles. "To having all we ever wanted in life!"

It seems like a nice toast, so I lift my glass with the rest of the women and then glance into my cup to see what looks like pink lemonade. I'm thirsty enough to drink anything after three cookies, so I take a big gulp and revel in how good it tastes as it slides over my taste-buds and down my throat.

"This is the best lemonade I've ever had," the woman with short black hair says before pouring herself another glassful.

Next to her, a plain-looking young woman with light brown hair I'm guessing is around my age nods. "It is. I usually don't like lemonade, but this stuff is incredible."

I want to say we're probably just thirsty so that's why what I'm guessing is pretty ordinary pink lemonade tastes so refreshing, but as each woman around me raves about how good it is, I decide being different in this case isn't going to help me. I'm not here to make friends or find the way to get all I ever wanted, but it won't help me find Rina by making myself stand out as a contrarian.

Anyway, what does it hurt to let them believe this lemonade is the best drink they've ever tasted?

Everyone's tongue loosens with the snacks, and it doesn't take long for us to be comfortable enough to introduce ourselves. The woman who poured the lemonade starts first, and I learn her name is Bethany and she lives on a farm not even a mile away.

"My parents would kill me if they knew I was here, but when I met Charlotte this morning and she started telling me about this place, I wanted to see for myself if it's that great. All I can say is if everything else is as incredible as those cookies and lemonade, I'm in!"

Everyone laughs at that as they nod their agreement, and the woman directly across from her on the other side of the table is next to speak up. "Hi everyone! I'm Mary. I know. Who names their kid that in the twenty-first century, right?" she asks with a nervous chuckle.

The one I judge to be the youngest of us sits next to her and shakes her head. "I think it's a pretty name. You know, names our grandmothers used to have are all coming back into vogue nowadays. That's why my mother and father named me Anna."

She suddenly stops talking and turns her body toward Mary. "Oh, I'm sorry. I didn't mean to horn in on you."

Mary waves off any concern and smiles big to show off perfect teeth. "It's okay, Anna. Nice to meet you!"

Relief washes over the younger woman's expression, which now seems incredibly innocent, but she lowers her head to hide her face when she does. I watch to see if I can figure out what she doesn't want us to see, but her chin practically touches her chest, so all that's visible is the top of her head and the straightest part possible through dark brown hair.

The one next to her raises her hand as if we're all still in school and says, "Okay, I guess I'm next. I'm Cheyenne, and I guess I'm the exact opposite of them. My father says that my mother chose my name from some book he can't remember, but because she's dead, I doubt I'll ever know what it was."

Something about how easily she confesses all of that makes me think she's repeated those sentences many times in her past. Maybe kids in grade school made fun of her name, so she came up with a justification for why her parents gave her it that made everyone feel bad for picking on her. Or maybe she's joined other groups like this and that's her standard introduction.

Whatever it is, the way she mentioned her mother being dead causes a momentary pall to come over the group. I'm the only one who hasn't explained who she is, but now it feels awkward to just pipe up with my name and how I got here. So I wait for a little while and smile when Bethany turns to look at me as if she's decided it's time to move on from the brief sadness Cheyenne interjected into what had been a lighthearted time.

Everyone else follows Bethany's lead and looks at me, so I smile and say, "I'm Lara, and I guess I'm here because a girl named Melody saw me sitting on a park bench in Wilmington and started telling me about love. She asked me if I wanted to feel pure love, and here I am."

My introduction is technically true but leaves out the real reason I agreed to come along when Melody and Delilah asked me to join them. I can't afford to have anyone know the truth of why I'm here. Not if I want to find out what happened to my sister.

Mary looks across the table at me and sighs. "Lara. That's such a beautiful name. I bet your mother researched pretty names and chose that one when she first saw you."

A chuckle explodes out of me, horrifying her and everyone else around the table, so I quickly explain, "Oh, maybe. It's just that if you met my mother, you'd know she probably didn't do much research at all. I'm guessing she saw a movie one night right before I was born and remembered my name from some character."

Next to me, Bethany looks at me with nothing short of pity filling her eyes. "You don't know why your parents chose to name you Lara?"

I shake my head as four pairs of eyes stare at me like I'm some kind of alien. "Not really. My mother definitely had a reason for my sister's name, but she's never given any reason for naming me Lara."

Before I can change the subject, Bethany asks, "What's your sister's name?"

Damn. I let my guard down for a tiny moment and now I've gotten myself into a discussion I don't want to be in. Quickly, I think of a different name than Rina and a reason my mother chose it.

"Mina. My mother loved the book Dracula, so she always said she wanted to name her daughter that."

Anna nods like she understands. "My older sister has a name like that too. She got to be named Daisy because my father loved The Great Gatsby. I guess younger sisters get the short end of the stick, huh?"

I smile like I agree with her assumption that my sister is older than I am and look around for Nadine. As much as she makes me uneasy, I'd love for her to interrupt this little chat session so I don't have to make up any more lies. When I see her walking back into the building, I'm oddly thankful for her return.

Her arms spread wide, she smiles and says, "Ladies, let's get you introduced to some of the other people in our little group. I think you're going to really love meeting people just like you, people who believe that they deserve to have all they want in this life."

The other four women hurriedly stand and walk toward where she's waiting, so I follow them, even though I'm pretty sick and tired of this positivity thing she likes to preach. I don't think she believes it for a second, so to me it rings hollow.

None of what The Golden Light has to say means a thing to me. It's all puffed up words, and if I didn't think that before she reacted to little Kinley's mistake, I knew it by how hard she had to work to keep her rage under wraps. This group, whatever they truly believe, isn't what they claim, and I don't want to stick around long enough to find out what the truth is.

All I want to do is find Rina and take her home.

9

LARA

A NOISE that sounds like a chime or a bell wakes me, and I open my eyes after the soundest sleep I've had in years. I don't think I tossed or turned, and one glance down my body tells me I'm right. The sheets and blanket look exactly like they did when I laid down last night in this cabin with the other four new recruits from yesterday.

I didn't get a chance to look around much at all after the break with the cookies and lemonade. Nadine took us all to meet Kinley's mother and the other women whose only job it seems is to make treats for everyone here. Much of the rest of the day is hazy to me now as I try to remember what happened after that and for the time until we all went to bed, though.

Odd that I can't put together what I did for what had to be at least six or seven hours. I must have been pretty exhausted.

Everyone but Anna is up and chatting as I swing my legs out of the twin size bed and set my feet on the wood plank floor. They must be morning people. I stand up and stretch, loving how rested I feel this morning. Maybe all this positivity is more than just talk.

"Breakfast is in ten minutes, so up and at 'em, ladies!" a woman says in a perky voice that usually would irritate me so early in the day.

I look over and see a woman near the door I haven't met yet. Odd that there don't seem to be many men here. I don't think I've seen half a dozen yet. I wonder why.

Anna still lies in bed with the covers over her head, so I lean over and nudge what I think is her shoulder. "Time to wake up. It's like camp. They expect you to get up and eat breakfast when they call."

As I turn to straighten the covers and make my bed, I notice she doesn't move. She must not be an early riser. I get it. Normally, I'm not either. My usual day starts with me bargaining with myself that if I get up and do what I need to do to get to work on time, I'll give myself a treat. That kind of self-bribery is the only way I've found that works to motivate me to actually get out of bed before noon.

When I finish, I nudge her again. "Anna, time to rise and shine. These people seem pretty serious about attacking the day right out of the gate. Not that I don't get how you feel. Trust me. If I didn't sleep like a rock last night, I'd be right with you on staying in until lunch."

Once more, she doesn't move. I don't want to be the kind of person my mother is in the morning and throw the covers off her, but I worry if Nadine sees she's still asleep, she's not going to like it. I get the feeling she's up with the sun, that one.

"Come on, Anna. Maybe they'll have more of those cookies today. Those were tasty, weren't they?"

From the other side of the cabin, Bethany asks, "What's up, Lara? Anna still knocked out?"

I shrug as she marches over toward where I stand between our beds. "I've nudged her twice. I don't think she's into waking up this early."

"No problem. My brother used to be like this every school day. Weekends the kid was up like a shot at six a.m. sharp. Once Monday rolled around, we practically had to pry him out of the bed. I'll wake her."

I watch her lift the blanket and sheet to reveal Anna's feet and then begin to tickle them. "Wakey wakey. Time to greet the day."

She tries again with no success and then wraps her long fingers around Anna's toes. Turning to look up at me, she says, "Her feet are cold."

"Cold? It couldn't have gotten below seventy last night," I say as the other three women come over to stand around Anna's bed.

Bethany pulls the covers back from her face, and Anna's eyes stare straight ahead. My gaze moves to her chest to see if she's breathing. As second after second ticks by, she doesn't move.

She's dead.

Mary screams and runs away toward the door while the rest of us just stand there in shock. I want to look away at anything other than the frozen expression on Anna's face, but I can't. I just stare at her in utter confusion as to how someone so young could die not six feet away from me and I never heard a thing to let me know something was wrong.

Did she cry out in pain? I didn't hear anything. At least I don't think I did.

Frantically, I try to remember the events of last night when we all came to this cabin to go to bed, but nothing seems definite. I think I know we all walked in together and said goodnight before we all went to sleep, but I can't say for sure. I don't think I heard her in any distress during the night, but I can't swear to that either. It's like my memory after we had those cookies and lemonade is full of more holes than Swiss cheese.

The door to the cabin flies open, slamming off the wall, and Nadine marches in with four huge men behind her. They make a beeline to Anna's bed, and I can't help but notice all five of them wear blank expressions. You'd think they'd be more animated since they've just found out someone's died.

We all step back out of their way, and one of the men lifts Anna out of bed and carries her off without looking at any of us or saying a word. The other three men follow him, but Nadine stays behind as Mary sobs over on her bed.

"Ladies, it's time for breakfast. Come. You need to eat," Nadine says without a hint of emotion in her voice.

Bethany hesitates but begins to walk with Cheyenne toward where Mary's sitting on her bed crying. I don't move because it's like I'm frozen to the spot after seeing Anna's dead body lying there. I'm not sobbing like Mary, but at least I understand why she's reacting that way.

What I don't understand is why no one else seems to be upset in the least.

Nadine stares directly into my eyes, almost as if she's silently ordering me to follow the others, but I don't budge. After a few moments, she says in a flat voice, "Time for breakfast, Lara."

"I don't really feel like eating right now. I just saw someone dead in their bed, someone who was just six feet away from me all night. I hope you'll forgive me for not wanting to stuff my face."

Barely able to contain my emotions, I swallow hard to keep myself from crying, but Nadine doesn't miss a beat and says, "Regardless, you need to go to the mess hall for breakfast."

Out of the corner of my eye, I see Mary, Cheyenne, and Bethany watching our conversation and can't figure out why they aren't telling Nadine the same thing I am. We may not have all been best friends, but Anna died in the room we all slept in and all Mary can do is cry while the other two remain silent. I get that how people handle death is a personal thing, but for God's sake, at least back me up and tell this hard-hearted monster glaring at me right now that I'm not wrong for not wanting to eat at this moment.

None of them makes a sound, and all I want to do is scream. Maybe it's because I'm worried about my sister. Or maybe it's because I'm a goddamned human being and not some robot or some scared girl afraid to tell Nadine I won't act like nothing happened just to make her happy.

When I don't move to leave, she grabs a hold of my

left arm and sinks her fingertips into the flesh around my bicep. She's surprisingly rough, and instantly, I'm afraid of her.

"Let go of me! I'm not going to your mess hall to sit down and act like nothing just happened. Anna's dead! Do you think we can have a few damn minutes to process that, or is that not allowed in your shiny, happy people group here? This place is supposed to be about getting all you want out of life. Well, what I want now is a few minutes to mourn a girl I met yesterday who died right next to me!"

Rage flashes in her dark eyes, and when I try to get away, she tightens her hold on my arm. My emotions get the best of me, unraveling because of all that's happened this morning, and I can't stop myself from bursting into tears. I'm not a crier, but the pain of her hand squeezing against my skin and how badly I feel about Anna dying right there in the bed next to mine combines to make it impossible to not fall apart.

Nadine seems more annoyed by my emotional break-down than anything else and yanks me away from my bed, pulling me through the cabin and past the other women who stare at us in horror as we pass. She snaps at them to go eat breakfast before continuing on her way with me in tow behind her like an unruly child being dragged to the principal's office for misbehaving.

When we step outside, the sun feels like a shock to my system. I knew it was daytime, but for some reason I didn't expect it to be so bright out considering what I just went through seeing Anna dead. It feels wrong for the sun to be shining so brightly with her no longer able to bask in its rays.

I repeatedly try to escape Nadine's hold, but her hand holds me like a vice grip. People see us and walk by without even a raised eyebrow at the sight of her forcibly taking me wherever we're going. I try to make eye contact with every single woman who passes us, but none seem bothered enough to even do that for me. They just look straight ahead and give me a hint of a smile, as if anything is worth being happy about.

Is this how people are routinely treated in The Golden Light group? What the hell kind of place is this? How is everyone okay with a seeing a woman pulled across the center of this farm?

As much as I think that, I know the answer already. It didn't take me long yesterday to figure out Nadine is one scary person. Her reaction to poor Kinley's mistake proved that. No wonder not a single soul seeing this wants to do anything to help me.

With each step, I grow more fearful about where she's taking me, but I can't escape the feeling I've screwed up so badly I'll never be able to look for Rina. I want to feel regret for what I did back at the cabin, but I couldn't just see someone dead and then go gobble up a plate of pancakes with syrup and a side of bacon. I may not have known much about Anna, including where she was from or even her last name, but she was a fellow human being who deserved at least to have us take a few minutes to mourn her.

"You're hurting my arm," I cry out, hoping someone nearby will hear me and help.

Nadine looks back and glares at me again. "You need to learn how to behave."

A dozen smart ass remarks pop into my head, but I stop myself from saying any of them. Normally, I'd tell someone like her off. Then again, normally, someone like her wouldn't have grabbed me hard and practically dragged me anywhere.

This place clearly isn't what I'm used to, so in the hopes that I'll be able to get past what's happening right now and stick around this place long enough to search for Rina, I keep my mouth shut. If I can somehow fly under Nadine's radar after this, I might just be able to accomplish what I came here to do.

A large, white building far past the others on the farm stands in front of us, and I sense it's somewhere I probably don't want to see. Not that I have a choice. Her grip as tight as ever, she continues to lead me where she intends for me to go, never looking back at me other than that one time to inform me that I need to learn how to behave.

Who says that to a grown adult woman? I bet she's done this exact same thing to little Kinley at least once. That's probably why she was so terrified when she dropped the tray of cookies. Poor kid.

The door to the white building opens, and out come the four huge guys who came to get Anna's body a few minutes ago. Then they wore blank expressions, but now they stare at me with nothing less than pure rage in their eyes.

I begin to literally drag my feet in the dirt, digging my heels in to stop what seems to be inevitable. I know if those men get their hands on me, something terrible will happen.

"No! I don't want to go in there with any of you!" I scream.

Nadine spins around and flashes me a look of anger that makes me recoil in horror. She raises her hand as if to hit me, but before she can do anything, one of those guys grabs me and throws me over his shoulder like a fifty pound bag of flour.

I kick and scream, but it's no use. The last thing I see before another one of the men closes the door is Nadine sadistically grinning.

10

NASH

FOR FIFTEEN MINUTES, Micah has paced back and forth across the room ranting about how disappointed he is in the membership of The Golden Light. He hasn't said anything about what Adam did to Maren, but I'm guessing that's what brought this on. I never understood why he favored her so much considering she had pretty commonplace looks and an average body. In fact, nothing about her stood out to me as anyone he'd like, especially since I've noticed he tends to go for blond women with big breasts and Maren had mousy brown hair and practically nothing on top.

"How the fuck am I supposed to lead these people with all of this bullshit happening around me?" he barks at the wall before spinning on his heel and marching back toward the other side of the room.

I take this as a rhetorical question because I know for

sure he can't be expecting me to answer him. Even if he did, I wouldn't know what to say. I try not to get too close to anyone here because I've seen what happens when members turn to one another for company.

Maren and her little friend were a prime example, and look how that turned out.

He stops in front of me and folds his arms across his bare chest. I don't look away when his green eyes feel like they're seeing right through me, but I'd rather be anywhere else at this moment than right here with him.

"Tell me where it all went wrong, Nash. I need to know because if I can't figure it out, this entire dream of mine is going to go up in smoke."

Now that's not a rhetorical question, but I still don't rush to answer. I don't know how to answer him. From what I can tell, this dream of his got corrupted the second he let Nadine have a say in anything. The problem is how do I say that and not immediately get sentenced to the box for disrespecting one of the most important people in the group?

After what seems like forever with him staring at me and me staring at him, I open my mouth and slowly convey that idea as carefully as I can. "Maybe the focus should be solely on you instead of including others in leading all of us?"

I watch his eyes get big and immediately add, "It's just that in many organizations, diffused power can lead to confusion among the people below."

Christ, that sounds like bullshit meant to keep me out of trouble. I guess I could say I heard that somewhere, but the less Micah and everyone here know about my past, the better. I'd prefer them to think of me as merely muscle and nothing else.

Slowly, his eyes return to their normal size, and he nods his head. "That's an interesting point, Nash. I think you might be onto something there."

I begin to say it was just something that popped into my head, but before I can get even half of that sentence out, Nadine storms in through the door, slamming it behind her. As usual, she glares at me before fixing her focus on the person she came to see.

"Micah, we have a problem."

For the second time in the last few minutes, I wish I was somewhere else. I set my gaze on the floor and wait for him to order me to leave so they can speak in private, but instead, he begins to pace again.

"I don't want to hear anything more about problems today," he says as he passes me.

"Well, this is a big problem. Actually, we have two problems."

I watch his bare feet walk in my direction again, and then he stops dead right next to me. "Didn't you just hear me, Nadine? I said I don't want to hear anything more about problems today. What about that didn't register in your damn brain?"

A man my size rarely feels uncomfortable when people around them are about to argue. I'm big enough to hold my own with most, including both Micah and Nadine, but I swear I feel like I'm going to vomit from how nervous these two are making me right now. The tension in this room grows by the second, and I have the sense that if I look up, I'll see nothing but rage coming from both of them.

"Micah, do I have to remind you how much I have invested in this dream of yours? I wouldn't be here to tell you about an issue if I didn't think it was important to the integrity of The Golden Light."

The edge in Nadine's voice is unmistakable. I stare at Micah's feet and try to distract myself until he tells me to leave. That's got to happen soon because he's never before allowed me to stay for one of his meetings with her. She's the second most important person in the group, and I'm no one.

Seconds tick by without him saying a word to her or me, and I begin to wonder if he's motioned for me to leave and I didn't see it because I'm staring at the floor and his damn feet. As much as I don't want to look up, I don't have a choice now, so I slowly lift my head and it's worse than I expected.

I've never seen Micah so angry with Nadine, and she looks like she wants to slap him across the face. Since I'm never privy to their private meetings, I haven't experienced the two of them like this before. Maybe this is normal, but I have to work to keep the shock from filling my expression.

He turns to look at me for a long moment before saying to her, "Nash and I were just discussing management of the group. Perhaps I should remind you that I'm the leader of The Golden Light. Not you. Not those four men you keep yourself surrounded by nearly every minute of the day. No, me. People believe in what I say because I am the one who's important here. Remember that, Nadine."

The air around the three of us practically crackles with emotion. I don't return my gaze to the floor and his feet, instead looking at the far wall as I hope they forget I'm here.

Not that he's made that remotely possible since he chose to include me in his speech dressing her down.

Out of the corner of my eye, I see Nadine shaking from anger, and when she begins talking, I'm sure I'll pay for the mistake of not quickly excusing myself when she walked in. "You and Nash? Is he suddenly the person who's footed the bill for this group or the farm where we stand?"

As I stare straight ahead, Micah snaps, "Money is not what The Golden Light has ever been about! Money is merely a means to an end, Nadine. Real happiness is more than dollars and cents. I thought you knew that. Perhaps you should go meditate and see if you can remember what brought you to me."

And then things unravel even worse.

"I'll tell you what, Micah. I'll go meditate, and you and Nash can handle the fact that the new recruit you enjoyed last night died when she was returned to her bed, and now we have another one who's making waves. Do you want to be the one who has to deal with these everyday problems? If so, I'll be happy to spend my time meditating day and night, and you can decide who lives and who doesn't to protect what we have here."

I can't stop myself from looking over at her when I hear

yet another person has died. Even worse, it's a new recruit. Older members are easier to control. They've bought into what Micah is offering with The Golden Light. They believe every word that comes out of his mouth is touched by the divine. He's their leader, but even more, he's their god.

New recruits still have ties to their old lives, and they have people who will be wondering where they've disappeared to. This new death hard on the heels of Maren's passing spells trouble, as does the other woman who's new and causing problems.

The last thing I want to do is be involved in how to handle this new development, but I'm stuck here until Micah tells me I can go.

"That's three this month!" he bellows as he begins to pace again. "What is happening that we have people dying, Nadine? What did the girl have to eat last night? She wasn't in the box, so it must have been something else."

"The same as everyone else. Chantel's cookies and the pink lemonade for a snack a little while after the new recruits arrived, and then dinner like everyone else here. She got no more than anyone else. I don't know what happened, but we need to decide what to do with her now. Bury her in the same place as Maren and that other girl? Go somewhere else on the property and start using land there? And then we need to figure out what to do with the other problem. It would be better if she were dead, but considering that would be four in a month and another new recruit, we might want to deal with her another way."

Micah sits down on the floor and pulls his knees up to

his chest, burying his head in his legs. "I never wanted anyone to die. Never. This wasn't supposed to happen."

The sadness in his voice comes through loud and clear, and it seems to calm Nadine. She crouches next to him, stroking his hair like he's her child and she's eager to make him feel better.

"I can handle this, Micah. You've never doubted me before. Don't let whatever's on your mind today make you start."

He doesn't respond but lets out a heavy sigh. "I don't want anyone else to die. No more death," he says in a voice barely above a whisper, the agony he's feeling hitting me squarely in chest.

"It's okay. No one has to die, Micah. I'll take care of it. I'll take care of everything."

Her words sound so sweet and caring that if I didn't know how Nadine really operates, I'd believe she actually cares about Micah and how upset he is. But I know all too well that this act she's putting on right now has nothing to do with caring about anyone but herself.

He lifts his head and nods. "Okay, but Nash will take care of the girl who's been making trouble."

For a second, the tension that filled the room before returns with a vengeance. I hold my breath expecting her to explode at his suggestion, but then Nadine smiles and presses a kiss to Micah's forehead. "That's fine. We just need to make sure that she understands the girl's death was an accident. That nobody could blame us."

The two of them look over at me, and Micah smiles like he's finally happy again. Nadine's tight expression shows she's less than thrilled by his relying on me to take care of this latest issue, so I quickly look away from her when she levels her gaze on me.

She stands up and starts walking toward the door. "I'll get the guys to deal with the dead girl right now. Don't worry. It will all be okay."

When she leaves, Micah jumps up and comes over to stand in front of me. Gone is the man devastated by the news of another member's death. The person now standing in front of me looks happier than he has the entire time I've been here with him.

What the hell is going on?

"Okay, Nash. Here's what you're going to do. Talk to the new girl. Make her see what we're really about here. I know you can do it. Don't get rough with her, but make sure she understands she isn't to say a word about anything she saw here. Then I want you to bring her to me. Got it?"

I nod, unsure what's happening. Was all that sadness merely an act so he can keep control?

"Go, and know that you're helping me in ways you can't imagine. Do this, and you'll be a favorite of mine, Nash."

Once more, I nod, and then I bow before hastily getting out of there. Who knows what he may have asked me to do if I stayed even a minute longer?

As soon as I step outside into the summer heat, I breathe a sigh of relief, but that quickly passes. Only a few seconds later, Nadine seems to appear out of thin air, and she's nowhere as sweet as she was with Micah.

"I don't know what you're up to, Nash, but you're no

one here. Remember that," she says as she stares up at me with pure hate in her eyes.

"I don't think I'm anyone, Nadine. I only do as I'm told by Micah. I just need you to point me in the direction of the new recruit who's giving us a hard time."

She doesn't bother to answer me and simply points in the direction of the white building at the edge of the farm. "Whatever you're thinking you can do that my men and I can't, don't be fooled. She's a problem, and whether Micah wants to see that or not, she'll have to be dealt with."

Nodding, I turn to walk away, but she grabs my forearm to stop me. Surprised since nobody but Micah has ever touched me here at the farm, I look down at where her fingers sit on my skin and then up at her. As usual, she wears that flinty expression that never fails to make me think all I'd have to do is scratch the surface and I'd find a very dangerous person staring back at me.

"Whatever Micah thinks, I'm more committed to the success of The Golden Light than anyone else here. Including you."

I say nothing, and when she releases her hold on my arm, I walk away, sure there's not another person here I trust less. Whatever's going on, I sense I'm already too involved for my own good.

11

THE SOUND of the new recruit's terrified screams fill the air, so I hurry over to where Nadine's guys are holding her before they do something stupid and we have another dead girl on our hands. I throw open the door and see I might be too late. Three of them hold her down on a sofa while the fourth looms over her threatening to give her a taste of what real pain feels like.

Obviously, none of what Micah's ever preached has sunk in with these goons.

"That's enough," I bellow, knowing I'm likely going to have to deal with a hassle from them. Before they can start claiming they have the right to do what they want because their boss said so, I quickly add, "Nadine needs your help with the dead girl. You don't want to keep her waiting."

That's enough to make the three guys restraining the

new woman hurry toward the door, but the one doing his best to terrify her remains, likely upset I stopped them before he could really do some damage. She scurries away to the corner of the room while he stares me down. About my height of six foot three, he's bigger and may give me a run for my money if I have to fight him. Add to that the perpetually angry look he wears that tells me he enjoys hurting people, and I might be in trouble.

"I'm not done with her yet," he says in a low voice that resembles a growl you might hear from a trapped wild animal.

One glance at the girl tells me she's scared to death, but I can't let him think I'm here to protect her. He needs to believe I've got the same idea he has when it comes to her.

With a shrug, I chuckle. "Fine. Piss off your boss. No skin off my nose. I don't answer to her. All I know is Nadine looked pretty upset when she left Micah after telling him about the dead girl. You know how she likes to take care of things so he doesn't have to."

He stares at me for a long moment before narrowing his eyes to slits like he's trying to figure out if I'm telling the truth or just bullshitting him. Or if he wants to kill me. A loud groan escapes from his throat, and then he looks over at the girl cowering in the corner.

Worried he's still not convinced, I say, "I've never seen Nadine use a shovel. I bet she's already started digging the grave. Personally, I wouldn't want to be the guy who made her do that, but you'd know her better than me. Maybe she's enjoying that workout in this heat."

Whichever part of that makes him realize he better go

find his boss I'm not sure, but after throwing the girl one last nasty look, he pushes past me, giving me a shoulder check for good measure. Not a lot of golden light with that one.

I don't look back in his direction until I hear the door slam shut, but when I know he's gone, I turn my head to make sure, just in case he has a change of heart and likes the idea of hurting some innocent girl more than obeying his boss. After waiting a few seconds, I breathe a sigh of relief. Why the hell does Micah allow Nadine to keep those stormtroopers around?

That's above my pay grade, and I have more important things to deal with at the moment, so I turn my attention to the girl. I recognize her as the one who was looking around when she first got here. A pretty brunette, she had a curious way about her that was tough to miss.

Now she looks so small crouched in the corner with her arms covering her head. I can only imagine what those four did to her, but at least she's still dressed, so I'm guessing they didn't go as far as they have in the past with other women in the group.

As soon as I begin making my way toward her, she starts to cry. Shaking her head so her light brown hair swings, she sobs, "Please, I didn't do anything."

She's not looking at me, but I raise my hands anyway. "I'm not here to hurt you. I promise. You don't have to be afraid."

My words do nothing to alleviate her fear. She still won't look at me, and she keeps shaking her head.

When I get a few feet away, I stop and try to make her understand I'm not like Nadine's guards. "It's going to be okay. I know they scared you, but I'm not here for that. I just want to talk, okay?"

I wait, and finally after a few seconds, she stops shaking her head even as she continues to cry. She refuses to look at me, so I crouch down in front of her and softly say, "I'm not going to hurt you. Honest."

"You're one of them," she sobs. "You're all the same here."

"No. I swear I'm not. I'm here to help you."

That finally makes her look up at me, and I see her blue eyes are red and tears stain her cheeks. She studies me and then shakes her head again. "You look like one of them."

I nod, knowing she's not wrong. "Yeah, I can see that, but I swear I'm not. I work for the leader of The Golden Light. They're just some woman's henchmen. Totally different. Honest."

"Nadine. She's a piece of work," she mumbles as she wipes her tears from under her eyes.

As much as I know I shouldn't comment about Micah's favorite, I can't stop myself after the last couple days. "Yeah, she's a lot. Trust me, that's not what The Golden Light is about."

The girl takes a deep breath in and lets it out in a rush. "Oh yeah? I'm having a hard time believing that after all I've seen in the single day I've been here."

She needs to stop that kind of talk right now, or she's going to find herself stuck with those four bastards again. I give her a tiny smile and choose my words carefully so as not to frighten her again.

"Just a little friendly advice, but you shouldn't say things like that. Noticing anything is a problem here."

I've never said that to another person since I became a part of Micah's group, even though I've thought exactly those words more times than I want to admit. Instinctively, I look around to make sure no one heard me.

"Who are you?" the girl asks, tearing me out of my thoughts of how much trouble I could be in if Micah's cameras can record sound. I don't think they can, but I'm not sure.

I turn my head to look at her. "Nash. And you?"

She answers without hesitation, surprising me. "Lara."

Leaning in toward her, I whisper, "Well, Lara, you've unfortunately gotten the attention of Nadine, and you've seen what happens when you make that mistake. The good news is she's not in charge. Not exactly."

Lara grimaces. "That's comforting. What kind of group lets that sadist have any power?"

I wince at how loud that sounded. "I need you to keep your voice down."

"Why?"

Without moving my head, I look up in the direction of the camera positioned in the corner on the opposite side of the room from where we are. "I don't know if they record what we say, so it's best to keep anything you want to say to yourself unless you know you're safe outside. If you must, whisper it if you're inside."

When she moves to look over at the camera, I grab her face to keep her looking at me. "Don't. They're always watching. Never forget that."

She stares at me in terror until I drop my hand. "Why are you telling me this?" she asks in a low voice.

"Because the leader wanted me to come here to talk to you."

Leveling her gaze on my face, she whispers, "The same leader who records everything in this place and might have it wired to hear every word we utter?"

I nod, knowing how that sounds. "Yeah. It's complicated."

Lara leans forward and groans. "It's complicated is a social media status teenage girls post when they know everyone hates their boyfriend because he's a dick. It's not complicated to say something's wrong when you're an adult, Nash."

Oh, this woman is going to get into trouble if she keeps saying things like that. Clearly, the shit Micah has put into the food and drink isn't working on her like it should. That's going to make things more difficult than she can even imagine if she doesn't learn quickly to hold her tongue.

"Let's just say Micah told me he doesn't want you hurt, okay? So keep your mouth closed when we leave this building, and no more looking around like you did when you arrived. That made you stick out like a sore thumb, and that's not going to help you here. Do you understand?"

My little speech makes her sigh, and drawing her eyebrows in toward her nose, she frowns as all her defiance seems to evaporate. "I thought I was being sly. So much for flying under the radar."

"Is that what got you in trouble with Nadine?"

She shakes her head and sighs again. "No, and to be honest, I don't think I did anything wrong by caring about someone who died not six feet away from me. She wouldn't even let us take a few minutes to mourn poor Anna's death. What a monster. How would it have hurt anyone to let us have a little while to process that?"

I want to explain to her that attachment to anyone but Micah isn't permitted in The Golden Light, but I've already spent too much time whispering with her in the corner like this. No doubt he's been watching every second of our time together, so I need to get her over to him now before he becomes suspicious.

"We need to go. Remember this, though. No looking like you're interested in anything but the leader. His name is Micah. No speaking unless you're spoken to, and never say anything that sounds like you're curious about anything here. Everything is positivity and light. Got it? Paste a smile on your face and look like you're blissfully unaware of anything but true happiness. And when you meet Micah, bow and then say nothing unless he asks you a question directly, and then be as vague and contented as possible."

She stares at me in horror before whispering, "Bow? Are you kidding?"

I shake my head. This woman is never going to make it here.

"It sounds like I'm supposed to be a Stepford wife."

"Just do as I say, and you'll be safe."

As I stand up, she asks, "Why does he let her use her junkyard dogs like that if he's the leader?"

Looking down at her, I shrug. "No more questions. I

don't have answers you'll like. Remember, look content and say nothing as much as possible."

"He doesn't sound like much of a leader, but fine. I'll do my best happy girl routine."

Christ, if she keeps this up, she's not going to last a week here. Worse, I'll probably pay for her misbehavior since Micah thinks I can get through to her so she believes all that positivity he preaches.

Lara stands up and takes a deep breath. "I'm curious about something."

My frustration ratchets up even more so I want to lash out at her. "Did you not hear me? I just told you no more questions."

"You said no more questions because you don't have answers I'll like. That's fine. I'll take those. At least that will be better than no answers at all."

I close my eyes as a headache begins to form behind my eyes. Squeezing the bridge of my nose to stop it before it gets out of control, I mumble, "Fine. Ask your question. One."

"Has any new member who looks like me showed up here in the past week?"

When I look at her, I see genuine worry in her eyes. God, this is bad. She's here looking for someone she cares about, probably a family member.

I quickly run through all the new recruits I've seen come through in the past couple days but can't think of anyone who might fit. Not that I could tell her even if I did remember someone. I may not want to hurt Lara, but that doesn't mean I'm going to stick my neck out for her.

Life here is precarious enough. It's all I can do to keep

things balanced with Nadine acting out her sadistic fantasies on anyone who steps out of line and Micah looking to me to do what he needs so The Golden Light doesn't descend into chaos.

If Lara is going to survive here, she's going to have to do it on her own. I've done all I can. Now it's up to her.

With a shake of my head, I answer her before turning to walk toward the door. She's got a meeting with Micah, and if she's smart, she'll play it exactly as I told her to.

12

LARA

I FOLLOW Nash as disappointment fills me. I'm not convinced Rina isn't here somewhere, but if he hasn't seen her, maybe I'm wrong. She wouldn't be someone who'd just swallow all this mumbo jumbo about some light, though. I know my sister. She'd listen because she's craving something positive in her life, but I just can't believe she'd buy into the stuff these people preach. She'd ask questions, and in this group, that would make her stand out.

This place is a cult, and Rina Simpson isn't the type to give up everything just to walk around in a daze and pledge all she is for a few catch phrases that belong on a middle school inspirational poster.

As I walk beside Nash toward the door, I look him up and down and see an attractive man with short, dark hair and brown eyes that have a hint of caring in them. Like

Nadine's men, he's clean shaven. Big and definitely someone who can handle himself, he reminds me of that bouncer at that club Rina and I go to in Wilmington sometimes who took a shine to her. My sister liked him too, but for some reason, they never ended up going out on a date.

I study him for another moment or two and wonder if Nash believes all of this Golden Light nonsense. I doubt it, but he stays, nevertheless. Why?

Maybe he gets some benefit other than feeling that he can have anything he wants in this world. Whatever that is, he's clearly someone the leader believes in. This Micah person wouldn't have sent him to deal with me if he wasn't.

Nash stops as he sets his hand on the doorknob and turns his head to look at me. "Remember, no questions. Speak only if Micah asks you something directly. If you mess this up, I don't know what will happen to you, and I'd hate to see you have to deal with Nadine and her men again."

I want to say he could help me with that, but I keep my mouth shut and simply nod my understanding. Nash isn't my savior here. He's merely some guy following orders. I can't rely on him to help me once we walk out of this building.

Satisfied I know how to act, he throws open the door and we step out into the blinding midday sun. I squint and follow him down the stairs as the heat of the day hits me like a brick wall. Summer in the mid-Atlantic is always a bit humid, but lately it's been downright suffocating.

"Whew. Any chance this leader of yours has air conditioning in his place?" I ask as we walk toward a small group of women.

He snaps his head around to glare at me. "What did I just tell you? Woman, I swear you're going to get yourself hurt."

I lean away from him, a mixture of fear and embarrassment filling me. "I was just making small talk about the heat. I can't even do that?"

Nash nods his head to a group of women as they pass us and remains silent until they're far enough away they can't hear him. Looking down at me, he says, "Do not say this leader of yours. He's everyone's leader, including yours. If you don't get that through your head right now, you're going to have a very hard time here."

His words frighten me, as I suppose they're meant to, so I don't say anything more until another group of five women pass by. They slowly nod to him, and he does the same again. No words are spoken, but I can't help but notice this bunch like the last have that vacant look about them.

"Why are all those women wearing those tan dresses that look like feed sacks? And why do they look like zombies?" I whisper as we continue to walk together.

Nash doesn't respond. Instead, he gives me a dirty look. I guess I can't ask about the ugly clothes every woman here wears or why they look like someone's sucked out their brains either.

Frustrated, I ask, "Are there any men here who aren't like you or those goons who would have done God only knows what to me if you hadn't shown up?"

He doesn't answer, and when I begin to ask again, I see why. Another group of women come out from behind a rundown-looking building, and they look even more like zombies than the others. They don't even notice us as they walk by in the same direction as the last two groups did, making me wonder where everyone is going in this heat. I hope it's somewhere cool, or there are going to be more people dropping dead.

The memory of Anna makes me stop for a moment, and I take a deep breath in to stop myself from crying. I don't know why I'm so emotional about what happened to her. I barely knew the woman. We just met for the first time yesterday, for God's sake. She was barely more than a stranger to me.

Even as I tell myself all of that, I know the real reason why thinking about her dying while I slept just a few feet away from her tears me up. What if that happened to Rina? I'd hope someone would care enough about her as a fellow human being to mourn her passing.

Lost in thought about Anna and the horrible possibility that my sister has met the same fate, I don't notice Nash has continued walking and left me standing alone in the center of the compound. When I see him storming back toward me, I recoil in fear.

"What are you doing? Is it that you don't understand simple instructions? I told you not to do anything to be noticed, and not five minutes later here you are standing alone in the middle of the compound? It's like you want to be punished," he snaps.

Rage fills his dark eyes, and I see in him what I saw in those four henchmen of Nadine's. Why the hell is he so worried about what I do? Even as I silently ask myself that question, I can guess the answer. He'll probably get in trouble if I step out of line. I doubt it's because he's concerned for my welfare.

"I'm sorry. I was thinking about Anna and got lost in my head for a few seconds there. There's nobody around to even see me, so I don't know what the hell you're so freaked out about. Anyway, I doubt a single one of those women even noticed me. They aren't exactly looking sharp, if you know what I mean."

He shakes his head and then moves his eyes to look at all the buildings around us. "There are cameras everywhere, so you're always seen here. Never forget that. Not just indoors. Outdoors too. Wherever you are on the farm, you can be watched. If you don't remember that, then this is going to be the last time we talk."

"Why? Because you don't want to risk being seen with a troublemaker?" I ask sarcastically, tired of his stressing out just because he wants to save his own hide.

He leans down and gets into my face so I can see the yellow flecks that circle the pupils in his brown eyes. "No. Because you'll be dead. Now shut your mouth and keep it shut the rest of the way."

We stand there staring at one another for a long moment before he grimaces and turns on his heel. "Come on. Let's go."

As we walk, I look around, making sure not to move my head as I do so no one watching can see I'm checking the place out. It looks like that colonial farm we visited on my sixth grade class trip. Old buildings sit on the edges of a large open dirt area. The difference is that farm was

filled with male and female actors playing the part of
early American settlers carving out a new world. The
people here seem to be overwhelmingly female and
whatever they're playing at, it has nothing to do with
making a better life for themselves.

The women I've seen today all seem lost, like they've
been hypnotized to be docile. Not that it would surprise
me if that's happening. You can't exactly have followers
thinking and asking questions. What kind of cult would
that be?

I'm guessing Melody and Delilah have been
instructed to only find females to bring to this place. That
would explain why out of all of us who arrived yesterday
there were no men.

The memory of how much those two smelled like
weed pops into my head, and I can't help but wonder if
that's what's going on with all the women here. Mari-
juana doesn't make you that dopey, though, and as high
as Melody and Delilah may have been, they didn't look
like zombies like these women I've seen today do.

Nash slows down his pace, so I follow suit, afraid if I
don't Nadine might come out of nowhere and take over
for him. He may frighten me, but I don't have the sense
he wants to hurt me. That woman, on the other hand,
clearly enjoys inflicting pain on people. I saw it in her
eyes when she was threatening me. She was barely
holding herself back from lashing out.

He stops at the bottom of the stairs to another white
building, but this one has a different feel to it. Every other
building I've seen or been in since I arrived here was old
and reminded me of the cabins at summer camp. This

building seems far more modern with a front porch and the front door painted green.

Without turning to look at me, he says in a low voice, "Remember what I said. Speak only if Micah asks you a direct question. No smart answers."

"Can I ask you one more question before I go in?"

Exhaling a sigh like he can't hold his frustration in any more, he looks over at me and squints as a bead of sweat rolls down the side of his face. "Fine. Go ahead. I have a feeling I couldn't stop you if I wanted to."

That this man, at least a foot taller and a hundred pounds heavier than me, would say that seems bizarre, but I don't have time to make a comment on that. I've got far more serious concerns at this moment as I look forward at that green door.

"Will Nadine and her men be in there with the leader?"

Nash's expression softens, and he shakes his head. "I don't think so, but don't be surprised if they show up. She's closer to Micah than anyone else in The Golden Light."

"Closer than you?" I ask, even though I know the answer.

That gets me a smile and a chuckle. "Much. I'm nobody here. Just a guard who follows orders."

The flash of a memory from a history class in high school when we studied Nazi Germany makes me wince at Nash's description of himself. I want to believe he's not merely some mindless follower like all those people who allowed Hitler to run wild throughout Europe, but I don't know.

"Well, thanks for the information. I appreciate the head's up on how to act in there."

He turns his entire body to face me, and I see worry etched into his expression, especially in the elevens between his eyes. "Micah isn't bad. He cares about everyone here. I don't know where I'd be if I hadn't found The Golden Light. He can help you too."

For the first time since I met him, Nash sounds like a true believer. I'm curious what his life was like if this Micah guy and his cult of positivity helped him. He seems so confident and in control of himself. Maybe it was drugs. I can see that. They've gotten a lot of people far tougher than him in this world.

"Okay. Will you be coming in with me?" I ask as that look of sincerity fades away and the hardness from earlier returns.

Nodding, he sighs. "I will. I don't know how long I'll be staying, though."

We stand staring at that green door like it's a symbol for us to come in, and I say, "Well, thank you for everything, Nash. I won't forget what you said."

When his foot lands on the first step, he says, "Don't. It might be all that keeps you safe here."

I swallow hard and feel all the moisture suddenly leave my mouth as I follow him up the stairs to the porch. My nature is to ask questions. I've always been that way, even as a small child. Standing silently and not looking for answers are antithetical to who I am, so Nash has no idea how hard this meeting is going to be for me. I'm here to find my sister and bring her home, so all I want to do is ask about where she is. Pretending to be a happy and content follower of this positivity nonsense everyone here is so eager to believe may be the hardest thing I'll ever do.

But if that's how I must act to be able to stay here and snoop around for what may have happened to Rina, then I'll do it. I just need to keep out of Nadine's way, or the next time I'm guessing there will be no Nash to save me from what she commands her men to do to me.

13

Nash slowly opens the green door and stands back as I walk into Micah's home. Or maybe it's just where he meets with troublemakers. I'm not sure. All I know is the second I step into this building, I'm sure someone important is here.

Unlike the rest of this farm, Micah's rooms are furnished for true comfort. The sofa is expensive, and I'm pretty sure it's exactly like the one my mother told my father she must have a few months ago. He, being a thrifty soul, balked at eight thousand dollars for a single piece of furniture, no matter how exquisite she said it looked on the showroom floor. My mother's choice had been light tan, but whoever chose this one went with deep red.

The floor is new hardwood, not the kind in the cabin I slept in or in that building Nadine and her goons took me to with old wood floors with splinters. The walls aren't simple wood boards over studs either. These are sheetrock primed and painted in light tan, eggshell sheen, I guess. And hanging around the room are pictures in pricey frames of nature scenes that undoubtedly were taken by a professional photographer.

The leader of The Golden Light likes to be surrounded by nice things. Interesting.

The man himself sits in a chair that I swear reminds me of a throne. I wonder if he requires people to call him king too?

Out of the corner of my eye, I notice Nash's gaze isn't on his leader but focused on the floor. He appears distinctly submissive right now, and I'm not sure if I should be copying his behavior.

I can't deny there's something about Micah that's intriguing. Sitting shirtless, he almost seems to be showing off his muscular chest and abs. It strikes me as odd that he welcomes people like this, although I guess it could fit with the whole positivity thing. I certainly could understand if he was hot, but this room we're in right now is obviously air conditioned and quite comfortable compared to outside.

I look over at Nash to see him bow and feel my mouth drop open. So everyone has to bow to Micah? That doesn't sound like something a group based in positivity would do.

The leader smiles, and I can't help but admit he's quite attractive. "Nash, thank you for bringing Lara here. Did you two have a good talk?" he asks in a silky smooth voice.

Nash stands up to his full height and nods. "You're welcome. I think so. I hope we did, at least."

Nothing in his tone of voice or the words he's saying sounds like the man I've spent the last nearly half hour with. This man couldn't protect me from Nadine's men if he had a gun. They'd chew this Nash up and spit him out without breaking a sweat, even in the oppressive heat outside.

With a wave of his hand, Micah says, "Well, thank you, Nash. You may go now."

I watch Nash bow once more before leaving me with his leader. Clearly, Micah has a strong hold over him. Perhaps not total control, but close to it.

The door closes behind him, and then it's just Micah and me. I assume I'm supposed to bow, but something inside me makes that impossible. It's not a sense of rebellion as much as a disbelief that anyone would have to bow to a man in the United States. He's not royalty, no matter what that chair of his looks like, and I am not his subject.

He appears to wait for me to act like Nash, and when I don't, he nods like we're having some unspoken discussion and I've just informed him there will be no bowing from me. It's probably not the best way to start this meeting, but if he presses me on why I didn't do it, I'll play dumb and claim I thought only men had to bow.

"How are you doing today, Lara?" Micah asks like he knows me and truly cares about my welfare.

I sigh as I decide how to answer. I can't tell the truth. He won't take hearing I've come to his group looking for my sister well. I can't complain about my treatment from

Nadine and her henchmen. Nash said she's important here, which means she's important to Micah.

So I choose the least offensive route and say, "I was very hot until I walked in here. It's quite comfortable in this room. How are you?"

Instantly, I worry I've made a mistake being polite. No questions was the one thing Nash repeated over and over, and right out of the gate, I ask a question. Stupid Lara.

I quickly apologize for my misstep. "I'm sorry. I didn't mean anything by that. It's just habit to ask people how they are after they've asked me."

His smile never fades, even when I ask him a question. He simply stares directly at my face looking genuinely interested in every word I utter.

"Society has trained you well, I see."

As much as I want to ask what that comment means, I do as Nash said and keep my mouth shut. When I don't reply, Micah stands from his chair and walks over, stopping directly in front of me.

"I'm guessing you don't know what I mean by that. Do you?" he says, staring directly into my eyes.

His gaze is almost hypnotic, but I don't look away. "No, I'm sorry. I don't."

"You asked me how I was because it was habit. Not because you truly wanted to know how I was feeling. Not that you genuinely cared about my well-being. That's society's training you to be a good little soldier, not to offend anyone but not to actually be interested in anyone either."

As much as I want to disagree with him, I can't because he's not wrong about this. Modern society expects a surface level of empathy, but caring too much makes you appear soft and weak. So we all go around asking how people are and never really caring. How many times have I asked someone how they were and hated when they actually told me the truth? Nobody wants to know what anyone else is going through. That's a burden we never asked for. Just say you're fine, and then we can all move on with our day, right?

"But that's not all you're supposed to be, Lara. Caring about people is admirable. No one should ever shy away from truly caring about their fellow man. Merely asking how someone is simply because it's polite is useless. It does nothing for them and nothing for you. Neither one of us gained anything by that question. In fact, I believe it hurts our souls to be so disinterested in our fellow man."

I consider telling him what my father once said to me about manners being the lubricant of polite society, but I press my lips together and stay quiet as Nash told me to. I'm supposed to be silent and listen, and if that will help me locate my sister, then that's what I'll do.

Still gazing into my eyes, Micah continues. "Society doesn't care about you achieving the greatness you were meant to have, Lara. It cares about you conforming. That's it. Step out of line—neglect to ask someone how they are after they've asked you—and you're rude, and you'll have to be punished for that."

I want to tell him that's exactly what's happened to me this morning, but I decide not to. It's just that staying quiet when I have so much to say is hard.

"Society is wrong, though. You have so much inside you that society has pushed down or snuffed out. I can see it when I look at you. I bet you don't see it, though, and that's a true shame. Society has made you think your greatness is based on how you look or how well you follow rules, but I can help you see your greatness is based on something entirely different and more fulfilling than you've ever experienced."

Even though I know this isn't what The Golden Light is about, especially after spending time with Nadine, it's hard not to wish the world and this place could be exactly as he says. However, I sense he doesn't see the irony of what he's preaching while everyone outside of this room must follow The Golden Light's rules or risk being punished by his favorite Nadine. At the same time, though, I'm beginning to see why someone would find his ideas appealing. This man has a way about him that's nothing short of mesmerizing.

Since he didn't ask me a direct question or my opinion, I stay silent and wait for him to continue as I study his expression. He exudes confidence, which likely makes him more appealing than his good looks do. There's something else about him, though, that I can't put my finger on, something that makes it hard to imagine he's anything but that caring leader Nash described.

He takes a step forward so our chests are practically touching and inhales deeply, letting the air out through his nostrils. I imagine I don't smell as fresh as I'd like to in such close quarters with anyone after spending more than a day in the same clothes in temperatures that barely dipped into the low seventies last night and have to be up in the high nineties today. If I smell bad, though, there's no sign of disgust in the way he looks at me after taking a big breath in.

"I'm sorry about what happened with Nadine this morning, Lara. I know you were just expressing sadness over what happened with that girl."

I want so much to tell him that's exactly why I spoke out, but I simply nod and hope that's not stepping out of line. If only his buddy Nadine had understood why I was sad and wanted a moment to mourn Anna, none of what happened today would have been necessary. I don't know if he thinks that way, though.

He sighs and says, "You're a sensitive person. I can see in your eyes the truth about what the world has done to you. You've cared, and society has run all over your feelings. You've loved wholeheartedly, and people who were too damaged or too callous took that love and twisted it into something they could use against you. I know, Lara. I do. You have no idea how many people I've seen just like you. People who have so much capacity for love and the greatness that comes from that ability to love, and just like you, they weren't appreciated for how wonderful they are."

With every word he speaks, it's like he's breaking down my barriers, walls I didn't know existed and those I thought were needed because I'm an educated woman in modern society. All this touchy-feely stuff isn't supposed to be real, but he makes it sound so true.

No! I can't let myself get sucked into this kumbaya world of his. As much as I wish life was kinder and gentler, that isn't the case. Reality is what it is.

I can only hope Rina didn't fall for this feel-good stuff.

And then, just as I think I'm in control of myself, he cups my cheek, and it's like my body is instantly covered in warmth and love.

"It's okay to not be sure, Lara. You've spent your entire life dealing with what society has forced you to handle. You've built up defenses to make sure you don't suffer. I understand. I felt that way all my life until I found the light. All I had to do was let it in, and I instantly knew happiness like I'd never known before. I want that for you. Do you want that for you, Lara?"

The deep green flecks around his pupils seem to sparkle as I stare into his green eyes, almost as if they're part of this performance he's doing. Now I understand why so many people willingly join this group and follow him. The things he says make you feel like he has the answers to questions you didn't even know you had until he spoke them. Who wouldn't want to feel complete love and acceptance and find their greatness?

I'm not like them, though. I know this game he's playing. If he truly cared about the people here, he wouldn't let the likes of Nadine and her gang terrorize them simply for stepping out of line. That's not unconditional love.

That's manipulation, and I have a feeling he's an expert at it.

My goal coming here was to find my sister, though, so for the time being, I need to play his game. He wants to be the one to lead me to the promised land, and I need to make him believe I've bought into his system completely.

Micah waits to see me succumb to his sales pitch to follow him to find happiness like I've never know before, so I need to make it believable when I say yes. I open my eyes wide like I'm enthralled by his offer and nod. I imagine I look exactly like I did when I was twelve and that boy I liked asked if I wanted him to kiss me.

But just as I feel now, I knew then too that what was expected of me was sweetness and compliance. Micah and that pre-teen boy are the same. They want control but don't want to fight for it, so instead they use a softer, more seductive ploy. I doubt Donnie Cimino knew precisely what he was doing, but Micah does.

He cradles my face and leans forward to kiss me softly on the lips. My eyes remain open as I watch him enjoy the first taste of me, and when he pulls away, he smiles just as a conquering hero would. He's sure he's converted yet another unhappy female tired of the world taking advantage of her good nature, and all he's had to do was promise to give me the one thing that can only be found inside me.

There is no way my sister fell for this. No one will ever be able to convince me of that. She may be here because she likes the positivity these people espouse, but I cannot believe she's like one of those mindless zombies I saw walking around outside.

"Okay. Now that I know you believe as we do, I'd like to officially welcome you to The Golden Light. Please don't let what happened earlier stop you from achieving your innate greatness. Do you have any questions?"

Every cell in my body practically screams out that I have nothing but questions about what's going on in this place. I know better than to voice most of them, though. I need to act like I'm a true convert if I want to find out what happened with Rina, so I shake my head and smile.

"I'll have one of the women explain how everything here works. You'll be given a job that will accentuate your natural abilities, and therefore, increase your happiness. You've found a place where you can truly be your best self here, Lara. I'm so glad you've joined us."

Although Nash told me not to speak unless Micah asks me a direct question, I decide I'm going to say something and whisper, "Thank you."

My new leader smiles and sets his hands on my shoulders. "You don't have to thank me. That's what society expects from you, but that's empty and hollow. Unless you truly are thankful for what you've found here. Are you truly thankful?"

"Yes. I think I've always wanted what I've found here, so I mean it when I say thank you."

Micah studies my face for a long moment before nodding. "I think you do. I like that for you, Lara. Are you ready to experience true fulfillment and happiness like you've never had before?"

"I am."

14

THE SUN BEATS down on the women tending to the gardens that produce the food we eat here, and I can't help but wonder how they do it day in and day out. It's got to be at least ninety degrees already today, and we haven't even hit the hottest time of the afternoon. Yet they're out there without a hint of shade picking vegetables like it's a lovely spring day with a nice breeze and barely any humidity.

A twinge of embarrassment pinches at me for all the times I've complained about how Micah forces us guards to wear black T-shirts, black pants, and boots year round. Compared to those women out there in the scorching hot sun every day taking care of the gardens so we all can eat, my discomfort with the temperature feels petty and small, especially now as I watch them from the shady area next to one of the sleeping quarters.

Footsteps behind me tear my attention away from the gardens, and I turn around to see Adam coming toward where I stand. Damnit, I hate having to deal with him, and for that, I won't chastise myself. This guy's a jackass. I can't figure out why Micah keeps him around as a guard.

Then again, if he wasn't doing that job, I don't know what the hell he'd be here for.

"I want to talk to you," he barks as he stops a few feet away.

Well, I don't want to talk to you.

If I could say that and not get into trouble, I would, but I know better. Micah may never have said the actual words telling me to get along with Adam, but he's insinuated it enough times that I know I have to at least make the effort.

"What do we have to talk about?" I ask, instantly wishing I had chosen a better way to say that.

He gives me a look of utter disgust, as if I'm supposed to know what the hell his problem is now. Does he think I'm a mind reader?

"You should have backed me up on that Maren bullshit, Nash. You know as well as I do that she wasn't right in the head. Even if we got her into the car, she probably would have tried to drive us all off the fucking road at some point!"

God, he's such a whiner. Like some tiny woman was going to be able to do anything safely secured in the back seat of the car. It's like this guy lives his life in some ridiculous fantasy story where women who weigh nearly a hundred pounds less than us can't be handled easily.

I've got news for him. As much as I wanted her to get

back here safe and sound, I would have done whatever I had to in order to make that happen, and that includes knocking her unconscious if I had to.

Staring at him, I say, "I told the truth. Nothing more. You went over the line, man. She wasn't going to outrun me. I've got at least a foot on her, for God's sake. Add to that the temperature outside that day, and it wouldn't have taken long to catch her. You just got overzealous, something you need to get in check before the next time we have to work together."

Adam seethes, unsurprisingly, and then takes a giant step closer to me so our noses are nearly touching. Rage fills his eyes as he says, "I don't need to change a damn thing about how I do my job, Nash. Maybe you need to remember what we were trained to do and fucking do it once in a while!"

Spittle flies from his mouth as he tries to intimidate me, and it takes every ounce of willpower I posses to not roll my eyes and push him away. I want to more than he even realizes, but I know he'll just go running back to Micah and cry about how I disrespected him.

What a baby.

So instead, I take a deep breath in and slowly let it out through my nose to calm myself down. There's no need to do anything stupid with this guy. He takes care of that all on his own.

"I remember full well what I was trained to do, and it's not shooting down scared women in cold blood. You fucked that up. Own it. I'd think you would have had time to figure that out while you were in the box last night. I guess not. But don't come up in my face with your bullshit."

His eyes grow wide, and I know he's about to try to push me over the edge to do something I shouldn't. "Oh, I had time to think about things in the box. A lot of things. Like how some of us guards can't be trusted. I'd watch my back if I were you, Nash. You might be one of his favorites now, but we all know how quickly that can change. And when it does, I'll be there to give you a taste of your new reality."

Adam storms away before I can say another word, but that's probably for the better. There's no point in arguing with him. He just wants to fight. It doesn't matter that he's in the wrong for what he did to Maren out at that farm. Like always, he's a crybaby who can't accept any responsibility for his actions and wants to blame everyone but himself.

I know my status with Micah is only temporary. I don't need the likes of Adam to inform me about that. I've seen how people rise and fall around this place. Other than Nadine, nobody who's ever been a favorite of the leader is still enjoying that position with him. Some have fallen only a little in his favor, while others have tumbled so low that they aren't part of The Golden Light anymore.

That fact never leaves my mind. The worst part is no matter what I do, it can't change the reality that when it's my time to suddenly be out of favor, it will have little to do with my behavior and mostly to do with how Micah feels that day.

Such is the reality of this place.

Before I head back to see how his meeting went with

Lara, I take one last look at the women in the gardens and silently hope the ones responsible for making sure they get enough water are doing their jobs today. We can't handle another death around here so soon after Maren and that new recruit last night.

As I STAND at the door wondering if I should knock or just wait until Micah summons me, I hear him call out, "Come in, Nash!"

Then I remember the cameras. Looking up, I smile as I silently wonder how I could have forgotten everything around here is seen. Stupid. You'd think I'm new here.

I open the door and quickly scan the room to see him sitting alone on his chair. Relief washes over me, and I step inside happy to only have to deal with him. I don't know why I feel that way, though. I've never experienced anything like this before with one of the women he's chosen to show interest in, so why is it happening now?

"Come, come," Micah says as he waves me toward him.

Stopping before him, I bow and wait for him to speak. Unlike other times, he remains silent for so long that I lift my gaze to see if something's wrong. He looks like he always does. He's smiling and looking at me with no hint of anger or unhappiness in his eyes, so what's going on?

Before my mind can start racing with possibilities, Micah laughs and says, "You know why you're one of my best guards, Nash? Because you never make the wrong move. Rise and talk to me about what's happening in our world today."

I do as he commands and say, "The women who tend to the gardens are hard at work. It's quite hot out there today, so I hope the ones whose job it is to bring them water are just as hard at work."

Before I can continue with what I've seen since I was last here in his rooms, he holds up his hand to stop me. "Are you worried about them?"

The memory of a time when another guard mentioned something about a group of workers here on the farm and Micah lost his mind on him for making it seem like he's not caring for his followers flashes through my brain. The Golden Light can be incredibly capricious, and at this moment, I can't tell by the blank expression he wears if he's about to explode on me for doing the same thing.

I don't say anything for a long moment before taking a chance that he won't be upset if I nod, but I make sure to smile as I do. "I worry about anyone working in this heat. It can be quite overwhelming if you don't keep hydrated."

That sounds like I'm some guest on one of those TV talk shows where they bring on people who sound and look like doctors but they're really just charlatans acting like medical professionals. I'd rather be far more straightforward with him, but I've learned that's not always what he wants.

Micah nods like he's mulling over what I've said and then tilts his head back to look up at the ceiling. "Do you believe I take good care of my flock, Nash?"

His question hits me like a sledgehammer to the center of my chest. He feels I've stepped over the line by saying I was worried about the women in the garden. Dammit! Now he's asking me a question I can't answer to his satisfaction. If I say yes, then he'll demand to know why I think those women would be in danger in this heat.

And if I say no...

Well, I don't want to think about what he'd do if I answered that way. No one has ever said no to Micah that I know of and was here the next day.

So I answer as I believe but also as I must. "Yes."

He's a master of making people wait to see how he's going to react, and he seems to be in rare form today. I don't look away, not wanting him to think I'm lying, so we stare at one another for what seems like an eternity until finally he smiles and I notice it goes all the way up to his eyes.

"I appreciate your concern for your fellow believers, Nash. You're right to worry. Those women take care of a very important job here at the farm, and they must be protected. I'll be sure to check that they're getting enough water."

I let out a sigh of relief, but then he adds, "I hope that eases your mind."

An edge at the bottom of his words makes me wonder if he's being sarcastic or truly cares about how I feel. Whatever his intention, he didn't ask a question, so I don't say anything.

"What else is going on today?" he asks, again smiling like he's happy.

Eager to move on from the earlier topic, I explain how lunch was mini chicken pot pies and I think all the guards enjoyed themselves. It's not much to report, but most of my day has been devoted to handling the new recruit with the problem.

I don't mind being his eyes and ears with everyone, but when there's not much to tell him, I get the sense he thinks I'm slacking off, or worse, keeping things from him. Micah has a habit of always believing the worst in people, despite the way he appears to the rest of his group.

He nods and steeples his fingers in front of his face as he hums. When I finish giving him the boring news of the day, he looks up at the ceiling again.

"I want you to keep a close eye on the new girl Lara."

"Okay."

I want to ask why, but I think I know the answer already. I'm not his only spy, and one of my fellow guards has seen her acting oddly since she arrived.

When he lowers his head again to look at me, he grimaces. "I don't think she's truly one of us."

My stomach clenches, and I have to work to keep my expression calm. Those words are the kiss of death for any member of The Golden Light. Lara has no idea the trouble she's already in.

Worse, now he's got me associated with her, and that's not a good thing for my place here.

"I'll keep a close eye on her. I'm sure Nadine will also, so if she's no good, we'll know soon enough," I say far more aggressively than I usually speak to him.

I'll take the reprimand if it means he thinks I'm actively working to help him root out the troublemakers in his flock.

He surprises me when he shakes his head and frowns.

"Nadine has strict orders not to bother with her in any way. We won't find out anything by terrorizing her. Better to let her think she's safe so she behaves in the way she truly wants to. I think she trusts you. That's why you're the perfect person to watch her."

As much as I don't want to disagree with him, I hurriedly explain she couldn't possibly trust me. "I may have been less intimidating than Nadine and her men, but I doubt she trusts me. I've given her no reason to."

Micah smiles. "I know, but I got the sense she liked you. You're not difficult on the eyes, so it might be even more than like. Encourage that. I want to know what she's really doing here."

I nod and pray that the fact that I already know the truth of why she's here isn't written all over my face. "Okay."

"By the way, did I ever tell you that I know how to read lips, Nash?"

My blood runs cold at his question. Is he saying he knows what I said to her when we were alone earlier? I've never known for sure if the cameras placed all around the farm can record sound, but now I'm thinking they can't so he's figured out a way to know what everyone here is saying at any time.

I shake my head. "No. That's a very unique skill. Did you know someone who was deaf and that's how you learned?"

Every word out of my mouth signals how afraid I am right now. I know better than to ask Micah questions, but I'd rather take his wrath for stepping out of line than let him think he can't trust me.

He doesn't answer at first, and then a maniacal laugh explodes out of him. "No. I was just joking. I can't read lips. I liked that you thought I could, though. That's another reason why I like having you around. You never doubt me. That's a trait I wish every one of my guards had."

I smile even as I feel like I'm going to throw up from the emotional rollercoaster this meeting has been. "Thank you."

The words taste like ash on my tongue, but I say them because I know I must. He likes how appreciative I am and stands up from his chair to pat me on the shoulder.

"You really are one of the best, Nash. Don't change a thing, and you'll go far here. Now go see what you can learn about our new member while I check on our garden girls. We don't want them dying out there in the summer heat, now do we?"

I don't answer since I believe his question to be rhetorical. Bowing, I receive his approval to leave and get the hell out of there as quickly as possible. He doesn't follow me as I thought he might to make sure the women get enough water and instead walks into the room adjacent to the one I was in, closing the door behind him.

15

I STEP out into the stifling heat and humidity and instinctively look over toward the gardens, but then I turn my attention to the other side of the compound where the mechanics work on the bus. As much as I hope those women are being given water, I can't focus on that.

You learn very quickly around here that caring too much for anyone will get you nothing but trouble.

As I stand on Micah's porch and scan the area in front of me for any sign of Lara, my mind drifts back to those first days after I found The Golden Light. I had no idea of what the truth was then. All I knew was when I really listened to Micah talk, I felt like I had finally found home.

My hands shake as the idea of scoring something fills my head, but I promised the people at A Brighter Tomorrow that I'd really try to stay clean this time. I want to. I truly do. It's just so damn hard.

People begin to file into the tent and sit down on the empty benches that surround me. A pretty girl with blond hair and the bluest eyes I've ever seen in my life handed me a pamphlet when I walked out of the rehab center this morning, so I figured I'd check this Golden Light thing out.

It sounds like complete bullshit, but then again, thirty days ago I thought rehab was utter crap too. A month later, I feel pretty good, all things considered. I haven't had any junk in all that time, and it wasn't too bad. Yeah, I had a few bad days and even worse nights, but I got through it.

That girl said The Golden Light would make me see the world in an entirely different way, and I figure since that's what rehab did for me, why not listen to some people talk about genuine love? She said that's the focus of the group, which sounds pretty damn good to me. I mean, who the hell wouldn't want to experience genuine love?

I'm not holding out a lot of hope for that today, though. I can say this. If they think they're going to sucker me out of money or anything valuable, they chose the wrong guy. I don't own a single thing in this world. All I have is my body and my brain, and those aren't the greatest after all the shit I've shot into them.

But I figure I can sit through this meeting, and if it's garbage, I'll leave. No harm, no foul. I don't know what I'll do after, but I could go for something to eat. I have that coupon the center gave me for a free lunch when they let me go, so I can go to that diner they work with to make sure those of us who finish the program at least get a hot meal on our first day out.

After that, we're on our own. Oh, there are a bunch of places I can get help if I need it, but I'm hoping my girlfriend will be happy now that I spent the month in rehab, and we can get back to living our life together.

"Have you ever been to one of these things?" someone next to me asks in a low voice.

I turn to my right and see a man I'm guessing is maybe twenty-three or twenty-four. He might be older than me, but then again, lots of people say I look closer to thirty. Abusing your body for years will do that to you. His shoulder-length brown hair looks greasy, like he hasn't washed it in a while, and his skin looks almost gray the longer I stare at him. He's about half my size, but I'm bigger than most men, even after all I've done to myself.

Shaking my head, I shrug. "No. Some girl told me about this, so I figured I'd see what it's all about. You?"

He shakes his head so long, greasy strands of hair swing around his face. "Nah, but I figure if there are hot girls here, I might as well give it an hour of my time."

I smile and wonder if he can see in my expression how much I doubt any girl here, hot or not, would give him the time of day. Maybe if he took a bath and cleaned himself up a little, but then again, some of the people I met in rehab had hot girlfriends and wives and they looked like shit warmed over.

After dismissing him with a nod and a half-hearted smile, I look around and notice most of the people here with us are females. Maybe he's onto something with his idea. I'm not looking for a hookup or anything like that, though. I've got Caressa waiting for me, and once this thing is over and she's home from her shift at the sandpaper factory, she and I are going to have a reunion for the ages.

I get lost in thinking about how great it's going to be when she walks in the door and sees me sitting on the couch all clean and ready for her. Thirty days isn't a long time, but I owe her more than I can ever pay back for being willing to wait for me. She's a pretty girl with a great smile and a body any red-blooded male would love. She could have anyone she wants, and the fact that she stayed with me after all the shit I've done is something I won't forget. I went through rehab as much for her as for me, and tonight I'm going to show her how much she means to me.

A man's voice interrupts my silent planning for our reunion, and I look toward the stage at the front of the tent to see a man standing alone with his arms spread out wide. He's much smaller than I am and wears loose white pants and a pale green linen shirt that practically hangs off him. He reminds me of that hippie guy in rehab who was in charge of the yoga classes they made me attend. I warned him the first day that bendy shit wasn't easy for someone as big as I am, but he swore I'd love how yoga would make me feel. I didn't, but it wasn't as horrible as I thought it would be.

"Thank you for joining me, my children," the man on the stage says with a big smile as he tilts his head back to look up at the ceiling of the tent. "I'm Micah, and I'm so happy to welcome you to The Golden Light."

He runs his fingers through his long, dirty blond hair and lowers his head to look out at us. Something about the way he stares at the people in the front row for a second too long makes me wonder if he's doing some hypnosis thing. He can try that on me all day. It won't work. I found that out in rehab too. The lady who tried it said it probably had to do with my being Irish. I'm not sure about that since it's never done anything good for me before, but maybe she's right. All I know is she couldn't get me to go under, no matter what she tried.

"*Do you desire to have all you've ever dreamed of? What-ever it is, you can have it. You just have to believe.*"

Ah, okay. I know what this is. These self-help types all have an angle, and it's always money. Sorry, man. Your girl picked the wrong guy to give that pamphlet to this morning.

I look over at the guy with the greasy hair and see he's not paying attention anymore either. He's got his eye on a girl a few rows ahead of us who's looking back at someone and smiling. Weird how confident this gross guy is. I wonder where he got that from.

Whatever it is and whatever this guy in green shirt is offering, none of this is for me. Oh, well. I gave it a try. I'll have to make sure I tell my counselor about that since she stressed how important it is for me to keep an open mind now that I'm clean. She claimed the whole world would be different for me now, but I'm sorry to say I'm still not buying into this woo-woo stuff meant to make a person think they can have anything they want.

We can't. Reality shows us that every day. A person can't become a millionaire just by believing they can. If that were the case, the world would be filled with all wealthy people because speaking as someone who's been poor most of my life, none of us on the lowest level of society want to be there.

I stand up to leave and get only a few steps toward the end of my row before the man on the stage says, "You're leaving, but I can see greatness in you. Stay and learn what that is."

Looking around, I see he's talking to me. Worse, everyone is staring at me since he's decided to single me out.

When I don't respond and keep walking, he asks, "What's your name?"

I stop and sigh, not thrilled with being the focus of atten-

tion. Maybe if I tell him my name and that I need to leave, he'll move on.

"Nash. And I'm not the kind of person for this, but thanks."

But that doesn't stop him.

"You don't want to be happy and have everything you've ever wanted in this world, Nash?"

For a few seconds, I don't answer because nothing I say is going to stop him. I guess I could say I don't want to be happy and prefer to have nothing I want, but who the hell is going to believe that?

"Of course, I want to be happy. Everyone wants that. I just don't think this is for me, but thanks."

I take another step and then a second one before he says, "Nash, I think you're underestimating yourself. You have such greatness in you, and I'd bet you haven't even scratched the surface to see it yet. Are you afraid to find out you're truly someone deserving of love and respect?"

Rolling my eyes, I smile. "No."

"Then stay and find out what your greatness is. I promise you won't regret it, Nash."

Everyone around me starts nodding, and some actually try to encourage me to stay. What is with these people? We're total strangers. What do they know about my greatness?

I don't know what this guy's power is, but it's not working on me. Let him charm the rest of the audience but leave me alone.

When I get to the end of the row, I look up at him and shake my head. "I'm good. Thanks."

He frowns, and I swear I see hurt in his eyes. Jesus, dude. You don't have to put on the show for me. I'm not interested.

As I head toward the open flap on the tent, I hear him say,

"What about the rest of you? Are you content to be nothing in this world because society has determined you don't fit in? Or are you willing to embrace your greatness right now and join us in The Golden Light?"

I glance back and see nearly everyone in the audience nodding enthusiastically. Suckers. Embrace your greatness. Please. What nonsense.

Shaking my head, I try to stop the memories of what happened later that day from flooding my mind, but it's no use. The pain rushes through my body, settling in the middle of my chest, as I remember trying to open my front door and my key not working. Now I think I was so naïve, but I never thought she would change the locks on me while I was gone. She promised to wait for me while I was in rehab. I didn't think the woman I loved would turn her back on me in just thirty days.

I wince as the memory of staring through the window and seeing her sitting on the couch with some guy kissing and holding hands fills my brain. She replaced me and never even bothered to let me know. She could have left me a message I would have gotten when I walked out of rehab so I didn't make a damn fool of myself going back to an apartment that was no longer mine.

Rage filled me, and like every other time I felt something that hurt, I wanted to turn to drugs. I didn't give a damn about the fact that I'd succeeded in rehab and gotten off the shit. All I wanted was to get lost in a haze of feeling nothing but good. I didn't want to experience the pain of losing the only good thing in my life.

I couldn't do it. I couldn't handle it without shooting up.

After walking toward the old places where I knew I could score something to make me feel better, I couldn't get that man's voice out of my head telling me I had greatness in me. Nothing in my life other than making it through rehab pointed toward that being even possible, but those words echoed in my head.

Was he right? Did I have greatness in me? Beneath the stupid choices and the rage, was there something good inside of me?

So I walked back to where the tent was earlier that day, but it was gone. My heart sank. I'd blown my chance to find something better than drugs, and I wasn't going to make it through the night if I didn't have them.

I stood in that spot and watched the sun set behind the trees, sure that the next few hours would be my last on earth. I'd find some way to score enough to put me out of my misery once and for all. Fuck Caressa and her new guy. Fuck rehab and all its nice words that meant nothing.

Fuck the world.

And then in the midst of the worst moments of my life, I felt a hand touch my back, and when I turned around, the man from the stage stood in front of me smiling. No one else was nearby, which seemed odd since I had the feeling this guy liked a crowd close at all times.

"I'm glad you came back, Nash. After the meeting, I thought about you all afternoon. Whatever happened before this moment, none of it matters. All that matters is helping you find your greatness, and I know with all my heart that once you find the love you deserve, that greatness inside you will come shining through. Are you ready?"

Every word filled me with a blissfulness I'd chased for so long. All I wanted was to know what this greatness he saw in me was and how I could see it for myself.

He held out his hand and smiled. "Come, Nash. Come home and be with people who love you. Come to The Golden Light."

16

NASH

SUMMONED ONCE AGAIN to Micah's rooms, I stand alone waiting for him as he talks to a member of The Golden Light in another part of the cabin. As much as I know I shouldn't, I try to understand what they're saying, but it comes through the walls and door as unintelligible mumbling.

It's probably better that I can't hear what they're saying. I already know too much for my own good.

The door behind me opens, and I turn to see Nadine march in with a look of determination on her face. Great. Just what I need now. All I want to do is go back to my cabin and relax for the night. I've had enough of her for a lifetime.

"What are you doing here?" she asks in her usual icy way.

For a moment, I consider not answering her and

instead waiting for Micah, but I know that will only result in more problems. "Micah wanted to speak to me."

That gets me a disgusted grunt, but thankfully, she continues on her way to the door on the other side of the room. Good. Go bother Micah and whoever he's talking to and leave me in peace.

I only get a reprieve for a minute before she and the leader of The Golden Light walk back into the room. They're talking about something concerning the children here on the farm, but I try not to listen.

"The mothers need to be talked to, Micah. They need to make sure the children are kept under control."

Nadine stops talking for a moment, so I look up and see Micah with his eyes closed and pinching the bridge of his nose. She doesn't take any of that as a hint he doesn't want to hear what she has to say right now, though, and continues her complaining.

"You know, this wouldn't be an issue if you'd let me give the children what we give to their mothers. That's the reason why they're so unruly. Their mothers can't control them because they eat the food and drink the lemonade like everyone else, but the children don't. Not to mention it forces everyone in the kitchen to make special food for them that doesn't have the drugs in it."

Micah sighs and shakes his head. "I've made my decision on that, Nadine. The children will not get anything in their food but food. They need nutrients to grow, not drugs to keep them quiet. They're kids. They're supposed to be unruly sometimes. I don't want a repeat of what happened last summer. Do you hear me? Not another child will die on this farm."

As he says that, I remember that little blond girl who passed away last July. Micah and Nadine told all the members that she came down with a terrible flu that took her life, but all the guards knew she died because she got too much of the drug they give to all the women. I'll never forget her mother's wailing at the memorial service a day after her daughter died. It made my chest hurt to listen to that.

Nobody saw that member for a long time. I suspected she was quietly disposed of like all the others who've become a problem, but just last week I saw her smiling and happily telling other members she's due in just a couple months.

"Fine. I understand your feelings on this," Nadine says in a much softer tone that a moment ago. "I just wanted to keep you up to date on the issue."

Micah waves his hand and walks toward me. "There is no issue. They're children. Now what else do you have to tell me?"

I focus my attention on the wood floor as she sits down in a chair behind his. Sounding frustrated, she asks, "Don't you think we should do this in private, Micah?"

As much as I agree with her, I can't say a word to support her on this. I'd love to since I don't like knowing so much about what's going on behind the scenes on the farm. I much rather being simply a guard with knowledge of as little as possible regarding what goes on here.

Unfortunately, that isn't how Micah feels about the situation.

"We are in private, Nadine."

She doesn't answer him but clears her throat as if to remind him I'm here.

"No need to censor yourself around Nash. He's as loyal as they come. So what else do you need to talk to me about?"

Still staring at the floor, I can't help but notice she hesitates for a long moment before continuing. "Fine. The new recruits will need to give us their banking information and details on anything else they own. I usually do that, as you know, but since that includes that Lara girl, it might be better if you handle it this time."

Again, Micah sighs. "Yes, you're probably right."

"Don't forget you'll need to have them sign the papers."

Clearly tired of this conversation, Micah snaps, "I think I know how to handle it, Nadine."

I glance up and see her focused on me with a look that could kill. "Maybe we should have Nash here do it. He seems to get along with her."

The expression on my face is definitely not the placid one I wish I could wear at this second. Micah notices what must be horror coming from me and walks over to pat me on the back.

"Nash is too busy doing other things for me. I'll take care of the financial issues with the new recruits. Anything else?"

Nadine narrows her eyes in rage and asks, "What? What do you have him doing? I should know since I have to deal with any issues that crop up."

Just like the last time I had to be here with the two of them, I feel like I'm going to be sick. I have no idea what

Micah means when he says he has me doing things for him. Other than keeping an eye on Lara, nothing else has changed in my duties as a guard.

For his part, her question doesn't seem to faze him. He sits down on that favorite chair of his and closes his eyes. I get the sense that she may want to keep talking, but for him, this meeting is over.

"I need to speak to Nash alone, so you can go, Nadine. Get me the forms they need to fill out, though. I'll do that either tomorrow or the next day."

And with that, she storms out, slamming the door behind her in an uncharacteristic show of anger toward our leader.

I remain silent, waiting for Micah to speak, but he seems happy to merely sit and relax with me standing in front of him. I want to tell him how happy I am to not have to deal with anything concerning financial forms with any of the new recruits. I'd do it if he told me to, but hearing him say I shouldn't be given that task made me happier than I can express.

Finally, he opens his eyes and smiles at me. "I called you here because I wanted to tell you how much I appreciate all you do for me, Nash. As you probably know, everyday affairs here on the farm are far more complicated than they seem from the outside. In addition to making sure my people are cared for, the mundane details like who eats what and dealing with the new recruits and their financial duties to the group have to be taken care of. Between you and me, I hate that part. The mundane stuff, I mean. That's why Nadine is so important to me. She takes all of that off my shoulders."

He stops for a second or two before adding, "Well, usually she does. I don't want any more problems with Lara, so this time I'll have to take care of the financial issue. It's important, though. This place doesn't run on believing in ourselves and the greatness inside all of us. As much as I wish it did, in reality, The Golden Light requires the same things any large family does."

I nod, trying to remember when the last time I thought of all of us here as a family. Maybe if Nadine didn't walk around terrorizing everyone I might be able to bring back that feeling.

"You look tired, Nash. Is everything okay?"

Shaking my head, I smile. "I'm sure it's just the heat."

Micah's eyes open wide, and he leans forward as if he wants to tell me a secret. "Speaking of that, I made sure to check on the women in the gardens after you mentioned them before. They were fine, but it's good that you brought that to my attention."

Sure I need to do something to change his impression that I thought he hadn't been concerned about them, I say, "I only wanted to make sure they were given enough water. It gets so hot out in that sun all day."

Nothing comes out the way I intended it, but thankfully, Micah doesn't seem offended. "Do you know why I like you so much?"

I shake my head, and he answers, "Because you make me remember what The Golden Light is all about. And for that, I'm thankful, Nash."

What he means by that I'm not sure, but I smile, hoping he truly thinks of me in that way.

He looks up toward the ceiling and lets out a heavy

sigh before returning his attention to me. "I want you to know I took to heart what you said earlier about groups needing a single leader. I sense you disagree with my giving Nadine so much power."

Oh, God. Now we're moving into territory I absolutely don't want to be anywhere near. Discussing Nadine can't have any positive outcome. He thinks the world of her, and anything I say against her, no matter how true, will only come back to haunt me.

Quickly, I answer, "It's not my place to judge you. You're the leader of the greatest group I've ever been a part of. The Golden Light saved me, Micah. You saved me. When I thought I had nothing to live for, you showed me I did. I'm forever grateful for that and all that I've been able to find here."

I watch his expression to see if I've successfully dodged explaining how I feel about Nadine. He listens intently, obviously pleased by the way I answer, and when I finish, he gives me a big smile.

"That right there. That's why I like you so much, Nash. I'm trusting you to keep an eye on Lara for me. Do you have anything to report?"

"Not yet. She's been busy doing what she was told to do, so I hope she's made it over the bumpiness from her first couple days here."

"Good. Good. I like the way you think. Go ahead and enjoy some time to yourself. We'll talk tomorrow."

I smile and bow. "Thank you, Micah. Have a good night."

"You too, Nash. If anything happens, I want to know

immediately, though. I don't care what time it is. Understand?"

"Yes."

Micah spreads his arms out wide and sighs. "You're a good soldier. Oh, by the way, I wanted to let you know that Ramon is no longer with us."

Sure the shock from hearing that news is written all over my face, I nod, even as sadness fills me over Ramon. He was a good guy. I thought he'd work out here.

I walk outside as I wish I knew what happened to him. Nobody leaves The Golden Light, so either he did something to himself or Micah and Nadine had him eliminated. Not that I'll ever know.

That's how things work here. One day you're the favorite, and the next, you don't exist.

17

LARA

"TIME TO WAKE UP! We all need to be in the meeting tent in fifteen minutes!" a woman I've never seen before announces from the doorway to the cabin before walking out.

I look around at my fellow sleepers and watch them jump out of bed like the place is on fire. Bethany gives me a disapproving look as she makes her bed.

"You better get moving, Lara. You don't want Nadine to see you still in bed."

For a moment, I consider telling her exactly what I think of Nadine and her damn henchmen, but I keep my mouth shut. I don't get the sense any of the women in this cabin with me have any issue with Nadine or anything else that goes on here. Why I have no idea. They seemed like such good people that first day, but in no time, they've become very comfortable with the ugliness that's been shown to us since we arrived.

Without responding, I get out of bed and quickly straighten the sheets and cheap brown blanket. None of us say a word as we prepare to go to the meeting tent. This is our first time going there since we joined The Golden Light, so I have no idea what to expect. I'm guessing Micah is going to put on a show, but what that will entail I haven't a clue.

I look down my body at the dress they gave me yesterday. Boring and tan, it's perfectly utilitarian. Nobody would ever see me wearing this and want to hit on me. That's probably the reason for it, though. There don't seem to be many men here at the farm, and other than Micah, I don't get the sense any of the others are allowed to even think about us women here.

Then again, I wouldn't put it past Nadine's goons to do much more than merely think about women on this farm. They act like they have free reign over everything here, so why not the females? I shudder at the thought of what they do when they decide to bother with us, though.

As I'm thinking that, Nadine walks into the cabin like the ray of sunshine she always is. Every time this person is in front of me, all I can think is she looks like she belongs in some women's prison ordering beatings of anyone who dares to step out of line.

She immediately focuses on me and says with a huge grin, "You ladies are in for a real treat today. Our leader is at his best when he's preaching. Hurry up and get ready and meet me outside as soon as you can."

Nadine seems downright joyful today. Maybe she ran over one of the little children on her way here this morning. I can see that making her as pleased as punch.

Mary catches my attention and gives me a tiny wave. She smiles back at me when I wave at her, and I can't help but think even in these ugly, tan dresses, she's beautiful. There's something about her warm brown hair and blue eyes that make her seem like the girl next door, even in her stupid Golden Light uniform.

As everyone else hurries outside to obey Nadine, Mary stops at the foot of my bed to wait for me. "I've been wondering if we'd ever get to see Micah talk. Yesterday at lunch, the women talked about how mesmerizing he is when he preaches. I'm looking forward to this today. Aren't you?"

I don't dare tell Mary what I'm really feeling about having to be part of Micah's captive audience this morning. She's kind and seems to want to be my friend, but trusting anyone here is a bad move.

So instead, I lie and pretend I'm just as thrilled to see Micah preach his special brand of believing. "I'm thinking it's going to be very interesting! I've spoken to him before, but that was one-on-one. This, I'm sure, is going to be even better!"

If I continue smiling and being this up, someone's going to mistake me for one of Micah's cheerleaders. Mary doesn't pick up on my lying, though, and grabs my hand in her excitement.

"I know! He looked at me when I was walking back from lunch yesterday, and I swear it was like God himself paying attention to me."

My cheeks hurt from smiling, but if I stop now, she's going to know I think she's nuts for what she just said. Comparing Micah to God seems a bit much, but that tells me Mary is pretty much lost to this cult. Too bad. I like her. I'm not going to be happy seeing her walk around in a blind haze like some kind of Stepford wife.

I give her hand a tiny squeeze to make her think I'm just like her. "We better go. We don't want to be late to our first meeting. I wonder where it's at. I don't remember seeing any meeting tent here."

She thinks about it as we walk outside but doesn't say anything. It's odd that I've never seen this meeting tent, but then again, maybe it's something they put up and take down whenever meetings happen. Still, Micah and his people seem to own this farm, so why not leave it up all the time?

Questions like that are why I'm never going to fit in with these people. I doubt Mary or Bethany or any of the others here have even considered something like why the tent doesn't stay up all the time. Maybe it's because I write for the magazine, but they don't seem to question anything here.

Nadine scans the group of us, making sure to glare when her gaze meets mine, and when she sees we're all here, she waves us on to follow her. "Come on. We don't want to be late. Micah has some very important things to tell us today."

As always, a question forms in my mind. What is so important that we needed to wake up and immediately go to listen to him talk without having any breakfast? I guess that's not the most important meal of the day here.

I obviously keep my thoughts to myself as we follow Nadine. I know better than to look around as we walk through the center of the farm and past Micah's private quarters, but I'm curious as to where her guards are today. They're always nearby, so what's happened to them this morning?

For a few seconds, I revel in the thought that something bad happened to them. I'd especially like something terrible to befall that one who Nash practically had to convince not to hurt me the other day. For him, I have no problem wishing the worst would happen.

Beside me, Mary whispers, "It's such a beautiful day out, and I had great sleep last night. I've never slept as well as I have since I arrived here. What about you?"

I think about it for a few moments and nod. "You know, I don't know when I've slept so well either. It must be all the fresh air we're getting. Like when I was a kid at summer camp. They'd run us around all day, so when it was time to sleep, we practically collapsed into our beds."

As I say that, I lower my voice so I don't get Nadine's attention. I'd like just one day to not have her focused on me. Not that I wish her to notice anyone else. I don't think Mary could handle what I went through with her men.

Bastards. They better not do anything to her.

At the back of the farm a white canvas tent appears like it grew out of the land overnight. I've seen this area of the compound before, and never once did I see a tent. Strange that they don't leave it up all the time, but maybe taking it down is someone's job here. Being productive seems to be a very important part of being in The Golden Light.

Nash stands at the entrance to the meeting tent, and my gut reaction is to smile because I know him. He immediately narrows his eyes, as if to tell me to stop right now. I don't know why my recognizing him would be a problem, but I tighten my lips so I look miserable and look straight ahead as we pass him on our way inside.

I quickly count ten rows of wooden benches arranged on the grass and a stage maybe a foot high in front of where we're going to sit. Behind me, women file in and take their seats, but Nadine points at the bench closest to the stage for us. I guess we get a front row seat to Micah's performance this morning.

Mary nudges my arm as we walk toward where Nadine wants us to sit. I look over at her and see worry in her eyes.

"What's wrong? Are you okay?" I ask as we take our seats.

"I'm feeling a little lightheaded," she whispers. "I'm sure I'll be fine."

My instinct is to ask for a cup of water for her, but I quash that as quickly as it enters my mind. Not that it matters. I don't see any water she could have anyway.

Nadine walks over to us and stops directly in front of Mary. Glaring down at her, she asks, "What's going on? Are you sick?"

I press my lips together to stop myself from answering for her, and Mary looks up at her and meekly answers, "I think missing breakfast is making me lightheaded. I'm sure I'll be fine."

To my shock, Nadine pats her gently on the shoulder

and smiles as she says, "Oh, not to worry. We'll be eating something before Micah speaks, so you'll feel better. I'm sure of it."

Sure someone has hidden the real Nadine away and replaced her with an actual caring human being, I stare down at my lap to avoid her noticing me at all. The last thing I need is her paying attention to me, even if this is a nicer version of her.

One of the women at the back of the tent announces she's got delicious cakes and lemonade for everyone, and I feel Mary's relief practically come off her in waves. She may be better at this obeying business, but she knows as well as I do what happens when you step a toe out of line. I can see by how happy she is now that food is coming that she was afraid.

This place is messed up. A woman feels weak because she hasn't had breakfast, and she worries she's doing something wrong. If that's not wrong, then I don't know what is.

It only takes the woman with the cakes a minute or two to reach us, and we put our hands out for her to give each of us two. Behind her, another woman I've never seen carries a silver pitcher full of pink lemonade and plastic cups. She pours each of us a glass and hands them to us, never smiling or even making eye contact as she does.

Like nearly everyone else here, she's little more than a zombie.

I want more than anything else to ask Mary what she thinks of this place and how strangely so many of the women act here, but I don't dare. I've learned my lesson already. One time making waves and having to deal with Nadine's henchmen was enough for me.

We finish our breakfast and lemonade, and the woman who had the pitcher before now comes around to take our plastic cups. Nobody talks as we wait for Micah to appear, so I keep my gaze focused on my hands in my lap.

Curious, even though I know I shouldn't be, I turn around to look at the crowd behind us and see every bench filled with women dressed exactly like me. They stare straight ahead, their faces expressionless. Nash and the other guards stand in a line across the back of the tent. They too stare straight ahead and show no emotion in their faces, but it's a different kind of indifference, almost as if they've been instructed not to focus on any of us. Nadine stands on the side of the tent, and as I watch, her guards walk in and take their positions behind her. She smiles as she listens to the one who wanted to hurt me tell her something.

Knowing those two, it's got to be the news that someone weaker than them has been hurt.

I quickly turn around and face the front again, worried she or one of her goons saw me watching them. I need to remember what Nash said about not noticing anything here. It's just that it's my nature to pay attention to what's happening around me.

As I think that, I sense my brain getting fuzzy. It's like when I take cold medicine and my head feels like a balloon bobbing up and down a few feet above my body. What's happening to me?

I glance over at Mary on my right and see her staring straight ahead. She looks like she always does, or so it seems. Maybe it's the heat. It's got to be near eighty already, and we haven't even hit the warmest time of the day. Sitting in this tent isn't helping either.

Strangely enough, though, I'm not sweating. I should be if the heat is affecting me, but when I run my fingertips along my hairline and across the back of my neck, I feel no dampness.

Maybe they put something in the food or the lemonade. That doesn't make sense, though, because they didn't taste off at all. Like usual, the cakes were delicious, and the lemonade was the most refreshing drink I've ever had.

I bet they're pumping something into the tent to make us more relaxed. I wonder what it is. I've never heard of anything like that.

With each minute that passes, my brain has to work harder and harder to focus. Everything, not just my brain anymore, feels hazy and fuzzy. Like if someone took a sander and ground off all the rough edges of me.

My limbs grow heavier and heavier as I wait with everyone else to see Micah. I have to admit that I'm interested in what he has to say. I wasn't before, but now I'm eager to hear him talk. He does have a very intriguing way about him. I knew it from the first time I stood in his rooms and we spoke.

Then, as if he materializes out of my desire to see him, Micah walks in through the flap at the back of the tent, and it's as if every cell in my body is happy he's here with us. I've never felt this level of bliss. That's what it is.

Pure, unadulterated bliss. It's the best feeling I've ever experienced.

"Hello, my children," he says, his voice smooth and comforting, like a piece of silk against my skin.

He's shirtless and wearing black pants that have a sheen to them. He's also barefoot, and I notice the top of his feet are as tan as his upper body.

Everyone says hello back to him, so I join in, careful to make sure not to stick out in any way. Going against the grain here is wrong. I know that now.

Micah steps up onto the stage and opens his arms out wide as he tilts his head back to look at the top of the tent. His biceps flex and his chest muscles puff out so he looks even more attractive. I don't think I understood how appealing he is until this moment. His body is as beautiful as his face.

"It's a wonderful day for us to join in fellowship and pledge ourselves to making this world the best place it can be for each and every one of us. As I look out at your beautiful faces, I see people who are finally living up to their potential. Do you feel it? Do you feel the love I have for you and the happiness that's coursing through me for how wonderful your lives are right now?"

Everyone around me answers him that they feel his love, so I nod and answer too. "Yes! I feel it!"

Whatever this is I'm feeling, it's warm and safe, and for the first time here, I'm happy. I want to live up to my potential. I want to be better than I've always been.

"Good!" he says as he walks across the stage to stop in front of Mary and me. "I have so much love inside me for you, and I feel your love for me. It's like a beautiful, warm hug that makes me feel like I can do anything in this world."

I look at Mary and smile at how happy she looks right now. Micah stares down at her, and I hope she knows how wonderful she is. If Micah can see it, I know everyone else here can. That's terrific for her.

He reaches out his hand to take hers, and I swear it's like the Michelangelo painting on the ceiling of the Sistine Chapel. Pulling her up on stage, he beams a smile at her and she smiles back. It's like they're as blissful as they can be.

"Mary here is a perfect example of what we do here at The Golden Light. She came here earlier this week unsure what she wanted to do with her life, and now look at her. She's thriving here with us! That's the key, everyone. We all deserve to thrive. Do you want to thrive?"

The crowd around me yells yes, just as I do, even though I'm not sure where my answer is coming from since I feel so fuzzy headed. I do want to thrive, so when I say yes, I mean it, though.

"Look at me. I want to tell you that I wasn't always the man you see in front of you today. I was lost too, but The Golden Light found me. As soon as I gave myself over to that glorious feeling of acceptance, I was changed. My life became everything I've ever wanted. Do you want that for you?"

Of course, we all answer yes, and Micah says, "Then promise me you'll give all you are to The Golden Light! Say you will! Repeat it with me. I will give all I am to The Golden Light."

Mary gazes up at his face like she's never seen

anything so incredibly beautiful while the rest of us in the audience cry out, "Yes! I give everything I am to The Golden Light!"

I don't know how long this goes on because with each passing second I feel more and more relaxed. Like I feel nothing but the purest love there is. Micah praises all of us for being so wonderful, and I watch him take Mary into his arms and feel so happy for her. To have the leader of The Golden Light recognize you for your greatness is something all of us here can only wish for, but she's got it.

At the end of the bench, the woman sitting there begins to cry and then collapses to the ground. Nobody rushes over to save her, but I understand why now. She's simply experiencing love like she's never felt it before. Just as those girls who recruited me said.

For the first time, I understand. The Golden Light is pure love. I get it.

Micah kisses Mary on the lips and announces to the crowd that he has special work to do for all of us. That makes the women all around me cry out their thanks. Some fall to the ground weeping, while others simply hold their heads in their hands and sob at how happy they are.

When she sits down next to me, I take Mary's hands in mine and smile at her. "You are so lucky. He's seen your greatness. I'm so happy for you!"

She nods and touches her lips with her fingertips. "He kissed me. It was like having someone you've admired all your life notice you. I've never felt this happy, Lara. I want you to feel this too. Do you?"

"I do! It's wonderful. This is how we're supposed to feel every day of our lives," I say, enjoying her happiness right along with her.

I finally get it. Now I see what The Golden Light is all about and how good it is.

18

A WOMAN'S scream pierces the heavy, humid air, and I run outside with the other new recruits into the dark night to find out what's happening. We stop at the bottom of the stairs leading to our cabin and look around for a clue to who screamed and why, but it's impossible to see anything in the pitch black.

Beside me, Cheyenne whispers, "Maybe we shouldn't be out here alone. It's so dark, and God only knows what lives in those woods over there."

Another scream makes us all stiffen in pure terror, and she grabs my hand, squeezing tightly. "Oh my God! We need to go back in!"

Cheyenne begins to cry, so Bethany tries to make her feel better. "It's okay. Probably one of the women here saw a bug. You'll see. It'll be fine."

Nothing she says stops Cheyenne from crying, but I'm not surprised. I've never heard anyone scream like that because of a bug. It would have to be one of those giant Australian spiders that take up half the side of a house to make me scream like that.

In a tiny voice, she asks, "Where is everyone? Those screams were real, weren't they?"

I nod, but before I can tell her she's not imagining anything, suddenly, light after light turns on around the farm as the rest of the group reacts to the terrifying sound. I don't know why, but seeing everything illuminated doesn't ease my fears, and I tighten my hold on Cheyenne's hand as I lift my arm up to shade my eyes from the bright lights.

I see no other group members are standing outside like us, though. Didn't they hear the screams? They must have. Someone turned all those lights on.

Nadine storms out of a building at the other end of the compound and begins to march toward us. Terrific. Just what frightened women need. The camp nazi. Another woman I've never seen before follows her, and I brace for twice as much rage.

They stop a few feet away from us, and although no one says a thing, the sense of fear surrounding us grows now that Nadine has appeared. Cheyenne lets out a tiny whimper when the nasty woman herself looks in our direction, and I wish I could let her know she's not the one Nadine is glaring at, but I don't dare say a word right now. Something tells me if I utter a single syllable, I'm going to find myself in even deeper trouble than before, and the last thing I want to deal with is her four-man goon squad.

The other woman with her has a rounder face that seems kinder, so I focus on her and hope Cheyenne does the same. In the distance, I hear cabin doors open and see men begin to walk out of buildings at the edge of the farm. It doesn't take them long to join us, but they look as confused as we are about who screamed. In addition to Nadine's men, others I assume work for Micah appear with Nash and stop in the center of the compound.

"It's all right, ladies. Why don't we go to the mess hall and get something to eat? It will make us all feel better to have something in our stomachs," the new woman says with a smile.

I sigh, happy she'll be dealing with us instead of Nadine, a woman who I doubt has ever made anyone feel better with her presence. Cheyenne gradually lets go of my hand, and I turn to see she's no longer scared.

"Food does sound good," she says with a forced smile.

The woman takes her hand as she leads the way to our snack. "Exactly. I know when I can't sleep a little bit to eat helps."

Everyone agrees as we walk toward the mess hall, but I can't help but think nobody had any problem sleeping until some woman screamed like she was having her soul ripped from her body. I know I shouldn't be looking around, but I can't help it. That scream came from someone in pain, and not a single soul around here seems to be investigating.

Then out of the corner of my eye, I see Nash watching me. He looks concerned, but I can't imagine he cares that

I'm disobeying what he told me. He's one of Micah's men, no matter how much he wants to pretend he's not.

Maybe he's worried about the woman who screamed, but if it's that, perhaps he should start searching for her instead of staring at me. I hold his gaze the entire walk to the mess hall, and when I walk inside through the wood screen doors, I look back one last time to see him still watching me.

Even worse, Nadine can't seem to take her eyes off me either. I want to run out of this building and shake them silly as I yell, "I'm not the one who screamed! Why aren't you looking for her? You heard it just like we did, so what's wrong with you?"

The woman sets down a tray of little vanilla iced cakes, a metal pitcher of lemonade, and some red plastic cups in the center of the table as we all sit down on the benches. "Here you go. I'm Maddie, by the way. Please don't worry about the scream. We all have nightmares from time to time. That's bound to happen as we shed our old life for the new one we can get from The Golden Light. I'm sure everything's fine. These cakes are fresh, just made earlier today, so enjoy."

As I reach for one of the treats and pour myself a cup of lemonade, I can't tell if Maddie believes what she said about the woman who screamed. I've had terrible nightmares that made me sit bolt upright in bed drenched in a cold sweat, but never have I screamed like that or heard anyone make that kind of noise from a dream. I can't know for sure, but that sounded like a woman experiencing some kind of excruciating pain.

Then I look at the women around me at the table and notice Mary isn't with us. Where could she be?

It doesn't take long before all of us are laughing and happy once again, as we've always been together since we first got here. Well, except for when we found Anna dead. I close my eyes as my body seems to completely relax after a few bites of the incredibly moist cake and a few sips of ice cold lemonade. The people who bake here really are quite talented. I don't think I've ever enjoyed a piece of cake more.

Maybe Maddie was right. Maybe we just needed something in our stomachs.

I don't know how long we sit here because it feels like time is standing still, but after we all eat a piece of cake or two, Maddie comes back to the table and says, "Okay, everyone. Feeling better? Time to get back to bed."

No one argues, and we all follow her out of the mess hall into the pitch black night. I wonder why nobody left even a single light for us to get back to our cabin, but I feel so tired that I can't seem to form the words to ask the question.

Actually, I don't feel tired. I feel relaxed. More relaxed than I've ever felt in my life.

My feet seem to know the way across the dirt compound, but Cheyenne grabs my hand again after a few steps and whispers, "I wish they had left a light on for us."

I squeeze her fingers and smile, even though she can't possibly see it in the pitch black of night that covers us. "It's okay. We're good. It's just a few yards away."

She sighs and eases her hold on my hand. "I know. I've just always been afraid of the dark."

Her words seem to float through the air, nearly getting lost before they enter my ears. It's the strangest thing. I hear them, but it's like my brain doesn't seem to know how to interpret what she's saying.

When we finally reach the stairs up to our cabin, she lets go of my hand. "Thank you, Lara. I think I'm good as long as I hold on to the railing."

In my head, I answer her, but I don't know if the words actually make it out of my mouth. I must really be tired. Probably the adrenaline rush that happened when I heard that woman screaming finally wearing off. God, I bet I'll be able to fall fast asleep as soon as my head hits the pillow.

I take a deep breath in and realize I'm already in bed. How did that happen? I look up at the ceiling but can only see a faint outline of the white painted wood boards above me. I thought I'd fall asleep instantly. Everyone else has. Turning my head, I see Cheyenne in the bed next to me where Anna slept that first night. She's snoring away fast asleep.

Maybe if I count sheep. That's never worked, but I could try. One. Two. Oh, I didn't imagine them jumping over a fence. That's what you have to do, isn't it?

I start over again, picturing a white wooden fence like I've seen on TV. One sheep. Two sheep. Three sheep.

Finally, I start to drift off, but I feel a hand on my arm. It's heavy, and I can't push it away. I'm still very relaxed, but something inside me says I should be afraid.

"What…" I want to say more, but I can't get the words out.

"Keep your mouth shut and come with me."

I immediately recognize the voice. It's that Nash guy. What is he doing here?

Shaking my head, I want to tell him I won't go, but I can't speak now. Even worse, I can't move my limbs. I'm stuck here in this bed and can't fight him off.

"Come on!" he whispers angrily. "We don't have time for this."

I keep shaking my head but can't get a word out. After a few seconds, he shines a light in my eyes, and I want to close them or turn away to escape the brightness, but I can't move.

He frowns and turns off the flashlight as he groans, lifting me out of the bed. I can't fight back. I can't even squirm in an attempt to get away. What's happened to me?

Something is very wrong. I want to cry out, but I can't seem to speak. Did he do this to me? I didn't feel anything like a pinch that would indicate he gave me a shot of something.

I'm limp in his arms as he carries me through the darkness, but I know when he walks outside because I can hear the sound of the cabin door softly close. At least something in me is still working.

Nash doesn't say a word as he hurries to wherever we're going. My head lolls around like my neck can't hold it up anymore, and every few seconds, it bounces off his flexed bicep. My nose bumps into his skin, and the scent of soap fills my nostrils.

So I can hear and smell. I can't speak, and I can't move. I don't know if I can see because once he put his flashlight away, we've been in pitch darkness. I have no idea where we're going. Maybe back to Micah? I can't think of anywhere else.

It doesn't take him long to get to where he's taking me. I feel him walk up a set of stairs and hear him open a door, and a second or two later, he sets me down on a bed. I wait for him to turn on a light, but that doesn't happen before I hear the door open again. I strain to listen for any sign he's still here with me, but it's deathly silent.

I try to move my arms and legs—at least I think I try —but they don't budge an inch. I can't get away from here, and as the moments pass, fear begins to fill me. I'm in danger, although I don't know why. Did I say something wrong in my meeting with Micah? I don't think so. I thought he liked me and believed what I said about wanting to be a part of his group. Did I do something wrong when we went to see him talk this morning? I can't imagine what, although I remember very little of the day after we arrived at the tent.

How odd.

My mind races even as my body sluggishly refuses to respond to my silent, desperate commands. I feel like I wasn't able to think a few minutes ago, but now thoughts run through my consciousness, frightening me. I can't control what my brain is doing.

What is wrong with me?

The sound of the doorknob turning makes my entire body go on red alert, and a moment later, the door opens with a horrible squeak I didn't notice when we arrived earlier. I hold my breath, afraid to make a noise, but then Nash turns on the light and I see a tiny smile on his face.

"You're going to be okay. It's just going to take a little while for the drugs to wear off. They must have given you guys enough to handle an elephant."

I can't respond, but I want to scream that he shouldn't be so goddamned blasé about women being drugged. Then again, I get the feeling this happens a lot around this place.

Fucking crazy people!

Nash sits down in a chair next to the bed as I wish I could speak. Then again, with how my mind's racing at the moment, I might try to say something and all that would come out is gibberish.

What the hell did they give me?

I stare up into his eyes and silently plead for him to speak to me. He winces, like he dreads giving me what I want, but finally he sighs heavily and starts to talk again.

"Don't ask me to do more than what I've done so far. I shouldn't even have done this, but I'm not okay with what's going on."

I continue to look up at him, confused about what he's saying. Does he mean he doesn't approve of them drugging us tonight or specifically something that's being done to me? Am I in more danger than I realize?

Opening my mouth, I try to form the words to ask him, but nothing comes out. Nash simply shakes his head.

"Don't bother. It's going to take a little while. Just rest. They didn't give you anything that can kill you. It just makes you pretty much a zombie. Give it a few more minutes."

Tears begin to fill my eyes, but I don't know if they're because I'm happy I'm not going to die from being drugged or sad because I'm trapped in this place since someone wants me here under their control. A single tear rolls out of the corner of my eye and down the side of my cheek as I try to figure out who.

Nadine or Micah?

19

Slowly, the drug begins to wear off, thankfully. First, the ability to move my limbs returns, but as much as I want to get the hell away from this place, I don't trust my legs to hold me up quite yet. Nash doesn't seem to be trying to hurt me, so I might be safest right here for now.

I lift my left arm above my head and then lower it before lifting my right leg and setting it down onto the bed. Both sides of my body seem to be working. Now if only I could speak.

All of my other senses seem to be working fine. The woodsy scent of men's deodorant fills my nose, and when I unsuccessfully try to start talking, I can actually taste the chemicals in my mouth. It's disgusting, but at least it lets me know that sense is still functioning.

"It'll be just another minute or so, I'm guessing, since

you can finally move. Don't force it. You'll be back to normal in no time."

I draw my eyebrows in and frown to let Nash know how I feel about his casual opinion on my recovery. I may not be able to speak, but I damn well want him to know I don't appreciate how cavalier he's being about this.

He doesn't bother to say anything more or try to entertain me. Instead, he simply sits there watching me as if I'm some curiosity in a zoo or some shop that sells oddities.

Finally, my ability to speak returns out of nowhere. I open my mouth and words start coming out again.

"What the hell is going on here?" I croak out.

Nash reaches over to a table next to him for a bottle of water and hands it to me. "Drink this."

As much as my throat is dying for even a drop of refreshing water, the last thing I want to do is consume anything more here. I throw the bottle back at him, disgusted with him and everyone else in this crazy place.

"No way. You drink it first, and then maybe I'll trust it's not laced with whatever they gave me before."

The bottle bounces off his chest and drops to the floor with a thud. He bends over to pick it up without a word and holds it out for me again. His expression looks like he's already tired of having to deal with me. Too bad. I wasn't the one who shanghaied him and stole him away from his bed in the dark of night.

"I just took you out of that cabin because you were in danger. I could have done whatever I wanted to you for the last half hour and you couldn't have done a damn thing about it. Does it make sense that I'd be trying to drug you now? Drink the water. It will make you feel better and flush the drug out of your system faster."

What he says makes sense, but I'm still not sure I trust him. Then again, out of all the people in The Golden Light I've met so far, he's the only one who doesn't seem to want anything from me.

I take the bottle of water and tentatively bring it to my lips, hoping to God my guess about Nash isn't wrong. After swallowing hard, I'm desperate for water, so I tip the bottle back and take a big gulp. It tastes like water should, although I would have said the same thing about those cakes and the lemonade.

Before long, I've finished the entire bottle, but I'm still parched. Nash grabs another bottle of water and hands it to me without saying a word.

He waits until I drink that one and set the empty bottle on the bed next to me before asking, "Who are you here to find?"

After a night of waking up terrified, being drugged into a zombie, and then rescued and brought here, that's a hell of a question to start with. Nash waits for me to answer, but I've got a few of my own questions I want answered first.

"I'll be happy to tell you if you explain to me what the hell is going on here. Why is anyone drugging us? And why am I in danger? Is it from Nadine? Micah gave me the impression that he was going to make sure she didn't bother me again."

Nash blows the air out of his mouth until there's not a hint of breath left in his lungs. Staring up at the ceiling, he winces before lowering his head to look at me. "The drugs are to keep you all in line."

And with that, he sighs, like we've just had a long discussion and he's exhausted.

I wait for him to continue talking, but clearly he thinks we're done. He's wrong. I want some answers, and I want them right now.

"Uh, I'm not sure what's going on with you, but that generic answer isn't going to be enough."

Then it dawns on me. Is he worried his room is bugged like the rest of this place?

Leaning over, I get as close as I can to him without falling off the bed and whisper, "Is it that there are cameras recording here too?"

I'm stunned when he shrugs and shakes his head yet doesn't keep talking. So we can speak freely and still he thinks that lame explanation that told me little is going to cut it?

Nope. He's going to have to give me more.

"Okay, let me see if I've got this straight. You don't have any reason not to talk freely in this room, and still you plan to only give me that one sentence as an explanation? And you think I'm going to tell you anything?"

His expression falls as I stare at him waiting for him to start talking. It's like he's afraid of something, but if he isn't being watched or recorded, what's wrong?

Finally, he says, "I don't know exactly what they put in the food and drink to keep control over all of you. No one has ever told me that. I just know they do it. Better?"

I can't help but roll my eyes. I guess three sentences is better than one, but he still isn't telling me much.

"A little. I don't really need to know the exact drug, to be honest. I am curious about if everyone's getting drugged, then why aren't you ever dopey?"

He smiles and shakes his head. "They don't drug the men. Only the women. Guards need to be able to take care of any problem that comes up, so having their reaction time dulled wouldn't work."

Makes sense. You don't want your thugs to be slow on the draw. Someone might get mouthy and actually do some free thinking here.

"Must be nice. Okay, that explains the drugging. Who screamed? And don't tell me nobody screamed. It woke me and everyone else out of a sound sleep."

Nash shakes his head. "I don't know."

Something tells me he does know. Why won't he say who the woman was?

"Is she okay now? At least let me know that."

He says nothing, but in his eyes I can see the truth. He knows what happened to that woman. Maybe that's the reason he brought me here. I'd love to think he was watching out for me, but I can't know for sure.

"Well, if you can't tell me that, then can you explain why the hell I'm in danger? Micah made me think he didn't approve of what Nadine did. Was he lying?"

Tilting his head left and right, Nash groans. "Lying isn't exactly what I'd call it. Micah believes. One hundred percent. All in. Toward that end, he just wants to make sure everyone gets what he thinks they deserve, but sometimes that means Nadine and her guards have to get involved."

I level my gaze on his face in frustration. "You

certainly have mastered the art of using a lot of words to say nothing."

He exhales and says, "I don't know if he lied. He can be unhappy with what Nadine does and still allow it."

"So why am I in danger? I thought I convinced him I was a believer."

That gets me a laugh. "Not exactly. I don't know how much danger you're in, but you're definitely on his radar. He assigned me to watch you. That's not a good thing."

"Why? What did I do? All I did was say I wanted to grieve a girl's death. What the hell is wrong with the people here that a girl can die and feeling bad about it is a damn problem?"

The expression on Nash's face morphs into a look of confusion, and I know I'm wasting my time. Whether it's because he's a man or because he's been a part of The Golden Light for too long, my sadness over Anna's death doesn't seem to register in his brain.

"Whatever. So I'm in danger. Great. All of this because I wanted to find Rina," I say in defeat, sitting back on the pillow.

Suddenly, Nash seems interested in talking. Sitting forward, he asks, "Who's Rina?"

Tired of playing this game with him, I close my eyes and sigh. "My sister. I found something in her apartment that made me think she was involved in your group here, so I went looking for her. Those two hippie chicks who smelled like weed approached me in Wilmington, and I asked them if they'd seen her. One of them thought she did, so I came here looking for her."

"I don't know any Rina," he says, shaking his head

slowly. "She might be at one of the other locations, though."

That makes me sit bolt upright in the bed and stare at him in shock. "Other locations? Where? How many? Those two girls made it seem like this is the only place associated with The Golden Light."

He stands up and pulls back the room darkening curtains to look out the window like he's worried someone might be joining us soon. "No, there are a lot of places where people in The Golden Light can be sent. Anywhere Micah needs them to be to support the group."

"Like where? Are there other farms like this? Because I could have sworn there was one right outside of the town where I live. I was there the other day because another girl in town working at The Golden Light office said my sister might be out there."

Snapping the curtains closed, he spins around and stares at me with wildness in his eyes. "What farm? Were you in a blue Mazda?"

Now it's my turn to stare at him. How could he know that about me?

"Yeah. How did you know?"

Before he answers, I figure it out. How could I have not picked up on his voice? "You were one of those guys out there, weren't you? The other one was a real bastard. Is he one of Nadine's men?"

Real fear fills his expression, and he sits down on the bed next to me. I see in his eyes he's terrified, but of what?

"Listen to me, Lara. Don't tell another soul what you just told me. You won't live to get the hell away from here if you do."

"Why? That guy is one of Nadine's goons, isn't he? It fits. He sounded like he wanted to kill someone. That dude needs anger management stat."

"He did kill someone out there at that farm. Trust me, you don't want to let anyone know what you saw there."

"I didn't see anything. I heard a little bit of your conversation while I was hiding in the downstairs closet. That guy's a psycho."

Nash nods, but it's like he's not even listening to me anymore. "Yeah, and he's one of Micah's men, not Nadine's."

I wait for him to say something else, but he seems lost in thought, so I shake his arm to get his attention back on the immediate problem of me getting the hell out of this place and hopefully finding my sister. "Hey, they took my phone when I arrived here. Can you get it for me?"

He turns to look at me, wincing as if he's in pain. "Maybe. I don't know. You can't call anyone. The only place on the entire farm where you can hope to get a signal is in Micah's cabin."

"What about messages? Can I get them anywhere here other than his rooms?" I ask, thinking that if I can get a message to Mario that I might be able to get help for me and anyone else who wants to leave here.

"Sometimes. The internet is spotty at best here."

"Nash, I need my phone."

What I really need is to get the hell away from this place, but I get the sense that asking him to help me with that would be a waste of breath. Nash may not be as bad as the other people here, but he's no angel. Why he's helping me I have no idea, but I don't want to stick around to find out.

"Okay, okay. Let me see what I can do. In the meantime, I need to get you back to your cabin and back in your bed."

Pure terror rushes through me. He wants to do what?

"No way! I can't go back there. Just get my phone, and I'll figure out a way to sneak out of here tonight."

He stands up and begins pacing back and forth from the bed to the door. It's a small space, so his long legs barely get three strides before he turns around and comes back toward me.

"You won't get away tonight. This farm is miles away from another house, and there are armed guards stationed at posts around the perimeter. They don't bother to ask who goes there before they shoot."

"Isn't anyone worried about people dying out here? Someone is going to start asking questions at some point. Or aren't they thinking about that?"

Nash stops in front of me and shakes his head. "Trust me. They're worried about people dying, but that kind of death they could explain as a trespasser on private property. No, let me try to get your phone after I take you back to your cabin. If I can grab it, I'll find a way to give it to you tomorrow."

"But I'm in danger if I go back there. At the very least, they're going to try to drug me again if I stay. And exactly how do you plan on explaining where I was for the past hour. Someone's bound to have seen you bringing me back here."

"Don't worry. I've got that covered. At least I think I

do. You just need to get back to where you belong. What's your phone look like?"

I describe my phone and the black and pink case it's in as I silently pray he means he's really going to try to find it. I need to trust him, but I'm still not sure about Nash. I can't figure out why he's helping me or if this is some ploy by Micah to trick me.

"Okay, let's go." Crouching down, he wraps his arms around my legs, so I jump away, shaking my head.

"I have to carry you back."

"Why?"

"Because I do. Stop asking so many questions. I'm trying to help you here."

He again moves to sweep me up in his arms, and this time I don't react. Lifting me like I'm as light as a feather, he begins walking with me toward the door.

"Say nothing if anyone approaches us. Close your eyes if I tell you to."

I don't say anything to that because all I want to do is ask why. He knows these people better than I do, so I figure I should follow his lead, at least in this.

We head outside into the balmy night air, and I can't help but notice how dark this place is at night. Micah's cabin is lit up, but other than that, every other building is pitch black. I have no idea what time it is, and when I search the skies for any clue, all I see are stars.

Halfway across the compound, he tenses up against me, and I have to bite my tongue to stop myself from asking what's wrong. I find out soon enough when I hear someone walk across the dirt, and before he orders me to close my eyes, I squeeze them shut.

"Pretend to be asleep," he whispers, barely audibly.

"Who's there?" a low voice gruffly asks.

"Nash."

The man walks over to us, shuffling his feet across the ground so I imagine he's leaving a trail of dust behind him. My eyes closed, I sense a light being shined on my face and try hard to remain still and not react.

"What's up with this?" he asks with a chuckle. "Enjoying a little something on the side, Nash?"

I feel his chest expand against my body when Nash hums what sounds like disapproval at the man's suggestion he's been up to something with me. "You know that's not allowed. Micah ordered me to keep an eye on this one. I found her stumbling around looking for the bathroom."

That makes the man laugh out loud. Why, I have no idea, but maybe he thinks it's amusing for someone to not know where to go in the dark. Sounds pretty twisted to me.

"Better get her back. The guards will be doing the midnight search at any minute. You don't want to get yourself shot over little Miss Pisspants here."

His snide crack makes me wish I could sit up and slap his face. Nash merely hums again and starts walking once more.

After a few steps, he whispers, "You did well there. Nice to know you can listen when you want to."

When I don't respond, he chuckles. "Good girl."

That's too much to bear, so I whisper, "Don't push your luck."

I feel him walk up stairs and open my eyes to see him

open the door to my cabin. Nobody wakes when we enter, and a few seconds later, he sets me down on my bed. I don't expect him to say anything more since we have no idea who may be listening, but in a gesture that makes me think I might be able to trust him, he cups my cheek, letting his palm rest against my face for a few moments before walking away.

The sound of the door closing makes me stiffen in fear that someone has heard him return me, but as the seconds tick by and no one says a word, I begin to relax. Closing my eyes, I hope he can find my phone and not get caught.

Nash is my only chance to get away from this place, but if Micah or Nadine thinks he's helping me, neither one of us may be safe.

20

NASH

As I HURRY back to my cabin, I see Micah standing on his porch waving me over to him. My heart sinks, but I have to make it seem like I'm not up to anything but helping him. I just hope he buys the act.

When I get closer to him, he flatly says, "Come inside, Nash. Let's talk."

Damn. I know that tone of voice. I've heard it many times when he's upset about something Nadine has done, and most recently, I heard it when he found out what Adam did to Maren.

Knowing he may be able to see my face even though I can barely make him out, I force a smile and pick up my pace to get to his cabin quickly. He doesn't speak when I join him on the porch, but anger practically radiates off him in waves.

I bow, even though I shouldn't until we go inside, and

he turns on his heel to walk into the building without saying a word to me. That's not a good sign. I follow him into his cabin, and see he's already sitting on his chair by the time I close the door behind me.

The temperature in here is far more comfortable than my room or outside since the air conditioning keeps it at a very pleasant sixty-eight degrees. As usual, he wears only a pair of dark pants as he reclines against the back of his favorite chair.

Bowing again just in case he didn't see me do that outside on the porch, I wait for him to tell me to rise. He takes his time, but finally he says, "I want to talk to you, Nash. Stand and look at me."

I do as he orders, and when my gaze meets his, I see pure rage in his eyes. Even after all this time here, I still have to stop myself from asking what's wrong. I guess it's a normal defense mechanism.

He frowns and folds his arms across his naked chest. "James told me he saw you with that new recruit I told you to watch. How do you explain that when she was supposed to be in her bed for the past few hours?"

Knowing he's watching every tiny move I make, I smile and hope my voice stays level as I answer, "You told me to keep an eye on her. I was. When she and the rest of the new girls came out after they heard the screaming, I could tell Nadine and her men had a problem with her. I was afraid they might go too far and kill her, and I know you don't want any more deaths, so I got her away from them before anything could happen."

I don't take a breath the entire time I'm explaining myself, and I have to fight the urge to inhale deeply when

I finally get all the words out because I'm sure it will make me look guilty. Technically, I am, so there's that. Micah ordered me to watch Lara, not protect her, but something's changed around here.

And I'm not okay with it, even if I don't know what's going on.

He silently studies me while all of this runs through my mind, manipulating the empty space to do what he always does. Make people uncomfortable so he has the upper hand.

At first, that skill terrified me. I'd never been someone who could control himself completely either in speech or actions. Whatever I'd ever felt came out of me with a force I couldn't deny.

Then as I got used to life within The Golden Light, I admired that skill. The way he'd stare at someone and practically squeeze the truth out of them simply by staying quiet impressed the hell out of me. I wanted to be like him. I loved the idea of having that much power over people.

And myself.

Now I know it's more a trick than a skill, and I can see how hard he has to work at not saying anything during those silences. He's barely containing his curiosity at this moment because he likely thinks I was with Lara.

Micah takes a deep breath in and lets the air out slowly through his nose. His arms still folded across his chest, he purses his lips but still says nothing. Finally, he gives me a smile, but every muscle in my body tenses as I wait to hear what he has to say to my lie.

"Nadine definitely has a problem with her. There's no

doubt about that. You know how much I trust her, don't you? The Golden Light wouldn't be what it is today without her love and support, Nash."

When he stops, I wish I could ask if he means himself or this group. I'm a little hazy on what Nadine should get credit for, especially since she's become little more than The Golden Light's gestapo.

I don't ask, of course. Whatever I may feel about the changes that have occurred here in the past few months, I still know my place in Micah's world. I rank just above new recruits and nobodies. For the present, I'm one of his favorites, but that can change at any moment.

It may change tonight if he decides I've broken one of his rules, especially the one that forbids us guards from being with any of the women in the group.

The tension between us builds until I find myself holding my breath out of fear that if I dare breathe, I might admit the truth of how I feel and what I'm planning to do for Lara. Micah looks up toward the ceiling and then slowly lowers his arms to his side. I want to take the change in body language as a hint that he believes me, but I can't tell.

"You were right to be concerned about another death here, Nash. For that, I'm thankful. However, it doesn't look right that you were alone in your cabin with a woman. That's forbidden, as you well know."

I nod, still wanting to speak but unsure I can lie well enough to fool him a second time.

"You look worried, Nash. Unburden yourself. Tell me what's wrong," Micah says, sitting up in his chair and looking like he's actually interested in what may be bothering me.

Finally, I exhale but only little by little so he doesn't think something's off. As my lungs empty, I feel my mouth turn down in a frown and know those two lines my mother used to call elevens between my eyebrows have appeared. I'm sure I wear the look of a man troubled by something, but I can't tell him what's really on my mind.

So I do the only thing I can.

"I knew it was wrong to take her to my room, but I didn't want another death and you having to deal with it. I'm worried that there are some people here who've forgotten your teachings, and I don't know how to handle that."

Most of that is not so much a lie as a half-truth. He nods as I speak, but I know from experience with that too that it may be merely the precursor to Micah unleashing a torrent of anger because I've stepped out of line.

I wait for him to respond, my body on alert for whatever reaction he may have to my concerns. The Micah I met that first day would care that one of his flock is worried about what's happening around him. This version of him I'm not so sure.

His expression turns dark, and he lowers his head but says nothing. I wish he would recognize that whatever Nadine may have been to him in the past, now she's basically creating a police state here in his name. I don't doubt Adam has always enjoyed hurting others, but because she's made it okay to punish and kill people, he believed he was in the right shooting Maren.

Nadine's poison will only make things uglier here. I know it, but I can't say a word about it because Micah is practically blind to her faults.

He sighs heavily and then lifts his head to look up at me. Sadness fills his expression, and I don't think I've ever seen him look so miserable. I hate that I had to be the one to say those things that made him so unhappy, but someone had to or things would only get worse.

"You'll spend two hours in the box, Nash. I'm sorry to have to do that, but rules are rules."

And with that out of the way, he stands up and walks into the other room.

I look around for any guards to come take me away to serve my punishment, but no one comes. After five minutes or so, I walk out of his cabin expecting someone to take me to the box. It never happens.

My feet seem to have a mind of their own, and I walk straight across the compound to where I know I must pay for my crime. I could just walk back to my room and go to bed. There's no one around to force me to go into the box.

Still, I know the rules. I deserve what's about to happen to me.

In the darkness, I see a light flicker on in the cabin directly in front of me where I'll serve my two hours. No doubt, Harker is preparing the box for me. I look around one last time before I make my way up the five steps to the front door, still confused why there's no one here to make sure I do as I must.

That's the thing, though, isn't it? I've always been a good solider, the kind of group member who doesn't deviate from what I know is right for myself and the rest of The Golden Light. So, of course, Micah doesn't think he needs to rouse anyone from their cozy bed to escort me to the box.

But what does it say about me that I've not only agreed to help Lara but also lied to the one person I've believed in and trusted above all others long before she arrived the other day? If Micah had even a hint about all of that, he'd know although I appear to be the same Nash I've always been since he saved me that night, something's changed in me.

I stop at the front door of the cabin and look down at the doorknob barely visible in the darkness of the night. I've only experienced the box once before when I got into it with one of Nadine's men. That time I needed to be punished for pride. Now I'm being punished for what appears to be a wrongdoing.

As I walk inside and see Harker, I know that's not the truth. I'm being punished for going against everything I believe in. Micah may not know that, but I do, and two hours isn't enough to pay for my sins.

"Where's your guard?" Harker asks as he waves me toward the six foot by six foot metal container at the back of the building.

I shake my head as I wonder if the man in charge of enforcing punishments for The Golden Light has lost weight. Always a thin man, he looks emaciated now.

"None needed. I know what I have to do."

He nods, and I see the skin around his chin dangle like it doesn't want to stay connected to his bones. It reminds me of that movie where a monster was wearing a man's skin. They called it a meat suit, I think.

Best not to think of anything like that as I go to spend two hours sealed in the box. The mind has a terrible way of taking a thought like that meat suit one and running with it. And two hours is a long time to be stuck with something like that filling your head.

"Two hours, Nash. Anything you want me to know before I lock you in?" Harker asks and then chuckles.

I shrug, not understanding the joke. He's always been an odd guy, but I'm thinking having to punish people all the time might be getting to him. He's forced to sit in this place every hour, day and night. He's brought his meals, and he sleeps in a back room just feet away from where people scream out in agony when the darkness and silence of the box become too much for them. That has to affect a person.

"Okay. Then see you in two hours," he says without a hint of care for what I'm about to go through. "Have a good time."

He jerks the steel handle on the door and opens the box for me to walk in. The stench of urine hits my nose immediately, but I don't hesitate to keep moving toward the center of the container. Maybe he should focus more on cleaning this thing instead of making lame jokes. It can't be that hard to hose the place down every so often.

The faint hint of shit passes by my nose for the briefest second before I turn my head to look back at the door as he slams it shut. For a long moment, I stand perfectly still in the complete darkness, but then I hear the bolt slam across the metal beneath it, locking me in. The memory of how terrified that simple sound made me the last time I was in here flashes through my mind, but I push it out, replacing it with a thought I've used since I was a kid and something bad happened.

Me sitting on the front steps of my childhood house watching the sun set with my father. He called them the stoop, and he took great pride in those red brick steps leading up to the brick porch. Whenever he sat with me there, he'd pat the bricks and smile. "It took me three weeks to build this, and it's the greatest thing I've ever done in my life."

That time I use whenever I need to distract myself included the most beautiful sunset I've ever seen. The reds and yellows mixing together to form the most perfect orange color no human could ever reproduce and the purples that joined in just before dusk rolled in made me happy. It was the kind of happy that just thinking about it can get you through anything bad that happens in your life.

I concentrate on that memory as my stomach wants to purge my dinner because of the smell of urine all around me. It threatens to ruin my beautiful sunset thought, but I won't let that happen. I don't blame the people who couldn't help but piss themselves in here. This place is scary. It's dark, and many people fear darkness, but worse, it's just you in here, and the mind can play some pretty nasty tricks when there's nothing but the blackness of this box to occupy your thoughts.

My father's boasting about his work on the brick porch and steps echoes in my head, an amusing reminder of a time long gone from my life. We left that house a few years later when he died and my mother couldn't afford to pay the mortgage and feed three children plus herself. The apartment we moved to had none of the sweetness of that house, and I quickly try to stop myself from thinking of what our lives turned into in that place.

But it's no use.

She went from a happy wife and mother to a depressed single woman with three kids to take care of, morphing into an alcoholic by the time I was twelve. My two younger sisters and I survived the best we could, but that's all about we could do.

Survive.

Not thrive like our teachers kept telling us was important for children. No, we barely got by, eating as little as possible so we could hopefully have more for a future meal. My mother couldn't care for us. Hell, she couldn't even care for herself, so how could she do it for three kids who seemed to need so much?

Without my father, our lives descended into hell of poverty and sadness. Every day was filled with want. We wanted more to eat. We wanted clean clothes that the kids at school wouldn't make fun of. We wanted a mother who could pay attention to us.

We wanted all of that and more, but we didn't get any of it. What we got was growing up faster than we should have. What we got was a parent who barely noticed we were even in the same room with her most days.

I shake my head to make those memories disappear, but this is what the box does. I try so hard to bring that moment back with my father, those brick steps, and that incredible sunset, but the image of my mother sitting on that secondhand brown and yellow couch stained with piss and shit from when she was too drunk to even manage getting up to go to the toilet fills my head.

She was barely recognizable by that time after nearly a year of drinking herself into oblivion every damn day. Her beautiful brown hair that I loved to touch because it was so soft turned into a dry, gray, tangled mess that framed the face of a stranger. Gone was the sparkle in her green eyes that my father used to say reminded him of a cat's. In its place, a gloom settled in, joined by dark circles that made her look so old.

The woman I knew disappeared when he died, and a shell of a human being came into our lives. Hollow and unable to care for anyone, including herself, she let her misery dim that sweetness in her until all she became was an angry stranger who resented the entire world, including us.

As I wallow in those terrible thoughts, questions creep into my mind. Is she still alive? Or has the booze killed her? She was barely hanging on the last time I saw her, and that was years ago. Still planted on that awful couch, she pointed her bony finger at me and cursed me out for wanting to leave to find a place of my own. "You're an ungrateful bastard, Nash!" she screamed.

I left that day without saying goodbye, so angry she couldn't be happy for me and want me to succeed in this world. My sisters couldn't come with me, but I hoped they'd be safe and they'd learned enough in the years I was there that they could survive.

Macy didn't last long. Drugs and an abusive boyfriend drove her to an early death before she was even sixteen. I'll never forget standing at her grave with that cheap marker that had grass already growing over it, making her and everything she was slowly disappear from this world.

My younger sister Jenny was left alone with my mother and all her demons, and even though she graduated high school and moved away, the last time I saw her I knew that time she'd spent as the only soul responsible for my mother had scarred her. She was the oldest nineteen year old I'd ever seen. Her eyes showed how much she'd endured. In them, the ugliness of her life shone through, even when she smiled.

I don't want to think about any of this, but I can't stop myself. It's what the box does to you. That's the true punishment. It isn't being alone in the darkness. It's being alone with the thoughts you've tried so hard to push down to that place you don't want to ever think about so they never appear again that gets you.

That terrible brown and yellow geometric pattern from that hideous couch fills the space around me until it's all I can see in the pitch black. I know it's not real, but I slap the air in front of me to make it go away.

I'm surprised when it disappears, but then a low sound that reminds me of something metal scraping off another piece of metal begins to fill my ears. I try to decipher what it could be. I have no idea. There shouldn't be any sounds in the box.

There isn't. It's all in my head. What is that sound? Where have I heard that before?

Those questions occupy me for a minute or two as the noise grows louder and louder until it's all I can hear. I can't make it go away like I did with the vision of that terrible couch of my mother's. I shake my head and then cover my ears, but it keeps getting louder.

"Stop!" I silently scream, hoping that will make it disappear.

That only makes it get louder, if that's even possible. I thrash my arms around me in a desperate hope I can make it stop. But it doesn't.

I open my mouth to scream, but if anything comes out, I can't hear it over the metallic noise all around me. It can't just be in my head. That makes no sense. I thought it could, but it's not possible.

Is Harker making that noise? He must be, but why? Did Micah instruct him to torture me with this sound? Is that why he only gave me two hours in the box?

Finally, I can actually scream, and I bellow as loudly as I can to drown out that horrible sound. It isn't loud enough, so I redouble my effort, but I can't scream loud enough because every time I try, the noise gets louder.

Over and over, I let out an agonizing sound until my throat gets hoarse. I can't stop, though. If I do, the sound will drive me insane.

I don't know how long before I fall to the floor and curl up in a ball, still screaming as I lay on a piss-stained floor. This is nothing like the other time I was in the box. This time, Micah is truly punishing me.

And all I can think is I must deserve it.

21

I OPEN my eyes to see two women standing over me sponging me down. One has dark hair and a round face, while the other is a blond with a gaunt look about her. Both are strangers to me, which seems odd since there aren't that many people who live on the farm here.

The warm water slowly rolls over my skin, and I sigh heavily at how good it feels. I take a deep breath in, happy to not smell piss now. A blast of cool air hits my body, making goosebumps form, and I quickly glance down at my legs to see a white towel draped over my hips.

Looking around, I see I'm not in the box or my room. I don't recognize this place, though. Where am I?

When I make a move to sit up, the round faced woman gently pushes me back onto the bed by my shoulders. She's surprisingly strong for her small size, but she smiles at me when I lie back down.

"Micah insisted you relax, so please don't make this difficult. We don't want to upset our leader, do we?" she asks in an almost monotone voice, and I notice how her pupils take up nearly all of her eyes.

I don't answer since I suspect she meant that as a rhetorical question. Instead, I ask her what I need to know.

"Where am I?"

She slowly rubs a sponge over my forearm while staring into my eyes the whole time. If she didn't look like a zombie and if she wasn't a female member of The Golden Light, this might be sexy. As it is, it's awkward, but I don't look away because I want her to answer my question.

After a few moments, she smiles and answers, "Micah's. He had you brought back here after your time in the box. Are you feeling better now?"

Unsure what she's talking about, I shrug. "No better or worse than I did in the box."

That makes her stop caressing my arm, and she lifts her hand to cup my cheek. "It's good that you've put it out of your mind. That's better for you than remembering."

"Remembering what?"

She doesn't answer and returns to giving me a sponge bath on the top half of my body. The blond walks away after giving my right shin a final swipe with her damp sponge, and when I look around to see if anyone else is here to tell me what's going on, I see it's just the woman near my head and me.

Did something happen while I was in the box? I don't remember anything after I walked in. No, that's not true. I remember the smell of piss surrounding me. Harker really needs to step up his efforts at keeping the box clean. He has time, I'm sure. It's not like there's someone in the box every minute of the day and night.

The curious way this woman is looking at me says something happened to me in there, though. I could ask again, but it would be no use. She's a follower. She does as she's told, and she's clearly been instructed not to talk to me about what went on with me inside the box.

As I try to reconstruct the two hours I was in there, she finishes her task and steps back away from me. "All done. Have a day full of light and goodness, Nash."

I give her a forced smile since I don't know her name and watch her walk out of the room. When she closes the door, I swing my legs off the bed and sit up to get a better look at where I am. The walls are painted a pale yellow, and the floor is that oak hardwood Micah likes. Three pictures of sunsets in gold frames hang along the wall directly in front of me, and on the table near the door a picture of the farm as it must have looked before Micah brought us all here sits in a similar gold frame.

This place is definitely nicer than anywhere else members of The Golden Light sleep. Why did Micah have me brought here, though? Why not just have me taken back to my room?

I stand up, but my legs give out and I fall back onto the bed. Reaching down, I grab the towel to cover myself in case one of the women comes back. I can't imagine why I don't have enough strength in my legs to stand up. I haven't been doing anything strenuous enough to make them weak, so what's happening?

For a few moments, I try to collect my thoughts, but it's as if my brain stopped working when I entered the box. I can't recall anything after Harker closed the door and I was trapped in pure darkness.

What happened for the next two hours? And how long have I been in this room?

I try to stand again but far more slowly, and I'm more successful this second time. I still feel weak, but I'm able to keep on my feet. After wrapping the towel around my body, I pad over to the window, noting how the floor here isn't filled with splinters I'll have to yank out later.

When I pull back the white curtains, I see it's daylight. Quickly, I do the math and figure out there are at least five hours I can't account for between when I would have finished my time in the box and now. Have I been in this room for all that time?

"Good to see you're up and around."

I spin around to see Micah standing in the doorway, and the first thing I notice is he's wearing a shirt. He never wears a shirt. Why is he wearing one now?

He steps into the room and my eyes are drawn to his feet. He's got shoes on. What the hell is going on? A shirt and shoes?

"Yeah, I guess. I'm a little confused about things, to be honest. Like how did I get here? And how long have I been in this room?"

He holds his hand up and gives me one of his smiles that's meant to say, "It's okay, my child." Normally, that works, but losing at least five hours of my life has me a little freaked out right now.

"Micah, I need to know what happened to me. That

woman wouldn't tell me, but then again, that's not surprising since I'm sure she's doped up to high heaven. I need you to tell me what happened in the box that warrants me getting all this special attention."

His smile never fades, even though I'm very much out of line with all my questions I'm demanding to have answered. Walking over to me, he nods his head and answers, "You had a bit of a breakdown in there. Yes, I think that would be the correct word for it. Now let's sit down and we can talk about it."

Sit down and talk about it? Why does he sound like some shrink?

I do as he says and take a seat on the bed. He sits at the nearby desk and leans forward to set his elbows on his knees. At any moment, I expect him to start giving me a pep talk like he's a coach and it's halftime in the big game.

Except there are no other players.

"So how do you feel now?" Micah asks in that social worker kind of voice like I need to be handled with kid gloves.

"I feel confused and would like some answers as to what happened to me. I'm sorry if I'm overstepping my boundaries. I truly am. You know me, Micah. I wouldn't do this if I wasn't really in need of some answers to clarify what is going on here."

His smile grows as I finish speaking, and he says, "What's going on here is what's always been going on. I care about how you're doing, Nash. I hope you know that. I hope you believe it."

As much as I want to find out what happened in those

206 K.M. SCOTT

five lost hours and while I was in the box, I see he's trying to be nice, so I take a deep breath to calm down. As my father used to say, you catch more flies with honey than vinegar.

"I do, and I believe with all my heart that you care about all of us here, Micah. I love being part of The Golden Light. It's my home, and I care about you and all my fellow believers. I just want to know what happened to me in the box and for the five hours after that I can't remember."

For the first time since he walked into this room, his smile fades just a little but enough that the worry in his eyes becomes obvious. "You didn't handle the box as well as you have before, Nash. Things got a little wild, but not to worry. You're fine now. I made sure of that."

"You mean with the women giving me a sponge bath? It was nice, I guess, but I need to know what happened in the box because I can't remember. And what happened in the five hours afterward? Please, Micah. I need some answers."

Once more, he gives me a big smile, but now I know to pay attention to the look in his eyes, and they're still full of concern. But for what or who? Me? Did something terrible happen to me in the box? Did I do something?

"Of course, you do. Maybe you should eat something, though, first. You must be hungry."

His dodging my questions frustrates me, so I jump up off the bed, shaking my head. "I don't want to eat! I want to know what happened to me in the box and then where those five hours went."

Nodding, he sighs. "Actually, it was more like thirty

hours. You were in the box for the two hours ordered, but things got a little out of control, so I thought you might benefit from a nice rest."

His answer stuns me. I stumble backwards until I feel the mattress hit the back of my knees and then my legs give out. I collapse onto the bed shaking my head in disbelief.

"I lost an entire day? How can that be? Why?"

"You were out of control, Nash. The box did something to you this time, and you needed to have something to calm you down or you might have a heart attack. You're fine now, though, so you don't have to worry."

As I look down at my legs that just gave out, I have to wonder about his definition of fine. "I don't know what happened to me and my body doesn't seem to have the strength it should. Please forgive me, but I don't feel fine."

"Well, you will be. Just give it a little longer."

And with that, he stands up and starts walking toward the door. No answers. Nothing but nice words that said little and did nothing to make me feel better.

"Wait, where are you going? Can I go back to my cabin? I don't have to stay here, do I?"

He looks at me and sighs again. God, what is with all this sighing? Micah has never been like this. Something must be really wrong with me.

"For a little while, I'm going to need you to sit tight in here, Nash. You'll get to go back to your room soon. I promise. Until then, just relax. Try not to push yourself too hard to remember. That won't help anyone. If you're meant to know what happened, your mind will let you."

Before I can say another word, he walks out, closing

the door behind him. I don't know what to think about what just happened, but something feels very wrong about it.

I sit with my head hung, unsure about everything for God only knows how long, and then I realize I didn't bow when I saw him. I never forget to do that. I must really be messed up to remember to do that.

But why didn't he remember I should bow when I see him?

22

LARA

DAMN, where is Nash? I knew I shouldn't trust him. He's probably the reason I'm stuck outside in this hot sun today. Do I look like someone who knows the first thing about tending a garden? I've killed every living thing I've ever brought into my apartment, so if these Golden Light people think their version of a farmer is the job for me, they're crazy.

He warned me not to look around, but I can't help it. He should have appeared by now. I heard someone say he was the one making all that noise two nights ago, but nobody's said a thing since.

My stomach tightens at the thought that he got into trouble because he tried to help me. Or maybe he did something else that got him punished. Whatever it was, he cried out for hours, and everyone on the farm heard him. I told Cheyenne not to go outside to see what was

happening, but she didn't listen. I never moved from my
bed until morning.

Now she's missing too.

I pick a ripe tomato and gently place it into my basket
beside me on the ground as I wonder if maybe the two of
them are in the same place. Maybe he helped her with
something too and that's why he got in trouble.

"Lara, how are things coming?" Bethany asks from the
next row over.

"Good. Just picking some nice tomatoes. How about
you?"

She points at the head of lettuce in front of her and
grimaces. "I don't know if I'm supposed to pick this whole
thing or just some leaves. Do you know anything about
lettuce?" she slowly asks.

I have the feeling she sounds very different from the
first day I met her. That was less than a week ago, though.
Wasn't it? Why would she change like that in just a few
days?

Maybe it's all in my head, but it feels like time passes
very strangely here at The Golden Light. It's the drugs, I
bet. They distort everything.

Well, the joke's on them because I didn't eat or drink
much at breakfast this morning. Then I made sure to
hurry to the ladies' showers right after and stuck my
finger down my throat to throw up in a garbage can so
none of whatever they're using to dope us up stayed in
my system.

That's my plan for the rest of the meals I have to eat
while I'm here. I'm still holding out hope I'll get to escape
soon, but since Nash has disappeared, getting to my

phone might be a problem. I don't know where they keep them, and the last thing I want to do is pop up on Nadine's radar again. Once was enough.

As I reach down to pick another tomato, out of the corner of my eye I see Bethany crumble to a heap on the ground. I turn to look around for someone to help, but nobody is around. I can't just leave her there, so I climb over the row of plants to get to her.

Looking down, I can't help but notice how pale she is. We've been out in the sun for at least an hour, but she's as white as a ghost. I crouch down and touch her cheek. It's surprisingly cool, almost clammy.

"Help! Help! Someone help me!"

I search the area around us and see no one. Bethany needs help, but she's too big for me to lift on my own. I scream for help again, but nobody comes running out of any of the buildings.

Where is everyone?

Even though I know it's futile, I try to pick her up, but I barely get her shoulders off the ground. I'm not strong enough for this. I need to find someone to help me.

I lightly tap her cheek to wake her up. "Bethany, open your eyes. Help me get you inside so you can feel better."

She doesn't react, so I slap her face harder, but nothing happens. What's wrong with her?

"Bethany, I'm going to find someone who can help you. I promise I'll be right back."

Even though I know it's breaking the rules to leave the garden after being told explicitly that someone would come for us when it's time for lunch, I run through the rows of plants and up the dirt hill to get to the main area of the farm. I see not a single person anywhere, though. That doesn't make sense. There are at least dozens of people who live here.

I look around, but there isn't a soul here with me. Where are the groups of women acting like zombies? Where are all the men guarding us? Where are Nadine and her goons? There's nobody.

Where have they all gone?

"Hello? Where is everyone?" I yell.

No one answers. This can't be happening. I need someone to help me carry Bethany inside, and somehow all of these people have disappeared. Even Nadine and her jackbooted thugs are nowhere to be found, and at this second, I'd even take them showing up.

"Please! Help me!" I call out, but the silence all around me is deafening.

Well, if I can't get Bethany inside, at least I can get her some water. I don't know if that's going to be enough, but I have to try.

I glance back and see she hasn't moved, so I rush across the compound to the mess hall. Maybe if I'm lucky, there will be some people there who can help me.

But when I fling the screen door open, I see no one. No women sitting on the benches eating cookies and drinking lemonade. No guards watching. No one. How is that possible?

I don't even hear anyone in the kitchen preparing lunch, which is less than an hour away. Has something terrible happened here?

Running over to where the metal pitchers sit on a table ready for the next meal, I grab one and hurry to the faucet to fill it. I take one last look around the empty building and shake my head. Something is very wrong here.

I don't have time to think about that right now. Bethany needs help, and although I don't know if anything I can do will be enough, I have to try.

As I run back to the garden, water splashes out of the pitcher, landing on my legs. It's refreshing after being out in the blazing sun all that time. I lose my footing and slide all the way down in the dirt, like a snowboarder on a snowy hill, but I do my best to keep the water in the container so there's at least some left for when I reach Bethany.

Again, I look around to see if anyone's around, but I see no one. Whatever they're all up to, if Bethany is truly sick, it's going to be their fault. Who thought it was okay to leave two women out in the field alone in this heat?

Suddenly, I stop dead in my tracks at what I see. Bethany's gone. Swiveling my head left and right, I look for her or anyone who can tell me where she is. There's no one.

I'm completely alone here.

Then an idea pops into my head. If there's no one to keep me here, I can leave. I remember from the bus trip the first day that the main road had some good traffic, so all I need to do is flag down a car and get a ride back home.

I toss the silver pitcher down onto the ground next to the lettuce plants and tear back up the hill, silently praying to God I won't see anyone appear to crush my dream of freedom. With a glance at the cabin I share with the other new recruits, I run toward the gate barricading the farm from the road.

My spirit soars at the sight of no one there to stop me. This feels impossible, but I don't care. I'm going to escape this terrible place and return home to search for Rina. What I've seen in the few days I've been at The Golden Light makes me thankful she never came here.

When Mario reads my article on these crazy people, he's going to jump for joy. I bet he'll even make it the lead for that edition. That will make my parents so proud. Rina will love it too. She's always been my biggest fan when it comes to my writing. We'll go out for a great dinner to celebrate. Malcolm's is a nice place for a steak. She'll say it's too expensive, but with the bonus I'll get from having the lead piece in the magazine, I'll be able to afford it.

As I pass the gate, I feel invincible. Power courses through my veins, and I don't even care that the heat and the sun is slowing down my running. I just need to reach the road and get someone to give me a ride. If they don't want to go all the way back to Wilmington, they can drop me off at a bus station and I'll take it from there.

All that matters is I'll be free from The Golden Light.

Just a few steps more and I'll be away from this wretched place. My legs feel like they weigh a ton each, and my thigh muscles feel like they're going to explode out from under my skin, but I can't stop.

My head pounds from the heat. Sweat rolls down the sides of my face and into my eyes, making it hard to see. None of that matters, though. All I care about is escaping this farm.

"Lara! Stop!" a female's voice calls, but I don't look back.

I'm almost there. Just a little ways more. Once I make it to the road, I can flag down a car. As I think that, a fear that I won't be far enough away spikes in me. Nadine's men will be able to catch me if I don't keep running when I reach the road.

That can't happen. I can't finally get away and have them snatch my freedom away from me so cruelly.

I turn my head and see people running after me. Where did they come from? Even Bethany is with them. I tried to help her, and this is how she repays me? This is what you get for being nice. I should have left her lying there with her head in the dirt next to the lettuce plants. I would have been away from here by now if I had.

"Lara! Lara! Come back!" one of them cries out in desperation.

In my head, a single word repeats over and over. No! I will not go back. I will not be kept here against my will anymore.

They run so much faster than I can, though, and just before I reach the main road, I feel hands grasping for me. They claw at my clothes as they sob over and over, "Lara, come back! Come back!"

There are too many of them. I keep my gaze facing ahead, but they pull me backwards. They won't let me go.

Finally, a man's hand lands hard on my shoulder, and my body slows before I start falling to the ground. He's holding me down so I can't move. I thrash around like a wild animal, but it's no use.

He pushes me down so my knees hit first. Sharp rocks

stab at my kneecaps, and then his hand slams my head to the ground. Dirt fills my nose and mouth, and I begin to cry at how close I was to getting away.

I open my mouth to scream for him to let me go, but no words come out. My heart races as all their hands keep me down on the ground.

They got me, and now I'm stuck here.

23

"There should be a clock in this room," I mumble to myself as I continue to wait to be released.

I'm not stupid. I know what's going on here. I'm not Micah's favorite anymore. Once I tried to help Lara, he decided I wasn't following the rules. So now I'm just another one of his guards. That's why I'm still being kept here.

I pace back and forth across the width of the room, spinning on my toes instead of my heel when I get to the dresser on one side and the door on the other. Each time, I wonder if now is when someone is going to come back and release me.

When I reach the door again, I stop and wait, but nobody comes in. I did my time in the box. Why am I being punished like this?

A sound like footsteps coming toward the room

makes my heart skip a beat, and I wait to see who it is. Micah's probably still angry, so he'll send someone else to deal with me. That's fine. I don't care who it is who springs me from here. I just want to get out.

For the third time in the last few minutes, I look up at the spot on the wall where there should be a clock and sigh. I have no idea what time it is. It's still light out, and I'm guessing it's maybe midday. My stomach grumbles, telling me it's time to eat.

As I stand there lost in thought about what's for lunch today, a knock at the door startles me, and I spin around to face whoever it is that's about to come in. But all they do is knock again, so I yell, "Come in!"

I'm surprised to see Micah walk into the room. Quickly, I size up his expression. He looks sort of happy. Not ecstatic or anything, but not miserable or angry. That's something.

He's not wearing a shirt or shoes. At least that's back to normal.

I bow and wait for him to tell me I can stand, but he just starts talking again. Maybe he doesn't want any of us to bow anymore. Or maybe it's because he's planning to send me away?

That thought hits me like a punch to the chest. I've been with The Golden Light for so long I don't know if I can make it out there in the world on my own again. Would Micah really force me out just because of one mistake?

"I'm glad to see you up and around, Nash. How are you feeling?"

"Fine. I'd like to go back to my room, though."

He nods like he's considering my request and smiles. "I think that can be arranged. I just wanted to make sure you were recovered after everything. Are you really feeling better?"

Frustration builds inside me and threatens to explode out of my mouth, but I keep calm and answer, "I feel fine, Micah. I'm hungry, so when I get out of here, I'm going to get some lunch at the mess hall, and then if it's okay, I'd like to go back to my cabin. I'm sure I'll be ready for work tomorrow morning."

Holding up his hand like he wants to stop me, he shakes his head. "Let's not worry about getting back to work, Nash. That will come in time. For now, I'm just happy to see you feeling better. Your idea of grabbing some lunch sounds good."

Relief washes over me. I'm going to get out of here and back to my regular schedule, and nothing could make me happier. Once I get some food in my stomach, I'm sure I'll feel even better.

"Thanks, Micah. I appreciate this."

He pats me on the back and gives me a big smile. "I'm happy to help, Nash. Go eat and relax today. We'll get back to work tomorrow."

I don't need to be told twice I can go, so I thank him again and hurry out of the room. A long brightly lit hallway greets me, and for a moment I don't know which way to go. Where on the farm is this building that has enough space to fit a hallway this length?

None of that matters as much as my getting some lunch, so I go right out of the room and rush to where another hallway intersects this one. I see a door to the left and make my way toward it, still unsure where this building is on the farm.

It's strangely quiet here, like there's no one around but Micah and me. That doesn't make any sense, though. There are nearly a hundred people who live on the farm with us.

Then again, if they're all working as they're supposed to, I guess there wouldn't be much noise in the middle of the day. Still, something feels wrong.

I push the door open and step out into the hot summer day, happy to be free from whatever that was inside. He must have been pretty worried about what happened to me in the box to keep me cooped up for all that time.

Halfway across the compound, I notice no one is out but me. Did Micah finally realize that making those women work outside in the blazing hot sun is a bad idea? Maybe since he's worried about having any more deaths happen here he decided to keep everyone indoors today.

When I reach the mess hall, no one's around in there either. Strange.

I start walking toward the kitchen, but Micah walks out through the swinging doors with a tray of food in his hand. Pointing toward a table nearby, he says, "Let me get you settled. Sit down. I'll get you a drink too."

This is definitely odd. Micah has never served me once since I came here to the farm. Something must be wrong. Did he have a doctor come in while I was out of it and do tests on me? Am I sick?

Then the memory of every time Micah was furious with a member of The Golden Light flashes through my mind. He's going to get rid of me. My helping Lara was too big a transgression, so he's going to make me disappear.

I sit down on a bench and look down at my tray of food. I thought today was tacos, but this looks like Salisbury steak. Never my favorite, it looks like it's being drowned in brown gravy with mushrooms. I hate mushrooms.

Micah sits down across from me and sets a cup of lemonade near my tray. "There you go. Enjoy!"

His enthusiasm for such a terrible meal doesn't change the fact that I don't want to eat this. The peas don't look good either. The cook ruined them so they're not green anymore but a sickly color resembling baby puke.

That leaves the single piece of bread up in the far right corner of the tray. There's no butter, though, and as I look around for the bowl that's supposed to be on the table, I see nothing. Great. A dry piece of bread. Wonderful lunch.

"What's wrong?" Micah asks.

Shrugging, I pick up the bread and take a bite. "I thought today was tacos. I'm not a huge fan of Salisbury steak, and I hate mushrooms."

"Why?"

I look across the table and see him waiting for my answer. He's never been curious about my likes and dislikes before. Then again, I don't think I've ever mentioned not liking something around him until now.

"They taste like dirt. I don't want my food to taste like I'm eating it off the ground."

He laughs at my explanation, as if anything I said was funny. "I guess you're right. I never thought about it that way."

I finish the piece of bread, wishing it had some taste or a hint of butter to it. My mouth dry, I gulp down some lemonade. At least that's good.

"I wish there was something else I could give you to eat, Nash. I don't want you to go hungry, but that's all we have for lunch today. I think we're having fish for dinner, though. Maybe you'll like that later today?"

The way he's talking to me is surreal. He's the leader of The Golden Light. He is the light, for God's sake. He gives orders, and people follow them. This doting version of Micah confuses me.

Even though I know I shouldn't ask him questions since that's not allowed, I can't help myself. If he gets upset, I'll blame my breach of etiquette on feeling under the weather.

"Why are you saying things like that? You've never cared about my eating before."

My question gets me a stern look, but that passes quickly and is replaced by a far more pleasant expression. "I always care that you're happy, Nash. I'm sorry if you haven't seen that before."

I hurry to make him understand I'm not saying he's never cared. That would be tantamount to claiming he's not the leader he's always worked so hard to be.

"Oh, no. I don't think that at all. I just wondered why you were here eating with me. I'm sure you have far more important people and business to focus on right now."

Micah reaches over and pats the top of my hand as it

rests on the table. "I have nothing more important to do at this moment, Nash. I hope the lemonade refreshed you. It's a hot day out today, so keeping hydrated is important."

I smile and take another sip of my drink before asking him about how different he looked the last time he visited me. "Why were you wearing a shirt and shoes yesterday?"

"What do you mean?"

"You never wear those, but yesterday you were wearing both. I know it was a hot day like today, so it seems odd that you chose to start wearing a shirt and shoes. I'm just wondering if something's going on. As one of your guards, I should know about it if anything's changed."

He gives me a strange look like I've said something odd. Taking his time to respond, he answers, "I'm not sure what you're talking about, Nash. I often wear clothes. Society generally frowns on people walking around naked. I do have new sneakers, though. Is that what you mean?"

Why is he talking about society and what it expects? This is The Golden Light. We don't give a damn about what society thinks we should do to fit in. That's one of the main reasons why Micah began this group. We don't conform to what's expected of us, so we left society to come live here on this farm.

"I mean none of this makes sense. You don't care about society or wearing clothes. And stop acting like wearing shoes is perfectly normal for you. You never wear them or a shirt. What's going on here?"

He pats my hand again to try to calm me down. "It's okay, Nash. There's nothing to be raising your voice about. We're just having a friendly conversation, right?"

I pull my hand back and stand up from the table. "Stop acting like everything is the same as it's always been. You don't wear a shirt or shoes. Ever! And where is everyone today? Nearly a hundred people live here on this farm, but I didn't see a single soul coming over here. Where are they? What have you done with them?"

Micah looks up at me, and I see not anger but worry in his eyes. Why?

"It's okay, Nash. Just calm down. Everything is going to be fine. You said you wanted to go back to your room, so why don't you do that for the rest of the day until dinner?"

Shaking my head, I try to speak, but nothing comes out. It's all the better anyway since he's speaking riddles today.

I need to get out of here and find Lara. She should have been outside so I could see her on my way here. Did Micah have Nadine do something with her?

Just before I reach the screen doors, I turn around and start to ask him, but it's no use. He wouldn't tell me anyway. Nadine has some special power over him, and I have nothing that can beat that.

He says something about going back to my room, but I can't do that now. Something is very wrong here, and I need to find Lara. I promised her I'd get her phone first, though, so I need to do that before I get her so we can leave this place.

I step out into the hot sun as that thought fills my

mind. I've never wanted to leave here until now. This is my home. After finding my girlfriend cheating on me, I thought I had nowhere to go. I was lost, and Micah saved me. He made me see there was more to life and I could have all I want if I just believed in myself.

Where is that man now? What has happened to him? What happened to the promise of great things coming to us if we allowed ourselves to believe we deserved them?

Something has changed with The Golden Light, and I don't know what it is, but I can't stay here anymore.

24

LARA

I WAKE up and know I'm not in the bed I've slept in since I arrived here. Looking around, I see the walls are white and not wood like at the cabin.

Everything after the moment I fell to the ground near the gate feels fuzzy to me now. I want to remember, but it's like there's a wall between that information and every other thought in my head.

Oh, God! Did they feed me while I was out? That would explain the fogginess of my mind. Whatever they put in the food and lemonade everyone consumes packs a punch. Why everyone just lets it happen is beyond me. They have to know they're being drugged, and they're okay with that?

Sheep. That's what these people are. Sheep. They have a leader in Micah, and they follow him wherever he says they must.

Well, I'm not one of his flock. I refuse to let myself be one of his little lambs he orders around. I don't care if he sends Nadine and her thugs in to handle me.

I sit up and swing my legs off the bed, noticing I don't have any clothes on other than my bra and panties. My tan dress they made me wear sits draped over the chair in the corner, and my shoes are on the floor nearby. I shiver at the thought that some stranger undressed me while I was unconscious.

None of that matters, though. What I need to focus on now is getting out of this place, so I pad across the room to the window and look out. The view seems different than I expected. All I've seen of the farm is my cabin, the central compound, Micah's room, and the gardens in the field. This view of green grass and a courtyard in the center of a white building looks like it doesn't even belong on the farm.

Fear tears through me, and I grip the windowsill in terror. Did they move me to another location? Nash mentioned there were others. Is that why nothing outside this window looks familiar?

Oh, God. If they moved me, I won't be able to find him to help me get my phone. I missed my big chance to escape, so I'm going to need that to get away from here.

A terrible thought makes my stomach sink. Did he tell Micah and Nadine what I planned to do? Is that why I'm in this strange place?

I need to get out of this room and find my phone. If I can call my mother, she'll inform the authorities and this nightmare will end.

Slipping my dress over my head, I let it fall down my

body while I slip my shoes on. Wherever I am has to have a way out. I just need to find it, and everything will be okay.

That thought calms my nerves, and I hurry over to the door to begin my second escape from The Golden Light. When I try to twist the doorknob, it won't budge.

I'm locked in!

I bang on the metal door with every ounce of strength I possess as I scream, "Somebody! Anybody! Let me out!"

After yelling until I'm hoarse and nobody responding to my pleas, I return to the window. If I can't get out through the door, then maybe I can through the window. Pushing on the glass, I can't get it to open even an inch. It's like it's glued shut.

Frustration fills me as I pace back and forth across the room like a caged animal. Did I lose my one chance to get out of here and now I'm stuck in this place?

No! I can't let that happen. I will be free. Whatever happens, I will leave this wretched place.

When someone knocks on the door, I frantically prepare myself for whoever it is. I've got nothing to protect myself with other than a comb sitting on top of the dresser, so I grab it and swear to God I'll do whatever's necessary to stop them from keeping me here.

I watch as the door slowly opens and reveals Micah. He's dressed in his usual dark pants, but today he's wearing a tan shirt that reminds me of the shirts my father wears when my mother drags him on cruises. I guess it's a nice change from that whole messiah look he had going on before. As I study his appearance, I notice he's wearing Crocs.

Is it costume day at The Golden Light?

"Nice look. Who are you supposed to be?" I ask as he steps into the room.

My little bit of sarcasm doesn't seem to register with him. He closes the door, disappointing me, and sits down in a chair over near the window.

Trusting soul, isn't he? I'm guessing he's got guards stationed outside the door, so he can afford to be relaxed.

"Are you considering a new look, Lara?" he asks with a smile that seems out of place since he's holding me hostage here.

I shake my head, not understanding what he means by that question, so he points at the comb. Looking down at my hand, I see I'm holding it like a weapon. He sees that too, I'm sure, so why did he bother with that new look comment?

Maybe I'm not the only one feeling sarcastic today.

"I want to leave."

My words come out like a proclamation some statesman might make to end a war. They allow no room for argument or discussion. I do not want to stay here any longer.

Micah, however, doesn't interpret them the same way. He tilts his head left and right and slightly frowns, as if he's weighing the idea I've presented and wants to find the best way to let me know it's not going to happen. Then he sighs, like dealing with me is such a drain on his energy.

"Well, that's something we can talk about. What's making you unhappy enough to want to leave here, Lara?"

I don't know why he's doing this social worker routine with me, but it's only serving to make me angrier than I was when he walked in here. Mocking his sigh, I take a step toward him and glare down into his eyes.

"Because you won't let me leave. Now I want to go. Right now."

This time, he doesn't bother to pretend like he's thinking about it and immediately answers, "You know that can't happen. Why don't we sit down and talk about how you're feeling today?"

God, this man infuriates me! I don't know which Micah I hate more—the one who acted like he was Jesus Christ walking on water or this one with his kumbaya attitude.

"You're already sitting down," I snap.

He smiles like I said something funny and nods, but I know he doesn't agree with anything I'm saying. It's all part of his act to make people think he understands their pain. Well, he doesn't understand mine. How could he? He's the cause of my damn unhappiness.

"I know you wish things were different, Lara, but I know if you talked about what's on your mind, you'd be a whole lot happier."

Waving my hand around, I study him in disgust. "What is this whole thing you're doing today? You look like you belong on some island, although the black pants might be a tad too hot for tropical weather. And what's with the Crocs? Seriously? Since it's not Halloween, I can't imagine what you're going for with this. I think I actually liked the misunderstood prophet look you were sporting before, Micah."

My insult doesn't have the effect I hoped for. Maybe he's not bright enough to know I was being rude. I wasn't exactly subtle about it, though, so whatever he's smiling about now probably has nothing to do with what I think of his appearance.

"You seem very interested in what I'm wearing today. Do I remind you of someone and that upsets you?" he asks in a clinical way I think I despise the most.

Even more frustrated than before when I couldn't get that damn window open, I flop down on the bed and roll my eyes. "No, you don't remind me of anyone and that's upsetting me. You're the one who's pissing me off with all your quiet talk and offers to discuss my feelings. I want to get out of here! What about that isn't registering in your head? I don't want to talk. I want to leave."

"Maybe we can discuss another topic. What about how you're feeling after this morning?"

What does he mean? Did something happen this morning that I don't know about? Is he talking about my near escape?

"I'm feeling fine. I'd be feeling even better if I wasn't being held here against my will."

"Would you like something to eat? I'd be happy to escort you to the dining hall and sit with you while you have some lunch."

I shake my head as what he says baffles me. "What? Have you given up on the whole messiah thing and now you want to be my best friend? I already have one of those, so too bad for you."

"Who is your best friend, Lara?" he asks as he sits up straight in his chair.

For a few seconds, I debate whether I want to tell him the real reason I came to this place. He probably knows already. Nash likely told him what I've been up to the whole time I've been here, so there's no point in hiding it anymore.

"My sister. Her name is Rina. She's the reason I'm here."

Micah tries to give me a smile, but the corners of his mouth barely hitch up. "I know. I know, Lara."

So he's been on to me, but for how long? I bet Nash confessed everything after all that screaming he did. And to think I was feeling sorry for him. Bastard! Now I hope he did suffer.

"Well, then you know. Great for you. It doesn't change the fact that I want to get the hell out of here. I need to find Rina. I've decided she's not here, so if you don't mind, I'd like to go now."

"Would you like to talk about Rina?"

God, he's irritating.

I swing my legs front and back as I sit on the bed, something that reminds me of how she and I used to do that for hours in the bedroom we shared. Neither of us could ever sit still, even when our parents grounded us and sent us to our room. We'd talk and giggle about whatever happened that day, all the while swinging our legs with all that nervous energy cooped up inside us.

"No, I don't want to talk about my sister. She isn't someone who would ever come to a place like this. I know that now. I can't believe I ever thought she'd even consider coming here. Rina's too smart to buy into all this feel-good positivity nonsense."

Micah nods, but I know he's not really listening. He's hearing me and waiting for his chance to respond. He's one of those people. I hate having conversations with people like that. You barely get the words out of your mouth before they start yammering on about whatever's on their mind.

Surprisingly, he doesn't say anything for a long moment. I still think he's a selfish bastard, though. One time being polite does not a nice person make.

Finally, he asks, "Do you think you're like your sister, Lara?"

I can't stop myself from throwing my head back in laughter. "Do you mean do I buy into all of this self-help crap you spew here? No, Micah. I do not. I was barely able to pretend the first time I met you, but now I can't even muster up the acting chops to fake it. Neither my sister nor I would ever truly believe in all this nonsense you and your people spew here."

He frowns at my condemnation of all of this Golden Light silliness. Too bad. Maybe if someone had told him the truth about it in the beginning, there wouldn't be women out there being drugged day after day so they're willing to work for him.

I am curious about something, though. Where is his best buddy Nadine and her boys? Out terrorizing like usual?

"So, tell me, Micah. Where's Nadine today?"

Again, he's quiet for a long time before he asks, "Nadine?"

Why does he want to play this game with me? He

knows damn well who Nadine is. Why act like he doesn't understand the question?

"Yeah. Your girl Nadine. She's got to be lurking around here somewhere. She always is. You told me you wouldn't let her harm me again, but I think we all know you don't have that kind of control over her. Or maybe it's that you don't want to be the bad guy and prefer her to do the dirty work of scaring people. Either way, she's a shitty person, and you're a shitty person for letting her behave like that. You know, just in case nobody's ever told you that before."

With that, he stands from the chair and walks toward the door. "I'll leave you be for now, Lara. Someone will bring you lunch soon since I'm sure you're hungry. We'll talk later."

"I don't want to talk later!" I scream. "I want to be let free from this place."

Shaking his head, he softly answers, "You know that's not possible, Lara. You're here because you need to be here."

I jump off the bed and rush toward him. Grabbing his arm, I look up into his eyes and hope he understands how desperate I am right now. If I had an actual weapon, I'd kill him and get the hell away from this place today.

He looks down at me with pure terror and tries to yank his arm away. I can't let him go before I say something else, though, so I hold on tightly to keep him there so he must listen to me.

"I don't need to be here! I know I have greatness in me. I knew that before I came here. Just let me go. I don't want to be here with you and all these people who believe every syllable you utter. I don't belong here. Why won't you listen to me?"

Micah plucks my fingers off his arm one by one and sighs. "You're so much worse than I thought when you got here. I want to help you. I truly do. I just don't know if you can be helped. God help me, but I don't know if you can."

"I don't need help! Why do you keep acting like I need this? Just let me go. Please!"

He shakes his head and hurries out of the room as he mumbles something about me not having a grasp on reality. Is he kidding? I know what's real. I haven't been consuming all that drug-laced food and lemonade he's been feeding everyone. I'm as clearheaded as I've ever been. Things don't get more real than how I feel right now.

And then, right before my eyes as the door slams shut, I see Rina standing there staring at me. She's not here, though, so is this my imagination? Oh, God. Maybe they did give me some of the food without me realizing it.

"Rina, I don't know where you are, but I came here looking for you. I'm sorry I thought you'd believe any of this bullshit. I should have known better."

She doesn't answer but shakes her head as she backs away from me. In her eyes, I see pure terror. I turn around to see what's behind me that could be scaring her, but there's nothing. When I turn back around to face her, she's not there anymore.

My shoulders slump in defeat, and I sadly hang my head. It was all an illusion because of the drugs in my system. Damn Micah and his people!

All I want is to see Rina in person. Not a figment of my imagination. Not a dream. I want to see her in flesh and blood so I can know she's okay.

I sit down on the bed as an uneasy feeling settles into my brain. Rina isn't okay. I don't know how I know, but I do. Something bad has happened to her.

God, I need to get out of here so I can find her and save her from The Golden Light.

25

NASH

THE BUILDING where they hide the phones should be at the far end of the farm, but I can't find it now. That's crazy, though. People don't go around just moving entire buildings around, so I must be mistaken.

I take a deep breath in and let it out slowly. Let me think for a minute. I'm sure I can remember where it is.

Two women walk by and smile, which is good because that means Micah hasn't told the others to shun me or kill me. He was acting very weird at lunch today. And what's with the clothes he was wearing yesterday?

Something strange has happened here. I just wish I knew what was going on.

I shield my eyes from the bright sun and look around at the buildings in front of me. None of them look like the one where they hide the phones.

This heat is crazy today. I rub the back of my hand across my forehead to catch the sweat forming at my hairline. It's got to be in the mid-nineties already. I suddenly feel woozy. Walking toward the shade from the building to my right, I nearly collapse as the heat quickly saps me of all my strength.

Damn, that happened quick. It must be even hotter than I think today. But that doesn't explain how everything seems to be swimming in front of me. Or maybe it does. I'm not sure. All I know is I felt fine up until a minute ago.

Then a tiny flame of understanding ignites in my mind. It's not the heat. I only ate a single piece of bread and drank a little bit of lemonade, but that would be enough if they drugged it. That explains why my eyesight is playing tricks on me.

He drugged me. Guards are never fed that stuff. My heart skips a beat as reality sets in.

I must not be a guard anymore.

Closing my eyes, I hope this feeling goes away now that I'm out of the sun. Yes, I know it's not that making me sick, but it wasn't helping. Taking a deep breath in, I wish the air wasn't so thick, but beggars can't be choosers. I take a second breath in through my nose and let it out of my mouth, calming myself and actually making me feel better.

Okay, I can find that building. I just need to think.

A banging sound distracts me from figuring out where it might be, and I open my eyes to look around for where it's coming from. It sounds like someone's locked themselves in a room and they need help.

The problem is I don't see anyone when I scan the area. Am I hearing things that aren't there now? Knowing what those drugs do to the women around here, I wouldn't be surprised.

Ignoring the noise, I focus on finding the building I need to go to. I step out into the sun again and begin walking toward where it should be, but that banging makes thinking of anything else impossible.

Where is that coming from?

Unable to concentrate, I backtrack and follow the sound. It grows louder with every step I take, so it must be coming from somewhere close. I look at each window but find no one.

Is this all in my head? Damnit, I shouldn't have consumed anything, but I was so hungry by the time lunch rolled around that I couldn't help myself. That was stupid, though. I know what they do to the food and drink here to keep the women under control.

I just thought I was safe because I was a guard.

As I try to determine if I'm losing my mind or not, a muffled voice joins with the banging noise. I look around again, desperate to find who's making the noise not only to help them but to know I'm not crazy.

After nearly giving up hope, out of the corner of my eye I see someone waving their arms in the window of a nearby building. I can't make out who they are, so I hurry over to see what's wrong.

I'm stunned to see Lara flailing her arms around her head and screaming at me. I can't understand what she's saying, so I move closer to the window through the bushes planted beneath it.

Her mouth opens wide and I can tell she's yelling something, but even next to the window I can't hear the words. She looks upset and frustrated with me.

"I'm sorry. I can't hear you," I say loudly, pointing at my ear to make her understand whatever she's saying isn't coming through the glass.

Her expression falls, and she shakes her head. I can't tell for sure, but I think she might be crying. Damnit, I have to find out what's wrong with her.

I tap on the window and smile as I point toward the nearby door. "I'm going to come in. Just wait, okay?"

Lara shakes her head, and I don't know if she's trying to tell me she can't hear me or I shouldn't try to come inside to see her. I can't stand out here not understanding what she's saying, though. She needs help, and I want to give it to her.

It's the least I can do for her now.

Happy to find the door unlocked, I walk into the building and knock on the first door I think could be her room. I get no response, so I knock again and then turn the doorknob.

Locked. Why is she in a room locked from the outside?

I grip the doorknob tightly and jerk it down toward the floor, snapping it off the door. Lara throws the door open and pulls me inside her room. "Shut the door! I don't want them finding you here!" she whispers before hurrying over to the window to close the blinds.

"What's wrong? Why are you in here?" I ask as I look around her room for any sign of cameras but see none.

Plain white walls, white industrial tiles on the floor,

and furniture screwed to the floor make this place look like a prison cell. Why is she being held in this room?

"I don't know. I nearly escaped this morning, but they got me and brought me back here."

She stops and lets out a heavy sigh. "Or maybe that was all in my head. I think it's possible they drugged me while I was asleep."

"I know. I think I got some of it too in a piece of bread. Or maybe it was the lemonade."

Lara's eyes open wide. "Don't drink the lemonade! That's one of the ways they drug the women here. Lemonade and those damn cookies."

She sounds frantic bordering on mad, but I believe her. "Okay. We're going to be okay. I don't think Micah gave me much. I'm much bigger than the women here, so the dose probably wasn't strong enough."

As she shakes her head, Lara asks, "Where is this building on the farm? And you should see Micah. Your leader has suddenly started wearing shirts and Crocs. Crocs! That's proof enough he's not some prophet who knows all."

The words tumble out of her mouth like an avalanche of sounds. Some I understand, but others make no sense. I've heard nothing of her nearly escaping. I think Micah would have mentioned that to me when we talked since I was supposed to be watching her.

"What do you mean you nearly escaped?" I ask as she paces back and forth across the room.

She stops and throws her hands up in the air. "I nearly got out! That's what I mean. I got to the gate, but then everyone appeared out of nowhere. When Bethany was passed out and needed help, I couldn't find a soul, but when I'm about to get my freedom, these people materialize out of thin air? I blame Micah. He did it. He let me think I was going to be free, and then he yanked it away from me at the last moment. I think the drugs are messing me up. I'm having a hard time remembering things correctly, but I know it's not me. It's the drugs."

I don't know what she's talking about, but she might be right about them drugging her. I'm convinced they're doing it to me too.

"You need to make sure you don't eat anything, Lara. That's how they get the drugs into your system. It's in the food and everything you drink."

She stops pacing and takes me by the hand to sit on the bed with her. Her eyes filled with concern, she stares at me for a few seconds before asking, "What happened to you? I heard you screaming for what seemed like hours the other night. What did they do to you? I thought you were one of Micah's favorites."

I hadn't thought about my time in the box for the past few hours, but her mention of it brings all those terrible memories rushing back into my mind. Shaking my head, I look down at the bed and mumble, "I'm not sure."

That's not the truth, but I'm not ready to talk about it yet. Not even with Lara, the only person I think I can trust in this place now.

She strokes the space between my thumb and forefinger with her fingertip, instantly easing my nerves. "It wasn't because of me, was it?"

I shrug and try to make it seem like I wasn't sent to the box because of helping her, but she sees right through my silent denial. "I'm sorry, Nash. You didn't do anything wrong. They shouldn't have punished you."

Nodding, I try to smile when I look up at her, but I can't fake being happy right now. "I know. Micah didn't even really want to do it. I think he just had to because if he didn't, he'd have guards spending time with women all over the place."

"Even though we didn't do anything together?"

"Yeah. I broke the rules by taking you back to my room. I'm probably breaking the rules just being here right now, but I didn't want you to think I forgot about getting your phone for you."

I stop for a moment and then say in a low voice that can't hide my embarrassment, "I just can't find the building."

"What do you mean you can't find the building?" Lara asks, a logical question since I've asked myself the same thing already.

Avoiding her gaze, I answer, "I can't find it. The building I thought they put the phones in isn't where I thought it was."

She doesn't say anything, so I add, "To be honest, I'm not sure where this is. I don't think we're on the farm anymore."

Lara gives my hand a squeeze that feels all too real. "What did they do to you, Nash?"

I hate the way that sounds, like I'm some broken creature Micah and his people have ruined. I'm not that man. I'm fine. They're just messing with me with the food and lemonade.

"Lunch. I think it was drugged."

"But you told me they don't drug the guards. Why would Micah let that happen to you?"

Looking up at her, I shrug even as I can't help but be worried if he's allowing that he's not going to stop when Nadine suggests her guys get rid of me. "I'm not a favorite anymore, I guess. Just don't eat or drink anything, okay? If you do, you're going to feel all messed up like I do, and I don't want that for you."

"I won't."

We fall into silence, and I wish I could tell her things are going to be okay. They aren't, though. I don't want to scare her, so I need to pretend, but I've lost all hope that Micah is the man I believed he was.

Lara wraps her arms around me, and for the first time in days, I feel safe. I close my eyes and revel in her head resting on my shoulder. I can't explain it, but it's like this simple act eases my soul.

I put my arms around her and let out a heavy sigh. For five years, I've lived here at the farm believing in Micah and The Golden Light. I sacrificed all human warmth for the belief that if I did everything he ordered of me that I'd find the happiness and fulfillment he promised existed inside me.

All I needed to do was believe in my greatness.

Now I know that wasn't true. I don't know if I possess any greatness. All I know is at this moment, all I want is to be here next to Lara. I didn't realize how much I'd missed the feel of another person holding me.

"We need to get out of here, Nash. The two of us. Come with me when I try to escape again. You don't belong here."

Fear spikes inside my brain at the mere thought of leaving. I haven't lived away from The Golden Light in so long I don't know if I can function in the outside world.

I nod, although I'm not sure I can do it.

"Do you think you can get my phone today?"

"I don't know," I answer, hating how pathetic that sounds.

How can I not know where a building is? Then again, I'm not even sure I know where I am. I've lost a day of my life, and nothing I've believed in for years seems to be true anymore.

Lara stands up from the bed and begins pacing again. "Then we need to devise a plan to get out of here tonight. Phone or no phone, I can't stay here any longer. If I can't eat or drink anything, it's quickly going to get to the point where I won't have the strength to run when I need to."

Quietly, I tell her what will really happen if she doesn't eat or drink for a few days. "They'll force feed you if you get to that point."

She stops dead on the other side of the room and stares at me in horror. "I won't let them do that."

I don't have the heart to tell her she won't have a choice. I've seen it before. Every so often, a new recruit doesn't handle the drugs well, but they never think that's the problem. They blame not feeling well on the food here, so naturally, they ask for something else. When they don't get it, they stop eating to avoid the discomfort.

What happens next is as horrible as my time in the box. Guards hold the woman down and jam a tube down her throat to force the food into her stomach. I've witnessed it, and the sound of the women's screams of terror will never leave my memories.

"Tell me when. I'll do whatever I can to get us out."

I've reached the point of no return. From this point on, everything about The Golden Light is on borrowed time.

26

LARA

OUTSIDE MY WINDOW, people walk around like everything's fine. I know they aren't, though, and tonight I'm going to leave this place and all its madness. Nash and I have a plan, and this time it will work.

It has to.

Every time my thoughts go to what may happen if they force me to stay here, I want to cry. I don't, though. I can't be that weak. Micah and Nadine may think they have control, but not over me and not over Nash. They could just let us leave, but since they've decided they won't, we have no choice.

At least Rina never got tangled up with these Golden Light people. I should have known she wouldn't fall for their crap, but I was worried about her. I bet she's back in her apartment right now on the phone with our mother listening to her complain about how she's tried to call me dozens of times and I never pick up. They'll both tease me about that the next time I see them.

I look around this stark white room and see nothing that's mine. They took everything from me, even my clothes, so when I leave here tonight, I don't have a single thing to carry with me.

That's probably for the best anyway. Running away doesn't really work when you have to drag a suitcase along with you as you flee.

Nash has been here for much longer, though. How is he going to handle leaving everything he owns behind?

A knock on my window tears me from my thoughts about how hard that's going to be for him, and I turn around to see him holding something up in front of him. I hurry over to see he's got a key in his hand.

I can't understand what he's saying, so I wave him in. A few seconds later, he walks into my room wearing a smile from ear to ear.

"Notice I didn't have to break that handle this time?"

"How?"

Nash dangles a keychain from his fingertip. "With this. It's a master key. It opens any door here."

My mouth drops open as shock fills me. "Where did you get that? I hope nobody saw you, or they're going to put you into the box again."

With more confidence than I've ever seen in him, he laughs and sits down in the chair near the door. "I was careful. Now we can leave without having to worry about all these locked doors."

It seems too good to be true, but I trust Nash. After what he did protecting me from Nadine and her guys, I have to believe he's not like Micah and the rest of them here.

He stands up and takes my hands in his. I no longer see fear in his eyes and know he's ready, just as I am.

"As soon as it gets dark, I'll come get you. We're going to do this!" he says with a smile.

Suddenly, I remember the cameras everywhere on the farm and look up toward the ceiling to search for a tiny red light. But there are none in this room.

"We are! See you in a few hours."

Nodding, he takes a deep breath and lets it out in a rush. "I wonder what the outside world is like now."

I hear the hint of fear in his voice, so I chuckle and say, "Same as before but with more cell phones. And more social media. You're a guy, though, so you probably won't care much about that. Don't worry. You're going to fit in fine."

Sighing, he nods again. "I hope. I guess I just needed to hear someone else say it too. Remember, when it gets dark, be ready."

He rushes out of my room, leaving me standing there with so much nervous energy I couldn't sit down if I had to right now. We're getting out tonight. With that key, nothing's going to be able to stop us. Nash is big enough to handle any of the guards Micah or Nadine will send looking for us. All we have to do is get to the gate and we're home free.

Mario is never going to believe me when I turn in my article on this cult. If he doesn't give me top billing in the magazine that month, I'm going to tell him where to stuff his staff writer job and find somewhere else that appreciates the kind of work I've done investigating The Golden Light.

FOR THE PAST THREE HOURS, I've nervously paced back and forth, unable to calm down because tonight's the night. Micah never came by again, which is good on one hand, but I would have liked to tell him what I think of this little group of his before I go.

He'll find out when my article goes live. Then he's going to have to explain what the hell has been going on here. How they drug people to keep them docile. How they promise to help people desperately searching for something good in life and give them nothing in return other than making them zombies.

Or worse.

I need to make sure I include information about the box in my article. I hope Nash can talk about it. The memory of his screams full of terror echo in my head as I think about asking him to tell me what happened there.

When I get done exposing everything ugly and horrible Micah has going on with this Golden Light garbage, he's going to be lucky if they only lock him up for the rest of his life. Then we'll see how he likes it when he's not the one holding the key.

I stop and look outside as the sun sets behind the nearby mountain, leaving oranges and purples behind to paint the sky for anyone lucky enough to see this beautiful scene. I can't wait to enjoy sunsets and sunrises and everything else I took for granted for far too long back home. I won't make that mistake again. I know now how precious freedom is.

No one is out. No doubt, they're all in their cabins doing as they've been told like good little sheep obeying their mighty shepherd.

A faint tapping noise pulls me away from the view outside my window, and I hurry over to the door. "Nash?"

"Yeah! You ready?"

I nod in response and watch as the door opens to reveal him standing there smiling at me. I show him my hands and chuckle.

"I've got nothing to take with me from this place, so I'm ready. Lead the way!"

Excitement courses through me when he takes my hand and pulls me out the door. We run down the hallway to where another one meets it, and he directs me to go down that one.

"It's okay. I went this way before," he whispers when I hesitate for just a moment.

I smile and start off again with him next to me. I want to ask where this building is because I'm sure it's not at the farm, but I don't. We can talk about all that we've seen with Micah and his followers when we're safe.

A door that leads to the outside appears halfway down the hallway, and my heart slams into my chest I'm so nervous. We haven't seen a single person yet, but I know at any moment someone can appear who will want to stop us.

When we reach the door, he drives his shoulder into it and it flies open. I expect to hear an alarm, but there's nothing but the sound of us laughing and our feet hitting the pavement as we rush outside into the warm night air.

I stop and look back at the building in disbelief. "I can't believe no one tried to stop us!"

It all feels too good to be true. No, I can't think that way. Sometimes, things are just easy. Not everything in this damn world has to be hard.

Unlike me, Nash isn't ready to celebrate so soon. Yanking me by the arm, he directs me toward the road leading to the gate. "We aren't free yet, Lara. Hurry up!"

I've never felt this alive in my life. It's as if every cell in my body is screaming for me to keep going because freedom is only yards away. Or at least I hope it is. I don't know what this place is or where we are, and in the darkness, it's hard to see much of anything.

But I know this is going to work this time. It has to. Nash is going to get me out of here tonight.

His long legs mean he can run faster than I can, so I struggle to keep up. He tightly holds on to my hand to make sure I don't fall behind, looking back at me every few steps as if to say, "Don't worry. I've got you."

Then in the distance, the sound of people sends fear racing through every inch of my body. If Nash wasn't practically pulling me toward the road, I don't know if I'd be able to continue on my own I'm so scared.

He smiles at me and looks over my head toward where the noise is coming from. "It's okay. We've got a head start. It's not far now."

I can't see in the dark, but I trust him. He's going to get me out of here. I know he will.

Tightening my hold on his hand, I push my legs to go

as fast as they can. I can't give up now. Not when we're so close.

"I see it!" he cries out a second later. "I see the road! Come on!"

My thigh muscles burn and my lungs ache from panting since I haven't run like this since high school, but I keep up with Nash and hope at any moment I'll see what he's seeing. "How far is it?"

He begins to laugh almost maniacally, and I can't help but join in. It's the sound of freedom, the sound of triumphing over the evil we've experienced here. They didn't break me. They didn't break him either.

We survived.

"I see it! Just a few more steps and we'll be there," he says with so much confidence that I want to jump up and down and congratulate us.

There will be time for that, though. Now, we just have to make it a little ways more.

27

NASH

LIGHTNING CRACKLES ACROSS THE SKY, and then a few seconds later, thunder booms all around us, startling me so I squeeze Lara's hand. The weather's been so hot these past few days that a storm is long overdue, but it couldn't have chosen a worse time. I'd planned on the cover of darkness to hide us as we escaped.

As all of this runs through my mind, a gunshot rings out, warning me the sentry guarding the perimeter of the compound knows someone's gotten out. Pulling Lara along, I hope to God my legs don't give out before we reach somewhere safe.

"I can't keep up!" she cries out when I tug her forward once more. "I don't have legs as long as yours."

Another sharp crack of lightning lights up the darkness, and when I look back at her, I see real fear in her eyes. "Just try. We need to cover more ground if we expect to make it."

We run our fastest down a dirt road that I silently pray to God connects to a main road somewhere close. My shitkicker boots aren't made for this kind of thing, but I push on as hard as I can. If they catch us now, I have no faith that Micah won't have the two of us killed.

"Do you know where we can call to get help?" she breathlessly asks.

I don't want to tell her there's no one who's going to open the door to two strangers in the middle of the night. She might give up, and I can't have that right now. Not when we're so close to getting away.

The sound of men behind us tells me we've got precious few minutes to reach the main road. At least there we'll have a chance to flag down a car. Not that I think we'll have any better luck with that than with knocking on someone's door to get help, but I can't focus on that now.

"We just need to get to the main road," I say, tugging her forward to stay with me. "Keep running! We can't let them catch us!"

I don't want to frighten her, but the sound of my voice is probably doing that for me. Thankfully, she can't see my face because if she could, she'd know I'm as terrified as she is.

"Nash, there are people following us! What are we going to do?"

At that very moment, a flash of lightning illuminates the sky, and I see the road up ahead. A car drives by, buoying my hope that someone will pick us up to take us the hell away from here.

Not that I have any idea where to go. I've been with The Golden Light for years. I don't know what it's like out in the real world. Lara does, though, so I can only hope in exchange for helping her get away that she'll help me out in the beginning.

My legs ache from running in these boots, and it takes everything I have to not groan in agony. I don't want to let Lara know I'm struggling, though. I don't think she'll keep going if she thinks I can't.

"Nash, they're getting closer! What are we going to do?"

The panic in her voice makes my stomach clench. I can hear them running behind us, their shoes pounding against the ground as they rush to catch us. It's only a matter of minutes, if that, before they reach us.

If only we can get to the road in time.

"Come on! It's not far now," I say in my best cheer-leading voice. "We're almost there!"

She has a burst of energy and nearly runs away from me, pulling my arm as she does. "We're going to make it!"

A gunshot echoes through the darkness. Terror courses through me as I push my body harder than ever before. Behind us, a deep voice barks out, "Stop! If you don't stop, we will kill you. Stop now!"

Lara tightens her hold on my hand, and I sense the genuine fear in her without her saying a word. I can't let them catch us. They will kill me, but I don't know if that's what Micah will do to her. Another woman dying might be too big a problem for him. My death won't be, though.

I have no connections outside of the group, so nobody will miss me.

As for her, she might not be killed, but her fate will be no better if he makes her one of his girls. Kept hidden away and used for his pleasure, they're forced to be little more than slaves.

I turn around hoping to see how far away the men are, but there's nothing but darkness without the lightning. Their voices threatening us come through loud and clear, though.

They're gaining on us.

We need to go faster, but Lara's right. Her legs aren't long enough. There's no choice now. If we hope to get away and find someone to give us a ride, we have to run faster than the men chasing us.

"When I stop, you need to get on my back. Don't waste time, or we won't escape them."

She lets out a tiny sob but says nothing. A few steps later, I suddenly skid to a stop and yank her back toward me. Just as I told her to, she jumps on my back and wraps her arms around my neck.

"Nash, oh hurry! I can hear them!" she cries in my ear.

I don't need to be told twice to get going. I know what the consequences of our attempting to escape will be if we fail. My feet take off like they've got wings on the back of them. I don't know where the strength comes from, but I don't feel any fatigue in my legs now. I only feel pure fear at the thought of what will happen to us if I don't reach that main road and find someone who will help us.

The sound of the cars' tires rolling over the pavement

fills my ears, thrilling me. It's not that far now. I just need to keep going.

"Nash, we're doing it!" Lara says, hope filling her voice.

Another gunshot rips through the darkness, but this time it doesn't terrify me. They're too far behind and running in the dark like we are, so their shots won't reach us.

Not yet.

I can't let up now, though. Just a few steps more and we'll get to the main road. I just have to pray someone will stop and help us.

"You can't get away, Nash!" a man bellows.

I recognize that voice. Adam. He's probably licking his damn chops in anticipation of catching me. I bet he's already got what he wants to do to me all planned out. No chasing after me just to shoot me down in the high grass like with Maren. No, he's a psycho. He's going to want to torture me for a little while before he finally puts a bullet in my head.

"Don't listen to him," Lara says in my ear. "We're almost there!"

My eyesight becomes bleary as we get closer to the road, so I shake my head hoping to clear it. I can't lose focus now.

Just a few yards more...

Lara begins yelling and flailing her arms above my head just before we reach the main road, and I'm stunned when a car pulls off to the side. I sprint over to it, spending the last of my energy to reach the dark SUV.

The window slowly lowers as I keep turning my head

to see how close Adam and his buddies are. Thankfully, they seem to have slowed down.

A man looks out from the driver seat, and before I can ask him if he can give us a ride, Lara exclaims, "Mario! What are you doing here at this time of night?"

Confused, I don't know what to expect him to say, but the man flashes us a big smile and waves us into his car. "I could ask you the same question. Jump in!"

I don't question how the two of them know one another and hurriedly get into the back seat. Lara climbs into the front seat, and we barely get the doors closed before her friend Mario is jamming his foot on the gas and slamming me back against the leather seat.

She turns her body toward him and slaps his arm. "I don't know what we would have done if you didn't come along. You saved us, Mario!"

"Timing is everything. So where were you two coming from?" he asks before glancing in the rearview mirror to look at me.

Something makes me feel like I've seen him before. That can't be possible, though. I haven't seen more than a handful of outsiders in my entire time with The Golden Light. The few times I left the farm to visit other locations for Micah didn't give me much opportunity to see people not in the group. Mario must have a familiar looking face.

"You wouldn't believe me if I told you," Lara answers with a laugh. "Someday after I give you my article I'll explain everything. Until then, I think I can speak for Nash when I say you literally saved our lives."

"Well, I'm happy to do it. Where can I take you?"

"Where are we?" I ask, but Mario doesn't answer.

Before I can tell her to not say too much, Lara blurts out, "My car is parked in Wilmington. I know it's a huge favor, but can you drop us off there?"

Wilmington? That's in Delaware. Did we get moved to a site outside of Pennsylvania?

As these questions fill my mind, I listen to him agree to take us wherever Lara wants, and then he says, "Why didn't you answer my call yesterday and again today? I've been worried about you."

"It's a long story, but suffice to say I'm going to need a new phone."

They continue to talk, catching up on all that's been happening in his life since they last spoke, and I feel myself begin to drift off now that adrenaline isn't pumping through my system. I take a deep breath and close my eyes, truly relaxing for the first time in God only knows how long.

Thoughts about where I'll go float through my mind, but they can wait for later. Right now, all I want to do is enjoy the feeling of freedom at it fills every nook and cranny of me.

28

LARA

AS MARIO TURNS off the exit on his way to Wilmington, I can't believe our good luck that he was on that road just when we needed him to be. Good old Mario. He may be the world's biggest pain in the ass when it comes to work, but he's always been a decent guy. I'm just glad he was the one to see us on the side of the road.

"How is Linda okay with your being out in the middle of the night?" I jokingly ask, knowing his new girlfriend keeps him on a pretty short leash. "I'm sort of surprised she's not with you."

He turns his head to look at me and smirks. "I told her I wouldn't be long. She'd only be in the way anyway."

I smile as how strange that sounds from a man who couldn't get a date for months after his wife left him. It makes me wonder if they're as serious as I'd thought. Mario's always been less a catch and more the kind of man a woman ends up with when she gets sick of the dating scene. He still drags around all that baggage from his ex after she cheated on him and ended their marriage, so any woman dating him has a hill to climb with all of that anger he can't seem to get rid of even now after more than a year since the divorce became final.

Poor Linda. I've only met her twice, but she seemed like a nice person. She's got that strange obsession with horror films she tried to discuss with me that last time, but since I can't watch scary movies without having nightmares for days afterward, the conversation didn't go far. Still, she appeared to care for Mario, so I figured to each their own.

As I notice he's gone the wrong way to get to Wilmington, I chuckle and say, "Hey, Mario. Did you get turned around in the dark? My car isn't anywhere close to here."

He smiles but doesn't take his attention off the road. "I know, but I have someplace I need to go. It won't take long."

Behind me, Nash makes a noise that sounds like a groan, so I look into the back seat and smile. "Feeling tired? We'll be to my car soon."

In the dark, I can't see his whole face, but his eyes flash a look I've seen before from him. He doesn't say anything, but he sits up straight now and looks out the window.

"What's wrong? I bet it's weird being away from the farm, isn't it?"

Beside me, Mario lets out a low chuckle. I want to explain what I meant, but it's too long a story to get into tonight. My boss will get all the details when I turn in my article. He probably won't believe the story, but I plan on leaving nothing out when I expose all that's going on with The Golden Light.

Nash doesn't answer me, but I have the sense he's uncomfortable now that Mario laughed at him. I wish I could tell him that's just the way he is. Nobody would ever accuse my boss of being a sensitive person, for sure.

Leaning through the space between the two front seats, I whisper, "He didn't mean anything bad. It's just how he can be sometimes. You feeling okay?"

Nodding, he looks out the window again. "Fine."

He doesn't sound fine, but I guess I can't blame him. We've had to escape from a crazy cult, been shot at as we ran down a dark road, and got lucky when someone I know picked us up. Talk about a rollercoaster of a night.

I turn back around as Mario pulls into a parking spot in front of a building I've never seen before. Typical brick like so many others in Delaware, it looks abandoned.

"Are we still in Pennsylvania?" I ask as he turns off the engine.

"Yeah. Hang out here," he says as he gets out and then slams the door.

"This feels wrong," Nash quietly says behind me. "Something's off about this."

I wave away his concern, shaking my head as I study his worried expression under the streetlight. "Not to worry. Mario's cool."

Nash looks around through the window and frowns. "It's the middle of the night. What's your boss doing driving down a road where practically nobody travels just in the nick of time to help us?"

"We're lucky?" I say with a smile.

"How well do you know your friend there?"

God, this guy really is a mess after spending all that time with those Golden Light nuts. Nash is going to have to work hard to learn to trust people now that he's out.

"He's not exactly a friend. He's my boss."

For some reason, that makes him lean forward, and I see genuine worry in his eyes now. "Where? Doing what?"

"Relax. It's nothing that interesting. He's the editor at an online magazine. Not exactly exciting, but it's not a bad job, at least for me. Mario complains all the time since he's got to deal with staff that can't seem to come up with any interesting topics for articles, but other than that, he's a good guy."

Strangely, my explanation doesn't make Nash feel any better. Instead of simply sitting back to wait for Mario, he shakes his head like he refuses to believe anything I've said.

"This is wrong, Lara. We need to get out of here. Now."

"Wrong? Where are we going to go? It's the middle of the night, and we're nowhere close to my car yet. Just give him a couple more minutes. It'll be okay. I promise. He'll take us to Wilmington, and then once I have my car, I'll take you anywhere you want to go."

In truth, I'm guessing Nash is going to want to stay with me for a little while as he gets back on his feet. I'm fine with that. It's the least I can do for the guy after he saved me from those crazies of The Golden Light. I'm not sure I'm the right person to help him transition back to living in society, but if he has no one else, I'm happy to step up.

Nothing I say eases him, and when another minute passes, he starts fumbling with the door to get out. "He locked the door. Why would he do that?" he asks, panicked.

"It's okay, Nash. Newer cars routinely have child locks. I'm guessing too many parents aren't watching their kiddos, so car companies thought they needed some way to keep the little angels in. I swear, if I ever even tried to open the doors while my father was driving, he would have pulled over and given me the spanking of a lifetime."

"It's not okay! Trust me, Lara. This is off. I can feel it. We need to leave right now," he says as he leans his body through the space between the front seats to unlock the doors on the driver's side door control panel.

His face just inches away from mine, I can see the terror in his eyes. I don't understand what's wrong with him. This is Mario we're dealing with. I realize Nash doesn't know him, but I do. Can't he trust me that I know someone's okay?

He sits back in his seat only to open his car door a second later. Stunned, I ask, "Where are you going? We don't even know where we are."

"I know we shouldn't be here. Say it's a gut feeling. Say it's intuition. Whatever you want to call it, this is not going to end well for us, Lara. Now come on. Are you staying here or coming with me?"

As he stands outside the car waiting for me, I think about what I should do. Yes, I trust Mario, but Nash has shown himself to be a good guy. He seems really unnerved about something, and although I think he's just experiencing some kind of jitters now that he's finally free of that farm and those people, I have to believe he's sensing something I'm not.

I just hope we don't end up walking for miles in the pitch black. Worse, I hope we don't get caught by that roaming posse of Micah's that was shooting at us just a short while ago.

"Fine," I mumble as I open my door and step out. "I want you to know that if you get me killed, I'm going to haunt you for the rest of your life."

It comes out funnier than I meant it to, but the horrified look on his face tells me he didn't get the joke. Taking me by the hand, he begins to hurry me down the sidewalk of whatever town we're in.

"We need to get out of here. Now. I don't know this area. Any suggestions as to which way we should go?" he asks, his head swiveling left and right as he looks for which street to take.

"Uh, no. I'm not from here, and this town, whatever it's called, is nowhere near my house or my car."

Behind us, Mario calls out, "Lara! Come back! Where are you going?"

I turn to look back, but it's too dark to see much of anything if you're not standing underneath a streetlight. Nash continues to walk quickly down the street, pulling me along to keep up with him.

"Lara, wait! Look who's with me!" Mario yells.

Again, I look back and standing next to his car I see someone who takes my breath away. Tugging my hand from Nash's hold, I turn my body around so I'm facing Mario.

And my sister.

"Oh, my God! It's Rina!" I say in utter shock.

Nash stops, but he's not as happy to see her as I am. "Don't go back there. Believe me. This is all wrong. What is your sister doing here in some small town in the middle of nowhere?"

I look at him and shake my head. "I can't go now. My sister, the person I was trying to find, is right there. How can you think there could be anything wrong with that?"

Rina steps up onto the sidewalk underneath a street-light, and my heart feels like it's soaring. She's okay. After all that's happened, she's safe and sound. Thank God.

Beside me, Nash whispers, "That's your sister?"

I nod, unable to stop smiling at how good she looks. All this time, I was worried for nothing. "Yeah. That's my baby sister," I say with a chuckle, knowing how much Rina hates when I call her that.

"Lara, listen to me. She's not who you think she is. Don't stay here. Come with me. If we run now, we'll have a chance."

What is wrong with him? How could Rina not be the person I know she is? And he thinks I'm going to leave my sister? Is he insane?

I look at him and see he's dead serious. Has he lost his mind?

"She's my sister, Nash. I think I know who she is. Come on. Mario can give us a ride to my car, and then if you want, you can stay with me. I'll probably go hang out with her for a while, but you're welcome to crash at my apartment for as long as you like."

He shakes his head. "I had no idea she was your sister. I've seen her dozens of times, Lara. She's one of Micah's women. She came to the farm about a month ago with a guy I now realize is your boss there. She instantly became one of the leader's favorites. Whatever you're thinking is going to happen here, she's not going to help you get away. She's in The Golden Light as deep as it gets. Believe me. She won't help us."

My mouth drops open as he says all of that. It's impossible. Rina would never get sucked into all that crazy nonsense. She's smarter than that. I should have known from the start she wouldn't be convinced by all that positivity crap and Micah's wannabe messiah thing he has going on.

"You're wrong. My sister isn't anything like that. You must have her confused with someone else."

"No, I don't," he says as he tugs on my arm to pull me away. "I've seen her, Lara. I told you I sometimes had to go to other locations when Micah sent me on errands. I've seen your sister with him. Come on. We have to go!"

What he's saying isn't possible. Even if Rina had somehow gotten involved with this group of crazy people, she would never have fallen for Micah's nonsense. She's too smart for that.

I look over at Rina and can't square what Nash claims is true. He has to be mistaken. There are millions of brunette women with dark eyes in the world. He must be thinking of someone else.

"You're confusing her with some other woman, Nash.

Wait until you meet her. You're going to like her. She's like me but sweeter."

Rina walks toward me wearing a big smile. "I'm so happy to see you, Lara! Come inside and meet my friends."

Looking back at Nash, I try to get him to understand. "See? She's just hanging out with some friends."

"Ask her who they are."

So he sees he's wrong, I ask her, "Who are your friends?"

Spreading her arms, she gives me an even bigger smile as she stops in the middle of the street. "They're people who helped me see things straight. They can help you too. You just have to come inside, Lara."

My heart sinks as I listen to her. She sounds just like all those women back at the farm. Oh, God. Is it possible Nash is right?

He leans in and says in my ear, "See? She's not the person you knew. She's one of them now."

I shake my head in disbelief. "No. I won't believe it until I hear it from her lips."

"Then ask her. Ask her if she's a member of the group. Then you'll see."

Mario waits on the other side of the street, and suddenly, it feels like the world has stopped. Part of me desperately wants to do just as Nash says and ask her that question, but another part of me is terrified to hear the answer.

"Lara, ask her, but she's lost. I'm sorry. I wish I didn't have to say these things. She's not the sister you remember. She's with Micah, which means she's in deep with

The Golden Light. You're not going to talk her out of staying, and if we don't get out of here, they're going to force
us back to the farm to punish us for leaving."

Looking over at Rina, I say the words I must and hope
her answer won't break my heart. "Who are your friends?
Are they from The Golden Light?"

She beams a smile, and even before she speaks, I
know Nash hasn't been wrong about her. "You know
about The Golden Light? Oh, Lara! I'm so happy for you.
Come in and find your greatness."

Tears well in my eyes. She's one of them.

Beside me, Nash says, "We have to go now. Come on."

I'm torn between trying to save my sister and knowing
if I don't go with Nash right now, he's going to be in
danger. I can't be the reason he spends hours screaming
from the torture.

Or worse.

I turn to face him, trying to figure out what to do. "Let
me just talk to her, Nash. I can get through to her. I can
make her see these people are messed up."

Sadness fills his eyes. "No, you can't. If she's with
Micah, she's too far gone. Listen to what she just said.
Come and find your greatness? That's straight out of the
leader's mouth."

From across the street, Rina says, "Your friend can
come too, Lara. All are welcome to share in The Golden
Light."

I glance over at her and can't believe this is happening. Or maybe I can. There was a reason I went looking
for Rina with these people. I think deep down I always
suspected she might fall prey to Micah's bullshit, even

though I tried to convince myself she was too smart for all of it.

"Lara, we have to go. We need to get away before he sends those people after us. Every second we stay here puts us in danger. I don't want to leave you, but I can't wait any more. What's it going to be?"

Second after second passes as I try to decide what to do. I owe Nash my life. He got me away from that farm. He saved me. Not Micah and his messiah posing. Not the women I was bunking with.

Nash.

But Rina's my sister. I can't just leave her here with these people. I have to try to get through to her.

"I'm sorry. I can't just abandon her," I say, hating the disappointment I see in his expression.

"I'm sorry too, but I can't stay here."

I watch him run away down the street into the darkness and feel a crushing sadness. I may not have known Nash for long, but after what we went through, it feels like we've been friends forever.

Now, though, I have to help my sister.

29

Nash

I run as fast as my feet will take me, searching each building in this small town for any sign of the police. If I can find someone to help me, I can get Lara to safety. I can't do it without the cops, though.

Two streets over from where I left her, I see a light on in what looks like an office. Since it's nighttime, I can only hope it's someone in authority and not just some workaholic lawyer who just happens to have an office in this backwater.

Bursting through the front door, I try to catch my breath before I explain what's happening. A man dressed in a blue policeman's uniform with a nametag on his chest that says B. Jameson stares at me in horror, like he can't believe anyone is actually bothering him at this time of night.

An inch or two shorter than me with big eyes and a

baby face, the policeman looks like he's barely old enough to get into a bar. I hope that doesn't mean he can't handle what I'm about to tell him.

"Can I help you?" he asks in a thin voice that seems to fit his small frame.

Still huffing and puffing from running here at top speed, I take a deep breath before letting it out in a rush. "I need help. A friend of mine is in trouble a few streets away."

The officer sits down behind his desk, the exact opposite of what I need him to do, and takes out a pen and notepad from one of the drawers. Looking up at me, he nods. "Okay. Tell me all you can about what's going on."

My heart beats wildly as I shake my head. "We don't have time for this. I told you my friend is in trouble. There are people trying to take her away."

Officer Babyface narrows his eyes like he doesn't believe me. "What do you mean trying to take her away? Do you mean a kidnapping?"

It's not exactly that, but I don't have time to parse meanings with this guy. "Yes! There are people trying to kidnap her. I just ran here from two streets over. Do you know anything about The Golden Light?"

His expression morphs into something close to disgust. "Oh, yeah. I know all about them. We've had three calls this week about their goings-on."

"Then you know they're no good. I need you to help me save her. You can't let them take her back with them."

The man leans back in his chair and studies me for a long moment. "Back? Is she one of them? Because if she is, I can't help you. The chief says they're considered a religion, so if she wants to believe in that stuff, she's more than welcome to. It's a free country."

Jesus, this guy and his freedom bullshit is going to get Lara taken by the time we get back there to help her. I know all too well how Micah and Nadine manipulate local officials to let them get away with practically anything they want under the guise of being a religion.

"She's not one of them! She's being taken away because she doesn't know any better," I lie, hoping that lights a fire under his ass.

He stands up and smiles. "Then I can help you with that. Two streets over, you said? I bet it's that new information center they just opened up last month. They say it's all about being positive, but we've had a number of people say they think there's something bad going on there. The only problem is you're the first person to say exactly what that is."

As he comes around the desk, I scan his body for any sign of a weapon but see nothing. Is this town that safe that the cops here don't even need guns? They better get smart quickly because with The Golden Light around, they're going to want some protection.

"You have a gun, right?" I ask as he heads toward the door.

The officer nods but looks over in the direction of his desk. "Yeah. Why?"

"Because you need one. These Golden Light people don't play around. They have weapons, so you better have one too."

His eyes grow big before he asks, "How do you know so much about them?"

Even though I hate to admit the truth, I answer, "I was part of The Golden Light until I escaped tonight."

"Escaped?" he asks as if I just admitted to jumping bail.

"Yeah. It's even worse than you think. I'll be happy to tell you anything you want to know, but first we have to go help my friend. She can't go with them. She won't make it out alive if she does."

That finally seems to get him to want to move, and he grabs his gun from his desk drawer before hurrying toward the door. "I don't have anyone to call for back up. We're a small force. We're not set up to handle kidnappings or anything like that."

My heart sinks at his lame excuses, but one cop is better than none. At least he has a weapon. Hopefully, we can get Lara out before Micah's men arrive. If we can't, one gun isn't going to be enough.

"It's two streets over," I say as we rush out the door.

"I know exactly where it is. As I said, we've been getting complaints. Mrs. Alastair said they were acting like hippies, but since she's like a hundred, I didn't think much of it," he explains as we hurry down the street. "Then another lady said they tried to convince her granddaughter to join them. That's when the chief told her religion or no religion, they have to follow the law."

With each step, I grow more worried that Officer Jameson and I are going to be no match for even Lara's sister and Mario. If only I can show her she can't help her sister now. No woman who's ever gotten involved with Micah left the group.

I break into a run and make it back to the car before

the officer. Lara is standing in the middle of the street talking to her sister and Mario, and for a moment, it looks like everything's okay. Then out of the corner of my eye, I see a flash of light and turn my head to see what it could be. As I feared, Micah's men have found us.

"Lara! Get out of there!" I yell just before a shot rings out.

Lara, her sister, and Mario run across the street and crouch down behind a car. Officer Jameson hides behind the corner of a building but screams, "You didn't tell me there were armed people. Get back here before you get killed!"

"Don't think you're getting away," Adam yells before taking another shot.

I run back to where the cop is hiding and scan the area to find a way to get to Lara. "They'll shoot us dead where we stand. Don't believe for a second they won't."

"What the hell are they shooting for?"

"Because I escaped and that means they want me dead. My friend too. Nobody leaves The Golden Light. Not alive."

His hands shake as he holds his gun in front of him. "How many of them are there?"

Good question. If this time is like the other times a member escaped, Adam's got to have at least four or five men with him. I have no idea if there are men in the information center where Rina was. If I had to guess, I'd say yes, but I can't be sure.

"At least five, I'm guessing. I don't know about at their center, but it's right over there," I say, pointing at the building where Rina came from.

He mumbles something, but all I'm focused on is seeing if Lara is okay. I can't find her behind the car, so all I can do is hope Adam and his men aren't aiming for her.

"Come out, Nash! You know how this goes. You just have to come back to the farm, and everything will be okay. Micah only wants the best for you. He wants you to find your greatness. That's it."

Officer Jameson looks at me and says, "I'm guessing you're Nash. Why do they want you back so badly?"

"Because I know too much to be allowed to leave."

"My chief is going to want you to give a full statement. You understand that?"

He says that like I'd hesitate to tell everything I know about The Golden Light. I'll be happy to confess everything I've seen and done. I want to make a fresh start, and if that means exposing Micah and every last one of them in that group, then so be it.

I nod my understanding of what he wants. "You get us out of this, and I'll tell you every last detail of what I saw there."

"Okay," he says in a trembling voice. "I don't want anyone to get hurt, so maybe I can defuse the situation. Stay here."

He steps out from behind the building and announces, "This is Officer Jameson of the River Crest police department. Put your guns away. This doesn't have to escalate. Let's have a calm discussion."

The silence that greets him doesn't make me feel any less uneasy. While Micah always stresses any dealings with authorities are to be positive, this is Adam in charge now, and if he'll gun down a helpless woman running away from him, I doubt he'll have second thoughts about killing a cop from some small town.

"Just come out of the shadows and let's talk."

I poke my head around the building and try to locate where Adam and the rest of the men are positioned, but in the dark, it's impossible to see. Officer Jameson takes another step out into the middle of the street, unknowingly risking his life.

He has no concept of how dangerous the people he's dealing with are. He thinks they're hippies wanting to live on a commune or a religious group dedicated to positivity. He couldn't be more mistaken.

This time, the silence is broken by a woman crying. It doesn't sound like Lara, though. Maybe it's her sister and she's making some headway in convincing her The Golden Light isn't what she thinks it is.

"Nash?" a voice cries out, and this time I do recognize it's Lara's voice.

"I'm here! You and your sister can come with me. It's okay. Officer Jameson will escort you over."

I wait for her answer, but I hear nothing. The officer looks back at me like he doesn't know what to do next, so I point at the car across the street. "They're over there."

He takes a few more steps toward them and calls out, "I'm Officer Jameson, ma'am. I'm here to help. Your friend says you're in danger. That someone is trying to kidnap you. Is that true?"

"Yes! My sister and I want to leave," Lara calls out.

Another voice sobs, "I don't want to leave! The Golden Light is my home. I won't go!"

Jesus, Micah really has his hooks into her. Rina

sounds far too gone to be helped, but I'm afraid Lara isn't going to leave her.

"Lara, you need to get out of there!" I yell. "You're not safe. They aren't going to let you go if you stay any longer."

I wait, holding my breath to see if she'll walk away. Officer Jameson looks back at me like he's unsure if he should do anything more, but I don't know what to tell him. He might be seconds away from being shot for all I know. Adam's not exactly a rational person, so at any moment he might just unload his gun and to hell with whoever he hurts or kills.

Another shot breaks the silence, and the cop runs back to where I stand behind the building. Obviously shaken, he gets his walkie talkie and finally calls for help.

"Chief, sergeant, anyone listening! I've got a problem over on Elm Street at The Golden Light place. Shots fired. I repeat, shots fired! I need help!"

The panic in his voice echoes through every word, but he truly has no idea just how bad things might get if Adam thinks he has a clear shot at either me or Lara. No doubt he's been told to make sure she and I either come back into the loving arms of The Golden Light or see to it we die before we can tell the authorities anything about what's going on in the group.

Officer Jameson's radio crackles with an answer from another officer telling him they're on their way. I just hope they get here before all hell breaks loose.

30

No matter what I say to Rina, she refuses to listen. All she keeps saying over and over is Micah has shown her how much true greatness she possesses and she can't leave him. It's like she's not even listening to all the horrible things I saw out at the farm.

Oh, God. Maybe Nash was right. Maybe she is too far gone.

I can't just leave her to these people, though. No matter what kind of brainwashing she's suffering from, she's still my sister.

Taking her by the shoulders, I shake her to try to make her see sense. Her eyes get big, like she can't believe I'm doing this, but desperate times call for desperate measures. If this is what I have to do to break that man's hold on her, then that's what I'll do.

"He isn't a leader or anything else. He's just a guy who

drugs women and forces them to work for him. He drugged me! If I hadn't been protected by Nash, his little minion Nadine would have had her guys beat the hell out of me. Or worse. And don't think Micah's only with you. From what I heard out at that farm, he's got dozens of you. Rina, you aren't this person. Forget these crazy things, and let's go home."

She shakes her head, and I know without even hearing another word from her that she's not going to leave willingly. Fine. Then she'll have to do so unwillingly, but I'm not letting her stay here for even another minute with these people.

"Why are you saying all these things, Lara? The Golden Light isn't a bad thing. It's all good," Mario says like he's lost too.

I stare into his eyes and feel like I'm never going to get them to see the truth. "What is wrong with you two? How is it you're fooled by this greatness nonsense? You just heard me tell my sister what I saw out at that farm. Don't you believe me?"

"You don't understand."

Arguing with the two of them is getting me nowhere. I'm going to have to force Rina to leave. I have no other choice.

In the distance, I hear the wail of sirens growing closer. Rina gets a terrified look in her eyes and turns to go back into the building. I can't let her do that, or I might never get a chance to save her again.

I grab onto her arm and clamp my hand down around her wrist. "No! You're coming home with me, Rina."

Terror morphs into something else, something far

more vicious, and she lunges at me, scratching her nails across my cheek. "I will not go! Micah is waiting for me. I need him!"

Her attack stuns me for a few seconds, and Mario yanks her away from me. Horrified by how lost she is, I try to reach her one more time.

I get into her face and hope to God there's some part of her that is still willing to understand me. "Rina, listen to me. You don't know what's really happening. It's nothing close to light or greatness. It's just a cult that's scamming people out of their life savings and drugging them so they work for Micah. Are you hearing me? Micah, Nadine, all of it is nothing but a cult!"

The sirens blare their noise now as two police cars skid to a stop at the corner, drowning out nearly everything else, including my pleas for my sister to see the truth. At the first chance she gets, Rina bolts away with Mario, the two of them so desperate to believe in Micah and all of the Golden Light nonsense that they refuse to hear a word I say.

I run after my sister and my boss and grab onto her shirt, desperate to keep her from going back into that building. She tries to twist out of my hold, but I clutch the fabric like my life depends on it.

"Stop, Rina! I can't let you go!" I scream.

The sirens end their wailing, but suddenly, a gunshot breaks the momentary silence. I turn around to see police crouched behind their vehicles with their guns drawn. Chaos explodes all around us with guns going off left and right. I push Rina to the ground as Mario hurries away into the building in front of us to protect himself.

I don't know how long the gunfight goes on because I bury my head in my sister's neck and pray to God a stray bullet doesn't find us. If we can just make it out of this alive, I know I can bring her back to reality.

Thank God Nash found a good hiding spot behind that building. I'm going need to thank him for getting the police here to help us. After this night is over, I'm going to owe him nothing less than my life.

31

Nash

FOR A LONG MOMENT, all the shooting stops. In the lull, I see Adam and follow his gaze across the street. He's not looking for me. He's looking for Lara.

Son of a bitch! Why didn't she listen to me when I told her we needed to get out of here? We could have been long gone from here by now.

A flash of lightning lights up the sky, joining with the cops' headlights to help me see where everyone is, and Adam's bloodlust shows as clear as day in his face while he watches for his chance to take a shot at her. I know what he's thinking. She's right next to one of Micah's women, and he doesn't dare do anything that could hurt her.

That killing her sister doesn't fall under that category shows how messed up these people are. How is it I didn't see that for all the time I was in The Golden Light?

Regret fills my thoughts, but I shake my head to force it away. I don't have time to feel that right now. That can wait for later. Now I have to make sure Lara doesn't get hurt.

Beside me, Officer Jameson practically quakes with fear. The poor guy. A small town cop like him has probably never experienced anything like this in his entire time on the job. He likely spends his nights fielding calls from old ladies complaining about their neighbors' dogs barking and boisterous kids playing outside too long after it gets dark.

"We've got nearly the entire force here," he says in a voice that barely hides how scared he is. "Any chance they'll just come peacefully now that they've stopped shooting?"

I shake my head, wishing I had a better answer for him than what I know is the truth of what's about to happen next. "No. No way. This is the calm before the storm."

From behind one of the police cars, one of Jameson's fellow cops calls out, "This can all stop now. Just put your guns down, and nobody will get hurt."

Looking at Jameson, I roll my eyes. "You guys don't understand. This isn't going to end just because you say it should. These are true believers, and Micah has told them not to come back without me and my friend."

"Micah? Who's Micah?"

"The leader of The Golden Light. They won't do anything to make him unhappy with them, and if they don't get us to come back, he's going to be furious. None of these people can deal with that happening."

The officer looks at me like he thinks I'm crazy. Maybe I was for a long time. I must have been to believe in Micah and everything The Golden Light represented.

But I'm not crazy anymore.

"Well, if they're wanting you to come back, that must mean they don't want to kill you, right?" Jameson asks with far too much hope in his voice.

I point toward where I see Adam standing with two other members of The Golden Light and say, "See him? He's a psycho. Nothing makes him happier than to hurt people. I saw him kill a woman in cold blood a few days ago because she tried to run away from him. That's what he wants to do with my friend. Lara is the one he's after."

Even as I say that, I know Adam will risk any punishment Micah can devise to gun me down too. He'll take the box or even whipping to enjoy the thrill of paying me back for what he thinks was my betraying him. He may be after Lara to keep her mouth shut, but he'll kill me just because he can and deal with Micah's disappointment.

Assuming the man I've served for years would be unhappy with my death, and that's not something I'd bet money on. To Micah, I've done worse than killing someone.

I've betrayed him, and for that, I have a feeling he'd gladly accept Adam killing me.

"So if we just get him, all of this will end?" Jameson asks, again sounding far too optimistic for the situation.

He just doesn't understand the mentality of The Golden Light people. I don't know how to explain it to him so he gets it. They don't just believe. They believe with every fiber of their being, and if Micah told them

Lara needs to be silenced permanently, they'll do whatever they can to make him happy.

Their leader has convinced them they're under attack by those who don't believe in him and all he teaches. All they see is the outside world threatening to take away all they love. For them, this isn't a simple matter of making sure people don't see the darker side of the group.

No, to them, it's truly do or die, as if they themselves are under attack.

"You can kill Adam, but the guys around him aren't any better," I say, wishing I could explain how truly devoted Micah's men are and how willing they are to kill for him.

My answer makes Jameson wince as if he's in pain. "We aren't used to this here. This is a small town. I've never even shot my gun the entire time I've been on the police force."

I want to shake him and make him see the time for thinking his little town was safe is over. Jesus, they should have been on red alert the damn second Micah and his crew set up shop here, but as usual, The Golden Light made it seem like all he wanted was to help people. That combined with people's fear of offending anyone when it comes to religion make it so easy for them to worm their way into this small town just as Micah has done everywhere he goes.

A gunshot breaks the silence, and I look down the block to see Adam smiling. My heart in my throat, I whip my head around to see if anyone was hurt across the street. Damnit, I can't see where she is!

"I need to get over there to make sure Lara's okay."

Jameson's eyes open wide with fear. "No way. I won't be able to cover you with at least three of them down there. You'll be like a target in a goddamned shooting gallery!"

Pointing toward his fellow officers down the street toward the corner, I ask, "Can't you radio them and ask them to cover me? I can't let her get killed."

Lara can't die. Not after all we risked to leave The Golden Light. I promised her I'd get her away, and no one, including that fucking psycho Adam, is going to stop me from doing that.

Before he can answer me, I hear three more gunshots and know my former fellow guards have decided they can get to her somehow. I can't let that happen.

I take a deep breath and say to Jameson, "They're focused on her now. They think they can get to her. I have to distract them. Just start shooting in their direction as soon as I come out from behind the building here. With any luck, they'll only nick me."

He doesn't get a chance to try to talk me out of it, and with my heart racing, I jump out from my hiding spot and race into the street. I don't get more than a few steps off the curb before Adam and his men start shooting again. Thankfully, they're focused on the other side of the street.

Out of the corner of my eye, I see someone move near the doorway of The Golden Light building. It's Nadine, and she's aiming for me.

"This is for Micah!" she screams.

From behind me, a shot rings out, and a second later, I see her drop to the ground. Glancing back at Jameson, I see him smile and wave me on toward the side of the street where Lara is hiding.

I'm almost there. Just a few more steps and I'll reach her.

32

LARA

WHEN THE GUNSHOTS STOP, I lift my head, but I can't see anything. Rina sobs uncontrollably into her hands, saying I've taken away the best thing in her life and that she'll never forgive me. I don't care if she can't as long as I know she's far away from those Golden Light bastards.

A tap on my shoulder makes me stiffen in pure fear, but then I hear a man's voice say, "It's okay now. You're safe. Are you hurt?"

I gently lift myself off Rina, making sure to keep a hold of her so she can't run away. Smiling at the officer, I answer, "I think we're fine. Just a little shaken up."

As much as I want to know if any of The Golden Light guys were hurt, I'm afraid to ask. He doesn't offer that information, instead focusing on helping Rina and me to his police car. I'm sure we're going to have to give statements, although I don't believe he'll get much out of my sister. It's going to take months, at least, to deprogram her of all that Micah Golden Light nonsense.

On our way to the police car, I look around for any sign of Nash, but I don't see him. The officer helps us into the car and then gets behind the wheel, so I ask, "Was anyone hurt?"

Before he can answer, I see other officers standing in a circle in the road. Craning my neck, I try to see what's happening, but there are too many men blocking my view.

"What's happening over there?" I ask the cop as he starts the car.

He looks in his rear view mirror and sighs. "Someone got shot."

As he puts the car in drive, I scream, "I need to get out! Please open the door! Please!"

The officer turns around to look at me like I'm crazy and shakes his head. "I need to take you to the station to get a statement. When we're done, you can go home."

"No! I need to see who got hurt. Please let me out! My friend was on the other side of the street!"

This time, he doesn't bother to say anything and simply gets out to open my door. I jump out and say, "Don't take your eyes off her, or she'll run."

I don't wait around for him to reply and sprint toward where the officers stand. I can't see who it is until I get up close to them. One tries to stop me from seeing who's on the ground, but I push him away.

"Who is it? I need to know!" I scream.

One of the other officers grabs me by the shoulders to stop me, and I see past him finally. He starts to tell me what happened, but I can't focus on anything but Nash's lifeless body there on the sidewalk. My tears make it hard to see anything clearly, yet I know it's him.

"Are you Lara?" the officer asks as I cry harder than I thought possible.

I nod, unable to speak I'm so utterly sad my friend hasn't survived after all he did to help me escape from The Golden Light. He had so much to look forward to, and now none of it will happen.

"He ran out into the street because he said he had to make sure you were okay. That's when one of them got him. I'm sorry."

"Please let me see him. I need to say goodbye," I say, barely able to get the words out.

Thankfully, he doesn't try to dissuade me from what I want to do and tells his fellow officers to let me pass. I stop next to Nash's body and crouch down to touch his shoulder as I see where the bullet went through his back and out his chest, leaving a gaping hole.

He looks so peaceful, exactly the way I wanted him to feel once he got to my place safe and sound. Nash didn't deserve this. After all he went through, he deserved a second chance, and I'll hate those Golden Light sons of bitches for taking that from him for the rest of my life.

"I'm so sorry, Nash. Please forgive me. I just wanted to get Rina out of here. I'm sorry I didn't leave with you when you asked me to. I'm so sorry," I say as I sob.

My tears fall onto his cheek, and I gently wipe them

away as I think about all he did for me. He didn't have to risk anything to protect me from Nadine and Micah, but he did and never asked for a thing in return.

For that, I owe him my life.

One of the officers softly taps me on the shoulder, and I look up at him knowing I have to go now. Turning back toward Nash, I whisper, "Goodbye, Nash. I'll never forget what you did for me."

As I stand up and turn to walk back toward the police car waiting for me, I see a body in front of The Golden Light building. Looking closely, I see it's Nadine dead on the ground.

Good. May she rot in Hell.

Six Months Later

Each Tuesday morning, I sit in this hunter green wingback chair in my therapist's office. He always begins on time, but today, he's running late, so I'm studying his bookcases to see what he likes to read. I see some classics like The Great Gatsby and Oliver Twist next to books about cults and psychology. Seems typical for a therapist, I guess.

Dr. Genero walks in and sits down across from me in a similar dark green chair like he does for every one of our sessions. He's wearing dark pants and a white dress shirt under a light blue cardigan, and I've decided since he wears this every time I see him that it's his version of a uniform. The color of the sweater brings out the blue in his eyes and looks nice next to his brown hair.

With a tiny smile, he asks, "How are you today, Lara?"

I never know how to answer him when he asks that, which he does to start every appointment. I'm fine. I didn't get hurt in the shootout, and other than some nightmares once in a while, my time at The Golden Light farm is slowly but surely becoming a distant memory.

So all in all, I'm fine.

Except I'm not, and I don't know what to do about that. I lost someone I cared about that night, and my sister is still a mess. I have so much hate in my heart for The Golden Light people that sometimes I can barely keep it inside. It threatens to explode out of me at different times, like when I try to talk to Rina and she refuses to even acknowledge I'm right there in front of her or when our parents suggest I should get out more, as if the most traumatic event of my life didn't occur only a few months ago.

So even though I shouldn't lie to my therapist. I say, "I'm okay."

"What would you like to discuss today?" he asks with that encouraging sound to his words I've grown to dread.

I'm not sure what he's hoping to hear. Maybe he's wishing today will be the day I'll finally break down and cry my eyes out in his office here. I hate to disappoint him, but that's not going to happen.

Not that I haven't cried. I cry myself to sleep most nights thinking about Nash and how much he sacrificed to make sure I was safe. He didn't have to find any police that night. He could have run away and disappeared, never to be seen again, and he wouldn't have owed a single soul any explanation.

Although I know my fate may have been very

different if he had, I can't help but wish Nash had vanished into the darkness that night. At least then he'd be alive.

"I'm not sure. Any ideas?" I ask with a forced smile, knowing the doctor is analyzing every tiny move I make.

He levels his gaze on my face, but I don't look away, preferring to stare into his very blue eyes. They're icy and almost flinty, especially for someone who seems to genuinely care about his patients' well-being. It's an odd contrast I can't help but be intrigued by.

"Perhaps you'd like to talk about something new you've been doing. How does that sound?"

I shrug, not unhappy to have that conversation. "Well, my story about what happened will be published sometime early next year. I'm pretty happy about that."

"Is that so? That's wonderful!" he says with a big smile that shows off his straight, white teeth.

It's a rare expression of excitement from my therapist, and I have to say it's a welcome response. My parents are none too pleased that I decided to write about what Rina and I went through. They claim it's going to humiliate our family. Rina just repeatedly says the book will be a pack of lies, although she never says that to me because she refuses to speak whenever I'm around ever since that night. Nobody seems to care that writing all that I experienced was therapeutic for me.

"I'm happy about it. At least one good thing might come out of all that happened."

We sit in silence for a long time before he asks, "Are you up to discussing how you feel about what happened with The Golden Light?"

Shrugging, I answer, "Sure."

For the past six months, he's asked that question, and I answer the same way every time. Sure. Then I try my hardest to hide my true feelings because I feel so fucking guilty about all that happened.

Today is different, though. When I woke up this morning, I told myself I'm going to give this therapy stuff a chance. Before all of this Golden Light business, I would have said with utmost confidence that I believe in therapy, but I've never given it any true effort.

That ends now.

"I'm wondering what your reaction is to all you went through," Dr. Genero says.

As I think about how to answer, I purse my lips to stop the words from escaping, but I'm not doing that anymore. I'll never find any peace if I keep everything inside.

"I feel so much that I don't know how to answer, if I'm being honest. I hate them for taking Nash away and stealing the second chance he deserved. I'm angry at what they did to me and everyone else there. I'm sad at all the people who suffered. I'm hurt that my own sister, my best friend all my life until she got involved in The Golden Light, won't speak a single word to me but lets anyone who'll listen know she hates me for taking her away from Micah."

"How do you feel about what the prosecutors are doing with his case?"

I have no issue with talking about how Micah and his goons, along with Nadine's stormtroopers, are having to pay for what happened. I find almost too much glee at the idea of them spending time in prison for all they did. I don't care about Adam having to spend the rest of his life in prison after agreeing to plead guilty in exchange for that sentence.

Well, that's not exactly true. I probably care too much since I'm sure he's the one who murdered Nash. I've avoided talking about it, even to my therapist, because I can't stop myself from relishing his punishment. It's the only happiness I can find in the situation, other than my book.

I take a deep breath in and let it out slowly before answering the doctor's question. "I'm not sure what I'm supposed to say. I don't pretend to be unhappy about any of it. I'd love to see them pay with their lives for what they did to Nash and me. And Rina. And all those poor people who believed in Micah. Since I can't get that wish fulfilled, I'll take whatever pain the justice system can give them."

He nods and asks, "Does that give you some relief knowing they will pay for their crimes?"

For a few moments, I think about that question and then smile. "Relief? No. I lost someone who gave his life to protect me, and my sister is a mess and might never get better. Nearly a hundred people, all women and children, took their own lives after Micah said to because he was afraid of what they'd tell the authorities. So no, I wouldn't call it relief. I'd call it just desserts."

Dr. Genero nods. "From what I've read about the drugging of the members, the torture of that box, and the treatment of women at that farm, I'd say you're lucky to have made it out alive."

I've told him very little about all of what went on at the farm, but the newspapers have shared the horrible details since some of Micah's men made deals with the prosecutors to get lighter sentences. "I have Nash to thank for that. I couldn't have done it without him."

My therapist says something else he's read about all that happened with The Golden Light, but I'm not listening. All I can think of is Nash and how much he sacrificed for me.

Sometimes at night when I close my eyes and see his face as clear as day, I wonder what could have been. I was planning to let him stay with me as long as he needed to get used to life outside of The Golden Light. Would we have ended up together? I don't know.

But if we had, I would have considered myself lucky to be with a man like him. He made mistakes and I'm sure the things he did for Micah would haunt him forever, but when he had the opportunity, he showed he was a good man. I can never pay him back for what he did for me.

"You mentioned last session that you didn't think Micah would get much time, but I read in the paper the other day he's going to be sentenced to ten to twenty years, and there will be subsequent trials for what he did to the women in The Golden Light and the suicides of all those people at the farm. How do you feel about that?"

I can't keep the smile off my face at the idea that Micah and his messiah complex will be getting to enjoy life around hardened criminals who most likely won't buy his brand of bullshit. If there's any justice at all, they'll treat him exactly as he's due.

And if that means he lives in abject terror for the next decade or two, I wouldn't be unhappy at all.

"Micah's sentence makes me think there's some sort of justice in this world."

"Is that enough?" Dr. Genero asks.

I close my eyes and picture Nash's face that first time we talked after Nadine's men terrified me. I know he truly believed in Micah and his teachings then, yet he still tried to protect me.

"Even though I can't be sure, I want to think Nash would be satisfied with Micah's sentence, so I try to believe it's enough. I don't know, though. All those women and children are dead, and the guilt rests solely with him. They would have never killed themselves if he didn't tell them to. So I honestly don't know if Nash would say he's going to pay enough for all that happened."

I don't know because I can't stop thinking about all the people who suffered at the hands of The Golden Light. Nash, Anna, Mary, Cheyenne, and that adorable little girl Kinley, along with so many others whose names I didn't know but who didn't make it out alive from that hellhole of a farm.

My therapist nods and starts talking about acceptance, but like so many times when I'm here forced to deal with what happened, my mind drifts to Nash and all he did to help me in my days at The Golden Light. We only knew each other for a short time, but he made the ultimate sacrifice for me, and I can only hope he's somewhere watching and approves of how I'm trying to make sense of it all. I may have never bought into Micah and his Golden Light garbage, but Nash showed me greatness can be found in the unlikeliest of places.

For that and everything else he did, I owe him my life. In that respect and only that one, Micah was right.

Nash did have greatness inside him.

LOOK FOR MORE BOOKS FROM K.M. SCOTT!

ABOUT THE AUTHOR

K.M. Scott loves a good story. A New York Times and USA Today bestselling author, K.M. has written dozens of books. In addition to romance, she's written cozy mysteries under her Anina Collins pen name. She lives in Pennsylvania with a herd of animals and when she's not writing can be found reading or feeding her TV addiction.

Be sure to visit K.M.'s Facebook page at **https://www.facebook.com/kmscottauthor** for all the latest on her books, along with giveaways and other goodies! And to hear all the news on K.M. Scott books first, sign up for her newsletter today and be sure to visit her website at **http://www.kmscottbooks.com**

ALSO BY K.M. SCOTT

THRILLERS

Now You Know How It Feels

The Neighbor

The Cult

HEART OF STONE SERIES

Crash Into Me (Heart of Stone #1)

Fall Into Me (Heart of Stone #2)

Give In To Me (Heart of Stone #3)

Heart of Stone Volume One

Ever After (Heart of Stone #4)

A Heart of Stone Christmas (Heart of Stone #5)

Return To Me (Heart of Stone #6)

Forever With Me (Heart of Stone #7)

Heart of Stone Volume Two

Hard As Stone (Heart of Stone #8)

Set In Stone (Heart of Stone #9)

Silent As A Stone (Heart of Stone #10)

Heart of Stone Volume Three

All of Me (Heart of Stone #11)

CLUB X SERIES

Temptation (Club X #1)

Surrender (Club X #2)

Possession (Club X #3)

Satisfaction (Club X #4)

Acceptance (Club X #5)

Complete Club X Series Box Set

NeXt SERIES

Notorious (NeXt #1)

Infamous (NeXt #2)

Ravenous (NeXt #3)

Ambitious (NeXt #4)

Flirtatious (NeXt #5)

Mysterious (NeXt #6)

Sensuous (NeXt #7)

Desirous (NeXt #8)

KING BROTHERS SERIES

Cruel King

Wild King

Broken King

CORRUPTED LOVE TRILOGY

If I Dream (Corrupted Love #1)

If You Fight (Corrupted Love #2)

If We Fall (Corrupted Love #3)

Corrupted Love Trilogy Box Set

K.M.'S BOOKS ARE IN AUDIOBOOK TOO!

BOOKS BY K.M. SCOTT WRITING AS GABRIELLE BISSET

BOOKS BY K.M. SCOTT WRITING AS ANINA COLLINS